PASSING OFF

by
Tom LeClair

THE PERMANENT PRESS
SAG HARBOR, NY 11963

Library of Congress Cataloging-in-Publication Data

LeClair, Tom,
    Passing off/ by Tom LeClair
        p.   cm.
    ISBN 1-877946-77-X
    PS3562.E2776P37   1996
    813'. 54--dc20   95-22746
                                                      CIP

first edition, 1600 copies December 1996

Manufactured in the United States of America

THE PERMANENT PRESS
Noyac Road
Sag Harbor, NY 11963

For Αλεξανδρος Μητρουσιας

Passing Off: A Season in the Greek Basketball Association

by Michael Keever

The Full Court Press
New York

Passing Off was originally published in Greece as *I Metavivasi*

Ermes

Athens

Prologue

Every coach has a keyhole view of the game. I'm supposed to fit, turn the lock, open up the room, and bring in the crowd. Break them down and coaches sound like those old philosophers I heard about when I went to Greece to play: everything moves, nothing moves, water, earth, fire the rock, and no air balls.

My first coach was my father. When he realized I was slightly walleyed, he told me, "Hit the open man." I trained my peripheral vision by bouncing the ball off the wall in the low-roofed room over our tractor shed. Before I hit organized ball, I carried my permanent scouting report: "He'd rather pass than shoot."

My high-school coach, Lee Kellogg, believed in speed. With the stopwatch he'd brought up to Vermont from Albany, Kellogg timed us touching the backboard twenty times, sprinting baseline to baseline, passing the ball back and forth twenty reps. "Run, shitkickers, run," he'd scream at us in the locker room, and we'd run our layup line full speed. When we put our hands together before the tip, we didn't shout "Go Black River" or "Presidents Rule" like other teams. We growled Kellogg's motto: "Speed kills." Coach tolerated my tricky passes because they reminded him of the city game, speed in a crowd.

Ray Matera recruited me at Boston College, where he looked in the keyhole and saw spacing. The first day of practice he gave us tapes and we measured the floor, the lane, the hoop, the ball, and each other's bodies. "If there is exactly the right amount of open space between players in our offense, their defense will fail." We practiced the same plays over and over, working the movements down to inches, precision screens, exact cuts, and pinpoint passes. "Function is fun," Matera told me, but I quit his slow-down game after a year.

At Memphis State, Danny Cater put a video cam up to the keyhole. When we scrimmaged, he had an assistant in the press box turn on the camera. After the suicides, we'd go in the locker, watch ourselves, and hear Cater's tale of the tape. It was a story with few words: "look," "see," "no," and "good." For Cater, words were just a pointer. "Tape doesn't lie." The facts were up on the monitor. Stop the tape, see the truth. Most of the Memphis players didn't believe Cater, not even when they watched game films. They'd stare at the two seconds of tape coach was running backward and forward, but they believed in themselves, in their bodies. They'd learned the fundamentals and pounded the Nautilus. They could soar. They'd listen to an assistant coach shout the usual wisdom—"Don't turn your head." "Don't dribble against a zone press."—but Cater's faith in video didn't reach them. "From image to act. No layer of language to throw off the imitation." After they left the room, coach took me through the tape again. The point who ran his TV show, I got extra tutoring in the Catescan, the way to find openings in crowded space.

Coach on the floor, I learned to coach myself. At six-three and one-eighty I'm too tall to be a darter, too small to post up most guards, and too thin to overpower anyone. I have foul-line to foul-line speed with the ball, I get a quick and long first step, and I can stretch out to the hoop though I don't get many jams. Speed kills, vertical kills. So can skill, what you can practice alone on a Florida driveway or in a high-roofed hay barn, shooting again and again, the same release, the same arch. Also what you can practice in your head in any room with electricity. After I learned my teammates and opposing teams from Cater's tapes, I had the State trainer take isolation footage of me and the man playing me. I'd read about baseball hitters finding imperfections in their filmed swings, swimmers comparing tape against the computer simulation of what their arms and legs should be doing. I studied the iso zoom for what I was giving away with a head turn or high dribble, what the man guarding me thought he was getting when I crossed over to my left or went behind my back, what I could take from him if he thought wrong, what I could do to him if he was made to think wrong. Sweat and pressure and sometimes adrenalin interfered with memory of these cues and clues. I didn't call them body language. The movements weren't something I read or heard. I perceived them all at once, like recognizing a figure or a letter. Tape made the recognitions usable. Tape didn't lie and somebody with my body couldn't afford to lie to himself. If I didn't see myself and my opponent neutrally, objectively, like a scientist watching blips run across his scope or screen, I couldn't use what I did see to "lie" to defenders the next time we met.

Over and over I ran the tape, looped and looped again through the recording, blocking out the words most coaches

8

would use for analysis, watching both bodies at once, editing away the extra limbs and irrelevant motions, searching the almost simultaneous lock of stimulus and response, re-recognizing the twitch that signaled advantage and the move that caused the twitch that sent the signal, rerecording in my brains the defender's mistaken dosage of fight or flight, translating the tape's information from my eyes and brains to my muscles, storing the knowledge as close to my ligaments and tendons and bones as repetition could insert it. Injected into cartilage and marrow, tape was the white player's substitute for soul. Fans used to tell me I had imagination, but what I really had was tape-enhanced memory, internal speed, perceptions ready for immediate recall, connection, and use, all a few milliseconds ahead of brothers without video aid.

Most of the players I faced were quicker or bigger or sometimes both. I used their physical advantages and confidence against them. The tape taught how they could be faked, misdirected, avoided, and embarrassed. The water bugs would dis me to my freckled face, I'd lay the ball out in front of them, invite them to make an easy swipe, and when they lunged I'd cross over and go the other way. The big guards I'd let body up to my skinny frame, feel the force they wanted to exert, let myself move in their direction, and then use my reverse dribble to leave them leaning into air. Deception sets up the high-li. At BC, Matera used to tell me the high-li was extra. "You must facilitate," he'd say. Sometimes the no-look or between-the-legs pass is intentional showing off: a little pastry for the beer drinkers. Other times I watch the tape and don't understand a crazy pass I've made. It looks both impossible and necessary, the only way to get the ball there, yet dictated by a situation I'd never seen before, mysterious. At Memphis, "T.V. Danny" Cater incorporated the high-li into his offense. My senior year I had one of the best assist-to-turnover ratios in the nation, and we went to the Final Four.

After graduation, I caught on with the Rockford Lightning in the CBA. Murray Jacobs was already inside the room, looking out at the fans. Murray believed in motive, desire, and will, in hate and fear, in using the crowd. He was perfect for the CBA, an organization of the failed or crazed, guys on the way down from the NBA, guys never going up. Murray gave a target to their manias. Before we even put on our sneakers, Murray sat us in the stands and explained what we were doing there.

"You all know how to play. Some of you are better equipped than others. You know this too. What you don't know is you're not playing for anybody. In the CBA, you will be playing to and against the crowd. Small crowds. Residents of the greater Rockford area. The high-school hopefuls in their untied high-tops. The former jocks if they're not working the night shift at the foundry. The divorcees with nothing left to do on winter nights. A family or two who won free tickets at Burger King. These people you can play up to. Keep them coming. You're their home team, the only thing that makes their home in Rockford different from a home in Grand Rapids.

"They will clap and whistle and call your names. But that won't be enough to give you will. No, you have to look for the guys in coats and ties, direct from the office. You'll hear the ties laugh and boo. You are minor league. They sit at their terminals and make numbers run faster and better than your brains can work. But no matter how much squash or tennis they play, no matter how much pussy they get in high-rise condos or airport motels, they know their bodies are left over, waste meat. Because you remind them, you are their enemy. They are your opponents. Their hate will fire your will. Play against them, and you will be complete. You may still be too short or slow for the NBA, but you'll be a player all the way through. All player, nothing left over. You can go to sleep at night whispering `Fuck you, ties.'"

I remember Murray's speech because I heard it three times. Some of the Lightning players were skeptical. They claimed the pride he promised was compensation for a high-school locker room and the thousand a month we were each paid. I liked Murray. He played up-tempo, the CBA scatter, lots of handles and responsibility for the point. And his audience orientation called for the high-li. I didn't want to hurt anybody in the stands. Hand out the assists, get a few baskets, and give the fans some fun, what they came for, something different to see and then see again on the ll:25 sports when they got home. Murray's view of the crowd got us into the playoffs my first season. The next year I led the league in assists, made the CBA All-Star team, and had ten days with the Celtics. My third year we won the championship, and we each got a ring worth $149.

My wife wanted to be back home in Memphis, so I took a job recruiting for Cater. Shooting tape of high-school kids wasn't like looking at the monitor. In fact, ever since Cater put me onto tape I've been kind of disappointed with life off the court. The game is quick and demanding, living on fast-forward. You can bring it back, though, slow it down, run and rerun, figure some tenths and inches. Leave the gym and you feel like you're doing knee rehab, running in waist-high water to recover lost speed. Slow as it is, the world won't reverse. Only the satellite cameras are keeping a record. They can scan the whole globe and read number plates, but you don't get to see your car. Reason to pay attention, you'd think, keep up the intensity, remember. With me, the opposite seemed true. I let it pass by. Run and erase, run and erase. "Low-Key," my Lightning team-mates called me on and off the floor. "Passive," my wife says. With the tape I'd slotted behind my eyes, I didn't have room for all those moving personal reminiscences some people can pull out of their hats, sleeves, and pockets. I wasn't interested in all those "critical decision points" TV editorialists talk about after the late sports. Language was to woof with in a game and play with on the long rides between games. Cater's tape confirmed what I learned as a kid in the shed: there wasn't much to tell anybody.

That was before I spent a year recruiting and before I went to Greece. When Ann and I first met and she discovered I was from Plymouth, birthplace of Calvin Coolidge, she called me "Cal" for a while: simple, silent Cal, the man who chose not to run, the last president you could trust. I hated whispering inducements into the ears of high-school seniors, surly hillbillies in Kentucky small towns, wise-ass black kids in Jackson and Birmingham. Elroy Hurd, Cater's top recruiter, called them "bones," short for boneheads who needed meat. Our only pleasure came at the end of the signing period when we could squeeze the bones: "We've got one scholarship left. You don't want to end up playing on that tile floor at the community college do you, Dwayne?" After six months of recruiting, I asked my agent, Marv Drinkman, to send tape overseas. Drink had to circulate tapes because he handled more marginals than any agent around: guards two inches short or a half step slow, the "tweener" forwards, centers who lacked heft, bodies that didn't quite fit the NBA. Most of Drink's misfits were still in the CBA, playing in Rapid City or LaCrosse or Sioux Falls, living in Day's Inn and eating at Wendy's, waiting for a shot at The League, what the brothers called "Elevation," that region way above the rim, high-domed stadiums with twenty-five-thousand fans, hotels with elevators climbing atrium walls, first-class leg room at thirty-thousand feet. We were known as "Drinkman's Ten-Day All Stars" because we got to the NBA only on the fill-in, try-out contract reported in the "Transactions" section of the sports pages: "The Boston Celtics have placed Derek Durst on injured reserve. Michael Keever, a guard with the Rockford Lightning, has been signed to a ten-day contract." The Boston papers said I looked like Danny Ainge with a John Stockton handle, but on the eleventh day Durst came back and I returned to Rockford. That last season I couldn't avoid the CBA code: put in more than three years for peanuts and you're both failed *and* crazed.

The third of August, Drinkman woke me up in the middle of the night. "I think I can jump you," he said. Drink moves players in the United States. He jumps them overseas.

"That's great, Drink. Where to?"

"Greece."

"No shit, but why are you calling me at three in the morning?"

"I just got off the phone with the GM at Panathinaikos. Greece is seven hours ahead."

"What did he say?"

"His playmaker just blew out a knee in a motorcycle accident. He's seen your tape and says you should help them. Key, you're not going to believe this. He goes for the high-li. You'll be the Greek Key. Zigzag. Come see me tomorrow. They're going to love you."

In his office, Drink explained the Greek league's rule on players from outside the country: each team could have one foreigner and one player from abroad who could demonstrate his Greek family background. Then he told me the Panathinaikos GM said Keever sounded like a Greek name to him.

"Gaelic," I told Drink. "Shortened from McKeever. My grandfather changed it when he got here."

"All right, Key." Drink was excited like he gets at NCAA tournament time. His right index finger was punching the chair arm like a remote. "It doesn't matter what you were. If your name has been changed once, we don't have any trouble changing it again. We get the photostat, do a little sleight-of-hand, and you have a Greek grandfather."

"Slow down, Drink. I don't get this deal."

"You remember Rome? Played for Auburn. His name had been changed from Romazalowski, something with a bunch of Eastern European consonants. We made it Romero, and now he's starting for Real Madrid. Double-figure rebounder."

"You're shitting me, Drink."

He rolled his chair forward and put his forearms on the desk. Drink was serious.

"Panathinaikos already has its American, James Henderson from Michigan. They're desperate for a point. They think you're Greek-American. If you're not, they can't use you. If you are, you could walk away with a $60,000 bonus."

Drink explained the bonus clause. American players get homesick and quit if their city doesn't have a McDonald's, so some owners overseas backload the money. I'd get air fare for myself and family up front, a monthly living allowance paid in drachmas, and the big pop in dollars at the end. But I had to finish the season.

"Henderson will do the lifting on the boards and you'll get the money."

"What's up with that? The big guys get the bucks here."

"You and Henderson would get the same monthly, say three thousand. But with the performance escalators I'll write in, you'll get the bigger dollar pop at the end. The Greeks want to bring back their native sons. Prove yourself and it will be more after the first year."

"And what if the Greeks find out I'm not Greek?"

Drink leaned further forward and picked up a pen. I could see he was preparing to sign me over the ocean.

"That will never happen, Key. They don't want to find out. The soccer teams have been doing this for years. South American mestizos are pretending to be white. Overseas everybody is somebody else. Fans see the NBA on television and want the League's 'fantastic.' Local teams have to compete, please the crowd. With you as a repatriating Greek, Panathinaikos gets two Americans. You'll be Greek as long as you can play."

Drink knew I wanted to play. I knew Ann wouldn't like this deal. She didn't change her name from Logan when we got married.

"Ann will never go for it."

"You got to think about yourself, Key. You're going to love

it over there. And if that's not enough, think about the Greeks. They don't see shit like yours live."

I quickly calculated Drink's 10 percent and suspected his concern for me and Greek fans.

"Ann's not going to like the paperwork."

"She'll never need to know. If she asks when you're there, just tell her Greeks add letters to American names to give them male or female endings."

"I'll have to think about this, Drink."

Drinkman leaned back in his chair and put his hands behind his head. Now I'd get the closer.

"It's late in Greece. The GM is in a hurry. Call me tonight. And don't forget: he thinks the high-li will put fans in the stands."

On the way home, I picked up a travel video of Greece. Ann and I had talked about Greece that morning before she went to work. Drink was always sending tape or saying he was sending tape, so there had been no reason to think about Greece before his call. When Drink sent tape to Peru, Ann found out about the cholera epidemic and the Shining Path before we heard the team thought I was a forward. Ann would go to the library on her lunch hour. When she got home, she'd have some information on Greece: companies doing business there, kindergartens for Sara, AT&T connections. "Anticipate," my high-school coach would tell me, "one fucking second, Keever. That's all you have to see ahead. Imagine just one second into the future and you'll be a player." I worked the seconds. Ann figured the months and years. She'd have information. For Ann, decisions involve thorough research, deliberate balancing, and careful projection. I'm the one with intuition. She'll list the pros and cons. As a professional con man with the ball, I resist the terms, the columns of "whys" and "why nots." Athletes make quick decisions. She'd want to exhaust risks and benefits. For me, it was simple. Playing was my benefit, my long-term goal. Shooters knock down thousands of goals and retire satisfied. It's harder for the playmaker to quit because his job is always all process, running the team, handling the ball, passing off. For the point guard, it's risk every second: avoiding surprise, preventing a turnover, holding the players together, controlling the crowd. Since leaving Rockford, I'd scrimmaged with the State kids and played some pick-up tournaments, but I missed the crowds, bringing fans into the game at home, keeping opponents' fans in their seats away, entertaining Rockford shut-ins on the cable, and performing nationwide on ESPN during the playoffs. For me, Greece was a last-minute break, a jump back into the action.

That night we sat on the couch and I rolled the travel tape. Greece was blue, white, and blue like its flag, blue sky, white buildings, blue sea, white beaches. These scenes, I knew, would remind Ann of her family's long summer vacations on the Gulf. As the muted tape skipped from island to island, I told Ann about the money. I stressed the bonus, how it would get us into the home market, a big down payment on the house she wanted to buy. She reported that Greece was a civilized place, that Athens had schools for foreign kids, that her friends agreed that the islands were "stunning." We talked about her job with the city. She could get a leave. We talked about my job. I'd be happy to leave it forever. Fly a commuter into some Appalachian shithole, jack my legs into a rental compact, and try to tape the recruit in a gym with sixty-watt bulbs. Talk to the kid's buzz-cut coach, who always overestimated his boy, hoping to ride him out of Shithole. Talk to the kid's parents, encourage them to teach their son how to read and write. Show the family the promo tape, the new Pyramid Arena with sky boxes, gowned graduates holding diplomas (I got mine in five years). Then, if everybody liked me, I'd get a few minutes alone with the "bone" to tell him what he wanted to hear— "We got some big-city women in Memphis. We need mountain boys to smarten up the bloods."—and to imply what I couldn't say: secret cash from the boosters, rapid rise to the NBA.

Ann and I talked about Sara, Ann's family, what kind of house we could buy, one with a two-car garage and level driveway for a hoop. With two service-sector salaries and credit tight, I told her, we had to leave the country if we ever wanted to buy a home here. I hated to do it, but I avoided mentioning the name change to Ann. I knew she'd refuse. I reminded her that Drink was expecting my call. Ann was uncomfortable with the pressure on. She dropped her chin and tilted her head toward me. I anticipated and beat her to the question she was always asking me:

"What do you want to do?"

She laughed. "I want to think about it some more. At least overnight. It could be good for all of us to live in another country. It might be fun."

"We don't have overnight."

"If I have to answer right now, I guess I'll have to say yes, I'd like to go."

She didn't ask me what I wanted. She knew. She knew the three years I was in the CBA and my shitty year as an assistant coach. Ann didn't need words then. Later she told me what "prologue" meant in Greek. Looking back at our talk that August night, I think she probably knew I'd play for the Shining Path if they had a team.

Chapter 1

Two weeks after I signed with Drinkman we were in the Athens airport with a sellout crowd of high-season tourists. After waiting an hour for our luggage and another forty-five minutes to pass through customs, we funneled into a line moving toward the lobby. Through the doors I could see bodies packed five and six deep against a railing. The Greeks were jumping, waving, shouting, crying. At the single gap in the railing, two policemen were trying to maintain a passage through the crowd, but people were pressing in from both sides, closing the gap just outside the railing. Out of the crowd, a short old man with thick arms and then an even shorter, heavy-hipped woman pushed past the policemen as if they were porters, scurried to incoming passengers, and clasped them in their tracks, stopping the line. Children ducked under the railing, darted forward, and jumped on arrivals. Passengers in front of us abandoned their carts and charged to the railing, where they embraced people who came pushing and shoving to the front. A man behind us rushed past us to the railing where he was beaten on the shoulders and then kissed on both cheeks by three middle-aged men who looked Middle Eastern. He pummeled them and kissed them back. The Greeks acted like fans welcoming home NBA champions.

Pushing a luggage cart with our six suitcases, I had enough weight to open a hole in the crowd at the rail and squeeze out into the lobby where I was tall enough to see young women holding up signs to welcome their groups. "Hotel Porto Rafti." "Hilton." "Aegean Cruise." I looked around for the Panathinaikos representative who was supposed to meet us. When I spotted a guy holding up "Key Tours," I said to myself, this team has some style: Key takes his high-li show on the road. I pushed over to the man and introduced myself. He shook hands and then looked at the clipboard he was carrying.

"Do you have a voucher?" he asked.

"Exile," I thought, Drinkman's term for Third World leagues. Drink has sent me to a team that makes me prove I'm me to get a ride into the city. I asked the guy if this was how all Greek teams treated their players.

"I'm sorry, sir. I do not understand. Do you not wish to take one of our tours? We offer day tours of Athens and longer trips to all important sites. Key Tours unlocks the secrets of ancient Greece."

That was turnover number one. Eventually, the tallest man with six suitcases, wife, and five-year-old daughter was spotted by a short woman with a sign that was a secret to me: KYBEPNOS, my new name in Greek letters.

Greece, we discovered right away, is not Italy, the leisure league you may have read about, that Danny Ferryland where big name players find a villa, car, and servant waiting for them. Furnished apartments were rented before we could see them, sometimes before we could call to see them. To find a place to live, we had to walk the streets looking for little "Enikiazete" signs next to doorbells. Our driver had suggested Kolonaki, which Ann's guidebook described as "an older section on the slopes of Mt. Likavitos. Resembling New York's Upper East Side, Kolonaki is dotted with embassies and chic shops and is home to a large foreign community." After five days, one basement apartment, and one flat available in a month, we rang a bell, heard English spoken back, and were shown into a fifth-floor apartment. Across the twelve-by-twelve living room were glass doors. Framed by the doors, as if it were a giant painting, was the Parthenon. We walked out onto the balcony, looked at half the city below, and Ann said, "We'll take it."

"What if it doesn't have a kitchen?"

"We'll cook out here."

"Or bedrooms?"

"We'll buy a tent."

We signed a lease and gave the landlady three months rent, but Ann refused to leave the apartment until I'd brought in our suitcases. Located between our hotel in the Plaka tourist district and Panathinaikos stadium, our new home did have a half kitchen, one bedroom, and a black-and-white TV. We didn't care because Kolonaki had everything we needed, we could walk almost anywhere else we wanted to go, and we were spending most of our time outdoors.

Like property, people in Athens move faster than in the States. The avenues converging in the city center are like four-lane drag strips, cars lurching away from lights, streaming through yellow, squealing into the crosswalk on red. Buses and trolleys have racing stripes. Midday looks and sounds like rush hour: streets jammed with cars, drivers honking and screaming, passengers waving out their windows. To speed through their overcrowded streets, Greeks are jockeys. Little sixty-year-old men, ties flapping in the wind, whip between lanes of stalled traffic on dirt bikes. Women ride sidesaddle behind their husbands or tuck their knees tight together on Vespas. Teenagers throttle minibikes as if they're trying to get donkeys to run. The real jocks, though, are the short young men hunched over huge Hondas and Suzukis, whispering to their handlebars.

In the Plaka, tourists walk slowly, rubbernecking, taking it all in, wary of being cheated, fearful of pickpockets. The morning crowds on the sidewalks in the rest of Athens are young men running goods into shops from double-parked vans, women with plastic bags bustling through the day's shopping, older men and boys hustling trays with small cups of coffee and large glasses of water to office workers, the workers themselves out on the sidewalks for something to eat on the go. Ten in the morning in Syntagma Square is like noon in Memphis, when people descend from their towers and scamper to lunch. The Greeks are darker, the men more casually dressed, the women classier, no pantssuits, and they all move closer to you than southerners, brushing shoulders or hips, steering through oncoming walkers with a slightly outstretched arm, placing a light hand on your elbow as they pass. They walk touching each other, turned toward each other, not seeming to look where they're going, because they're trying to be heard above the street noise. Like players pumping up teammates, Greeks holler in each other's faces, their mouths forming the words against the noise. The speech is noise, adding to the other noise, crowd noise in this densely crowded city.

"No savage quickness," Drink said about the natives, but they're fast even when sitting down. The first day Sara, Ann, and I sat in a cafe, she asked me why my eyes were flicking and fingers were twitching. I hadn't noticed. I was responding to the jerking heads and darting hands at the tables all around me. A guy off to my left was raising his eyebrows like the Lightning center signaling for an alley-oop. My hand wanted to float my beer bottle up over the back of his companion's head. The Greeks' constant gestures remind me of rappers' hand movements and finger codes, secret signs for the home-boys. Like young blacks in the States, Greeks are always shaking hands, bobbing and moving when they're standing still. Their motion keeps your eyes sharp, your body ready to move.

Even sitting down, I felt like I was on the floor.

My only problem was finding something to tape. While Ann was telling Sara stories about Athena the woman warrior, I shot the Parthenon but it didn't move. Although the figures in the museums were buffed, they were all white and posed. The statues of Athena and Apollo in front of the university were high in the air but pedestaled. We didn't see any of the Greek fishermen that danced on the travel tape I'd rented, Anthony Quinn Greeks. No crazy customs like Muslims bowing to Mecca, just this density of people in public space. The differences here are difficult to film. The light bouncing off the surrounding stucco and onto my balcony is like the high-intensity floods above the court, but you can't shoot into the light. The sun pleases my eyes, sneaks through cracks in the shutters in the morning, gets me up, somehow gives me appetite. Like the people, the food is dense. There are no air holes in feta. Olives come with pits. We were sniffing the pots in a taverna one night when we caught a smell we couldn't identify. The waiter tapped his head. "Brains, we cook brains." The Greeks are eating brains. There's a difference. I'll need a steady diet to learn the language. The signs on stores are alien squiggles, patterns I can't recognize, can't even sound out. We roam the streets, look in the windows, go in the shops, handle the products, touch the textures. Cotton or polyester? Wood or plastic? Feel the goods, rap the watermelon. One day Ann rapped and hesitated. The old guy with two teeth took it out of her hands and split it with a foot-long knife. It was tomato red. She just couldn't hear the color. At the supermarket I saw a woman smelling a can of coffee. Honey is identified by different habitats. Greeks can taste where bees live. How would I get that on tape?

I feel a subtle pressure. The air and light seem to surround me, things and people are closer together. It's a difference you have to sense. I feel I have my proprioception here. Ann said it's the only word I know as long as motherfucker. Ran across it in a phys. ed. class. It's the sixth sense, connecting the others, controlling balance, the key to every athlete's body. After our walks, when Sara and Greeks are taking their midday nap, Ann and I quietly balance our long-legged bodies on our six-foot bed and secretly take our second honeymoon, more moving density I can't tape. "Do you think there's something in the water here?" Ann asked. "It's everything," I teased her, "all the senses in play are good for the pro."

Even the language is dense. I sent Coach Cater a postcard of Greek script from ancient times, when words weren't separated. The writing looked like nonsense, the work of a child with alphabet blocks and a chisel. The language is still compressed, consonants impossibly rubbing up against each other. "M" and "P" together at the end of a word are useful: jump, pump, dump. But what are your tongue and lips going to do with those letters at the beginning of a word if your parents never spoke Greek? No other country uses this alphabet, speaks this language. I doubt I ever will. I don't speak that much English, a smattering of Afro-American. Ann is trying to learn Greek, but maybe I don't want to. Texture would become a text, motion X's and O's. The proprioception would be different then. Reading and listening could overwhelm the rest. I'd lose my touch. Food wouldn't taste the same. I wouldn't be able to smell Greeks passing me in the street. I take in a few words that seem like presents from Greek, signs of our connection, welcoming sounds. Running around looking for a place to live, jumping away from cars, lugging groceries home on foot, heaving our rugs over the balcony railing to air, I thought Greeks are like pentathletes. When I learned to count to five, I realized that "athlete" is Greek.

For Greek and American athletes, Coach Zikopoulos' one-eyed demand was suicidal conditioning. "To running faster and longer over other teams," he explained, "we must overtraining." Even before Coach Z introduced Henderson and me to the team, he made us all run the suicides. They are the secret all basketball players keep. No other sport does the suicides. If you haven't played basketball, you haven't seen them. They're not run before a game. They're not usually run before a practice. After practice, hangers-on or reporters don't stick around because the suicides are an inside story no one wants to watch or tape. Ten men, all stripped to skins now, line up along one baseline. The coach blows his whistle and the men, no longer players, sprint eyes down to the foul line, touch the floor with one hand, and sprint back to the starting line, sprint eyes to the floor to midcourt, touch down, and sprint back, sprint without looking to the far foul line, touch, and back, sprint blindly the whole floor, touch the other endline, and sprint back. The men rest, the coach blows the whistle, and they run. Rest, whistle, run, over and over, up and down, around and around. The men turn into bodies, large sweating bodies. They go out strong, an even line together on the first circle. Then the group starts to break up. They begin passing each other going to midcourt and on the third circle out the floor is crowded with bodies going in opposite directions, the big bodies sometimes colliding with the smaller bodies already coming back. On the last circle the bodies are strung out all over the floor, stabbing at the line, slipping in the pools of sweat, heads swinging, arms flailing, legs staggering on the long stretch home.

It is suicide not to run hard and suicide to run hard. If you finish last, you may run while the others are resting. If the coach catches someone dogging, the whole team will run extra suicides. If you go all out and finish in front, you feel you're going to die on the baseline. You stand doubled over, your lungs looking for air on the floor, or you throw your head back, chest heaving, gulping for any oxygen your teammates may have missed. You wish your nose was the size of your mouth. You wonder why you're here, why your ancestors came up out of the sea and became mammals. The air you get comes with the stench of sweat and garlic coming out of the Greeks' pores. In the September heat, sweat is pouring out so fast you're over-cooling, shivering in your own overheating. The sweat collects in your ears, burns your eyes, trickles into your mouth, puddles like sea water on the floor. Your lungs feel clenched in your chest. Your heart pounds in your head. You pray that it's the only sound you'll hear, that the whistle won't blow, that the coach will swallow his whistle, that the motherfucker will strangle at the other baseline, gasping like you, sweat coming out of his eyes. The whistle blows. Sprint, bend, sprint. Your stomach aches, your back aches, your arms and legs ache. You wish for a cramp, a painful knotted muscle, a reason to stop that the trainer can feel, hard evidence. You even consider colliding with another body, risking injury to one limb to stop the pain all over.

The suicides are called that because they're the absolute negative and because they go on and on. Running the suicides, you may be stretching tendons, increasing muscle density, expanding lungs, building endurance, preparing to run the fast break, but what the suicides are really doing is subtracting, little by little by little, taking off weight, shedding differences, cancelling pride, decreasing mind, diminishing instinct, forgetting the body's good sense. In the suicides, perceptions don't matter. No skills are involved, no teamwork. You're running for yourself, against yourself. No statistics, only the coach's count. No language, just the whistle. No place to hide, no crowd to keep you going. From the suicides there's no escape, no leaving early, because they're what you've chosen in order to play, to work, to be here, to be anywhere basketball is played for pay. Coach Z blows his whistle and you run and you make yourself run and force yourself to keep running harder and harder, slower and slower until there is no more air, no more water, no more energy inside. Then you crumple and vomit. I was the first. Nothing came up. I was on my hands and knees retching, turning inside out, but nothing was inside. The other bodies kept running. It was two more whistle blows before Henderson went down on his knees and splattered green bile on the floor. I lay on the sideline, a towel filled with ice under the back of my neck. I sucked an ice cube and wondered if twenty-eight was too old for the Greek Basketball Association. I'd been keeping in shape in the States. The big guys are supposed to go down first.

The trainer flapped a towel over my white, clammy body. He was my best friend in this country, the man with the ice.

"Zesti," he said.

I sucked the cube.

"Hot," he translated.

Zesty, I realized.

"Also the Nefos is bad today."

"Nefos? What's the Nefos?"

"The cloud, the pollution," he said, pointing up toward the open windows. "Outside."

So that's why the Greeks are still running. They're used to the weather inside the gym. That yellow cloud I see behind the Acropolis every afternoon is the Greeks' home court advantage in the Athens basin, this LA without the Lakers. I had run the suicides in full sweats in Vermont, in 90 percent humidity in Memphis, and under the master of loathing in Rockford. It might take a few days, but I'd catch the Greeks in the suicides.

Ahead in conditioning, the Greeks were far behind in team-work. "Fazbreaking, fazbreaking," Z yelled in English, z-ing the two words together for speed. Panathinaikos ran up and down, but it wasn't fast and it wasn't the break. "Broke," I heard Henderson mutter, "GRs' game broke." All of the Greeks were shooters—the fill-in point guard, the power forward, two kids about nineteen up from the junior team, and the substitute center. Petros was six-five and 280 pounds. The club found him working in a marble quarry when he was twenty-five. Petros had hands of stone and only one thumb. That didn't stop him from airing out fifteen-foot tiptoe "jumpers." Those first sessions, the Greeks would not give me the ball. Forwards rebounded, dribbled the length of the floor, and threw up fall-away baseline jumpers. If a guard got a long rebound or a steal, he'd run down and fire a three before his teammates could get into better position and he'd have to pass.

Only Henderson and Koko, the thirty-five-year-old starting center, didn't get their share of shots. Koko was from another generation, he said, when parents waited to see if a boy was tall before putting a ball in his hands. If Koko grabbed a rebound, one of the Greeks who could dribble would run to him and take the rock off Koko's hands. It would be up in the air before Koko could get down the court. Henderson concentrated on offensive rebounding. Watching the ball on its way to the rim, he figured the angles, calculated the bounce, carved his space, levered with his hips, pried with his elbows, pushed off with his hands, and then exploded up above the Greeks. The third day of practice Henderson cracked Koko's nose. "That moth-erfucker's too slow to live," Henderson said. Like most broth-ers, he must have grown up playing thirty-three in the school-yard, the ghetto game you don't see on TV. Five or ten black kids around one hoop. It's all against all, one on four, one on seven, one on whoever is out there. You have to get the ball yourself and you have to shoot it yourself. There is no one to pass to. No fouls are called. Make it, take it. Keep it, reap it. Miss it, kiss it.

Two of the forwards were named Papadopoulos. The one with touch I called "Pop." He reminded me of Chris Mullin, a six-six lefty, a little slow afoot but a quick release and nice rotation, a soft ball. He could drop it from the wing and base-line. Pop was a country boy whose English was limited to bas-ketball terms used in Greek: "tzuball," "bloke out," "passa." Pop never tied up anybody for a jump, rarely blocked out, and always shot. Defense, rebounding, and passing were foreign to him. I wondered if it was because Greeks didn't have words for them. The power forward was "Dop." He explained to me in excellent, British-accented English why he should get at least twelve shots a game. Give him time to set up and he could hit the three, but he had no feel from fifteen feet in. "Face-shy," guards call a player like Dop, afraid of getting his shot slapped back in close. He had good shoulders and a quick rise for six-eight. His hips and heart were too small to help Koko and Henderson much in the paint.

Kappa had played some point with another team. He said he was happy to have me here. Now he could shoot it out with Calphoglou for the number two slot. They were like stubby bookends, both six-one and thick. Kappa went to the rack, Lou buried the threes. Kappa could take his man off the dribble, Lou moved better without the ball. Kappa learned his English in tourist cafes, Lou had an American wife.

Coach Z wanted us forcing the break every possession and, if we didn't score, he had us running a motion offense. The "Panatholes," as Henderson called the Greeks, weren't moving without the ball. They were making me into a "bouncer," Drink's term for a point guard who pointlessly dribbles the ball waiting for something to happen. To get the most out of my shooters, make a team go, I need to handle the ball every transition, receive the outlet, push the pace, decide who finishes. If we don't break down the transition defense, I call the set, choose the option, distribute the rock, open up for the release pass if the play doesn't work, and when the shot clock goes under seven I make something happen. I'm the funnel point in the egg timer, twenty-four seconds in the NBA, thirty here. The ball comes to me from the other four and I pass it back. If I don't have the ball every possession, I lose my feel for the game's changes, who's on and who's winded, who wants it, who needs a get-back or reward, what the man guarding me expects, how the defense is shading or doubling. Nothing never happens on the floor. I need the control to have the knowledge. I need the knowledge to have the control.

With both and some movement off the ball, I can predict the future, the next second.

"Thousand-one, thousand-two," Kellogg used to say. "Break it up. If they can split the fucking atom, you can halve the second." Now the game clock in the last minute of a half registers tenths of seconds. With the help of tape, I'd been cutting up the second for years to help me predict the next second, perhaps a hundred next seconds a game, decision points when two-tenths of a second in the future can make two or three points difference on the scoreboard, their off-guard three inches short as he leaps toward my jump shooter, a defensive stopper just fingers late on my forward's back door cut, or the ball and hand meeting above the rim as if they'd been engineered by Raytheon, still at their instant of intersection before the rim-rattling jam that ends the alley-oop. My teammates didn't have to play in the next second, but they had to know I did. They had to give me the ball and trust me. Do what they always did or were supposed to do and trust that the ball would be there waiting. Their present, my future.

When Kappa ran the half-court offense, everything seemed to happen late, sequentially. When I was in charge, my passes were ahead of the players, a foot out of reach. Or the ball sailed through the air six feet from the nearest offensive player, an open spot where I thought he should have been. I hit Dop in the side of the head when he made a cut he assumed I wouldn't see. Then the players did everything with their eyes on me, which slowed their cuts. Dop had lost some face with that red splotch on his cheek. I wasn't going for any high-li. Just trying to figure the Greeks' movements, calculate the tenths. I'd had similar problems at Memphis and with the Lightning, but the Greeks and I were far from connecting. They were bouncers who became shooters when they got within thirty feet of the basket. Z cursed, the players fumed, and the GM sat at mid-court and talked to himself. I figured he was counting those future dollars he'd put in Switzerland.

Drink had warned me that foreign teams sometimes resent American players. "You'll be there to please," Drink said, "set the table." At the end of our first week, I asked Z if I could show the team some tape. It might help the players see what I could do for them. I would explain and Z would translate.

The next day I used the style Plaka hucksters had adopted to reach all those Spaniards, Swedes, and Japanese who shopped in English. Simple sentences and present tense: "I make you special price." I told the players that other teams had problems adjusting to me. I took the blame. But I told them, "We can help each other. I make special passes. You get better shots. You score points and I have assists. We win games." Henderson must have thought I was simple-minded.

How to explain the future second? As used to sequence as the Greeks were, it wouldn't do any good to show them subtle timing plays. I'd have to shine the high-li in their eyes. I turned on the tape. I'm crossing the center line with the ball.

The Lightning shooting guard, Jackson, is in the right lane even with me. I catch motion in the corner of my left eye. That should be Bix coming up the left lane, ten feet back. I turn my head slightly right. I never look left. I slow the pace just a little to let Bix make up half the difference. Their two guards are backpedaling, getting ready to set every coach's defense against the three-on-two fast break: one man meets the ball seventeen feet out to force the pass, the other waits a few feet behind him, moving right or left depending on the pass. Jackson and I are closing. Their front guard assumes I've never seen Bix. I let the guard push me right. Their back guard starts to cheat toward Jackson. The front guard is now so sure the play is going right that he edges into the passing lane, hoping to deflect the ball, save his partner from taking a charge or getting a foul. Both of them are leaving too much space on the left. I turn my eyes toward Jackson. Without picking up my dribble, I flick the ball across my chest to the left. Not too fast. I know Bix will be there but not exactly where. Bix will be there and is there, stretching a little to catch the ball, taking his last big step knowing the back guard who has wanted Jackson will be too late to step in for the charge. Bix slams it home.

"For three seconds I know number 34 will be there. He knows I know. The defenders do not know. Number 34 and I have a secret." I hesitated just a fraction. "It is the future."

"Why do you show this?" Kappa asked. "We know these things. Pass to the man open. It is easy three-man on two-man break."

Kappa didn't want to be the point. He also didn't understand it. I didn't argue. It looked easy to Kappa because the defensive players had been encouraged to think it was going to be easy for them. I used their anticipation. The no-look pass at the end made the take-off easier for Bix and made the pass-off look more difficult for me.

OK, Kappa, put this in your eyes. I forwarded the tape to the last few seconds. Anyone can see it's close because the defense is in our shirts. We're running a double-low for our center, Franklin. The options break down. The ball comes back to me at the top of the key. Gates is overplaying me tight right. I go through my legs, right hand to left hand, making Gates lean to my left but when the ball hits my left I reverse to go by Gates right. Their other guard steps over and slaps at the ball but I'm picking it up and taking my long last stride toward the hoop. Their forwards stay home. Deny the pass, their coach has told them. Make Keever shoot and let Webster, their shot-blocking center, clean him up. Good thinking, except it does open up some space here. I'm in the air now, the ball in my right. Webster will be coming from my left. Come on, Web, this is what they pay you for. When he goes up, I'll show him what he wants, just a taste of the rock to keep him interested. Then I'll switch it to my left and slip it off to my center, Franklin. Never leave your feet with the ball unless you know what you'll do with it. All coaches agree. OK, here comes Web. But what's this? Web's been listening to his coach. He's jammed Franklin half out of bounds before coming to me. Let's see now. I'm going to need some more time. Web thinks he's going to cuff this one for sure. I bring the ball back toward my body with my right. Tuck it in my belly. It's OK, Coach. I know what I'm going to do. Create in the air. I turn my back into Web. Where that rock? Come on, Franklin, get your ass in bounds. I'm coming down now, my back to Web and Franklin. I can't see shit. Be there. With Web hanging over me, still looking for the ball, I lay off a blind bounce pass on the floor. I don't know it, but the tape shows Franklin taking it all alone and gently placing it in the hoop, a gesture more insulting than a jam to the shot-blocking center who's been had. Like Coach Jacobs used to say, "Bring 'em to you, fuck 'em up."

I stopped the tape. Koko could have caught that pass, if he'd been ready. Dop could have made the shot, if he'd moved to the open spot. Kappa never would have made the pass. He and everybody else in the room knew it.

"Deception," I said, and looked at Z to make sure he could translate. He was blank. I tried "deceiving." Dop filled in the Greek word.

I continued with simpler language: "I trick other players into a false future. My players know what I will really do."

I knew exactly what I was going to do. I'd push the button, restart the tape. The camera will show Lightning players slapping me on the back and slapping palms. The scoreboard light will be flashing. The camera will pan across fans clapping, cheering, shaking their heads. In the locker room, Z was smiling, the GM was beaming. Out on the floor, we started playing together.

Chapter 2

Our first game was at home, what Henderson called "The Pit," because it's a sixty-foot deep hole in the ground under one end of the Panathinaikos soccer "stadio." On the left as you walk in the only entrance are fifteen rows of concrete bleachers overhung by the soccer bleachers. More concrete bleachers are behind the baskets on both ends. On the other long side to the right is a forty-foot wall with large banks of windows and a few bathroom-sized fans that suck in the Nefos. At floor level are two metal chutes from the lockers to the benches. The wall, chutes, center circle, keys, and sidelines are all green, a shade lighter than the Celtic Kelly. The pit holds eight-thousand fewer fans than the Boston Garden's old sellout figure of 13,909, but without separate seats the six-thousand Greeks are packed tight like college crowds and are on top of the action.

That first night a team from Salonika tried to fast break with us and we blew them out early. That gave me freedom to turn on the high-li for the fans. With two minutes left in the half, we come down three on one—Kappa, me in the center, Henderson on the right. The one is their center. He's had a tough time with Henderson. He won't mind picking up a foul. Three on one should be an automatic layup, but when the defensive man is as big as this guy you might as well pull up and take the 90 percent jumper. Kappa and Henderson aren't pulling up. They're timing their final strides to the hoop. The center will want the ball to go to Kappa. About an eighty-pound weight difference. I'm looking straight at the center. He definitely prefers Kappa. The center tries to fake me by dipping his shoulder toward Henderson. I fake taking the fake. I pick up the ball with my right hand and start it behind my back. Henderson's covered, sneak it off to Kappa. The center lunges toward Kappa. I knew he would. I bring the ball back out from behind my back, still in my right hand. I bring it out and look in the center's face. Wrong choice. I flip the ball up in the air on Henderson's side. He's in full flight. To balance the act, he catches it like James Worthy used to, one hand, and throws it down. The center still knocks Kappa on his ass. I take a quick look at the crowd. They're on their feet and throwing their palms at the center. I thought all those extended palms with fingers spread were Greek high-fives but wondered why they were aimed at the guy who'd been had. When I asked Kappa at the half, he gave me the finger. "It is like this," he said, shoving his hand up into my face, "but with all fingers."

In the States fans usually responded to the high-li with something like wonder. The Greeks go for the effect, rub in the humiliation. They want victory first, action second, and a well-played game third. Greek fans are loyalists. They don't come to the pit because there's nothing else to do in Athens. They've chosen one of the city's six teams, and they come early to show their support, screaming insults at the visitors during introductions. When Lou translated the fans' chants, I knew the pit was no place to bring a date or wife. Most of the fans are men between eighteen and forty who act like soldiers or veterans. The boys wear green scarves on their legs and arms, flap green capes after baskets. Some of the men carry green flags they wave at timeouts. Even during our layup line, the fans are hunched forward on the cement, impatient for something to happen. In the pit, they have nothing but the game to excite them: no ball girls, cheerleaders, animal mascot, dancers, band, clever PA announcer, instant replay monitor, or flashing scoreboard. The players are the whole show, and the fans sound like they all have front-row seats. After a few more tricks in the second half, I could hear them chanting "lefkos magos, lefkos magos" every time I handled the ball.

In the locker, Lou translated: "They call you `white Magic.'" "'Key' in the States," I told him and asked what the Greek was for "key." "'Klethei,'" Lou said and spoke in Greek to some other players. They started laughing and calling me "Klee." It sounded like "glee," the player's final reward, winning the last game, the championship, what every athlete waits for, the reason Michael Jordan wept. Glee is something most men never know after Little League, the experience many women miss. They have happiness, pleasure, fun, even ecstasy in some movies I'd seen. But not glee. I'd felt it only once, this high key, the total release completely shared with players, coaches, fans, all jumping and hugging and dancing together on the Rockford floor. The tape is jiggled like one of those amateur disaster videos, but the memory is inside, not just at some synaptic intersection, but all over, a feeling just beneath my skin as if glee were a chemical injected to check my whole nervous system. After my first win in the pit, "Klee" was close to glee.

For the Keevers and Panathinaikos, the first half of the season was often glee. A Greek game is like a college game, two twenty-minute halves, and the Greek season is like a college year, split in the middle with a month-long Christmas vacation. That first semester we all enjoyed being away from home for the first time. Sara giggled at her schoolmates' strange names and laughed at her parents' fumbling pronunciation of the Greek she was learning at school and on the school bus. The weather stayed sunny and warm throughout the fall, so Ann walked the city's sites with her Blue Guide and rode to the beaches south of Athens. We ate on our balcony or at outdoor tavernas in the Plaka. In the evenings, we reported the day's oddities and errors, Ann's being asked for directions by an out-of-town Greek, my ordering well-done "pedakia"—children—instead of "piedakia," lamb chops. From Sara I learned the colors, and from the newspaper Ann discovered the Greek word for "word" was embedded in her last name. On Sundays we'd take a taxi to Mt. Penteli and eat lamb from the spit or go to Voulagmeni Beach and rent a paddleboat. Gesturing at the panorama—purple mountains surrounding the blue sea and new hotels—Ann used Drinkman's highest compliment: "This," she said, "is the resort league." We took a bus tour to Delphi, where the future looked bright, and a hydrofoil to Idra, which looked exactly like the white villages on the travel tape. Although the island didn't have enough level space for a gym or enough people to fill the pit, Ann wondered if I could be traded to Idra in the spring.

Panathinaikos opened up six and one, my individual stats were good, and I showed plenty of high-li on Greek TV. The owner was so pleased with my performance and attendance figures he wanted to give me more money. On payday in November, the GM whiffled my stack of 250 thousand-drachma bills through his machine and then counted them by hand. I liked being paid in cash. When I was a kid, I got my allowance counted into my palm on Saturday mornings. Since then money had become invisible—scholarships, direct deposit checking, the Memphis State Athletic Department's Mastercard. Drachmas are substantial, in your hand, in your pocket. After I put the money in my bag, the GM asked me if I'd consider changing my citizenship. The owner wanted to see one of his players on the national team, and I'd have a better shot if I made a commitment to Greece. Panathinaikos pride would be worth an extra ten thousand this year. Ten thousand dollars? Dollars. Five thousand in the bank now, five thousand more when I made the team. I told the GM I'd need some time to look into this.

I asked my all-purpose advisor, Vassilis the trainer. A lumpy guy about forty with every trainer's walk—that brisk, short-legged, almost-a-doctor strut—Vassilis had studied at NYU and spoke English I could trust, even if he did sometimes pronounce "i" like "e," turning "live" into "leave." And unlike Lou, whose English was just as good, Vassilis didn't need the ball. In the CBA, trainers have game responsibilities such as keeping the shot chart or screaming "three seconds" at the refs every three seconds. Although Vassilis did double-duty as caretaker of the pit, during a game he just sat on the bench and waited for somebody to get kneed in the nuts. I taught him to shoot iso tape, and he coached me in Greek. For Vassilis, language was physical, even the words themselves: the Greek word for language, "glossa," meant "tongue." The English word "physical" came from the Greek for "nature." While being taped up or rubbed down, I learned the referee's "me soma" meant "with the body," and that "muscle" came from the Greek "mys," the mouse moving beneath the skin.

"You would have a better chance to make the team," Vassilis said, "and it would be good for you next year, if you want to stay."

"I've been thinking about that. How does this citizenship change work anyway?"

"You don't become a Greek seeteezen overnight. I'll have to check for you, but I theenk you start the process by signing a paper that states you want to count the months you've been leaving here toward seetizenship."

"When would I have to turn in my passport?"

"Not for years. You just start the process."

"What if I change my mind later?"

"You change your mind. You'll steal be a Yankee."

The declaration looked like a "ween-ween" proposition to me, money in the bank, but it wasn't a matter I could discuss with Ann. I didn't want her looking too closely into just who was eligible for the national team. And since Lou and his American wife hadn't invited us to their place, there wasn't much chance Ann would find out. Vassilis translated the document for me and I took it to the Alien's Bureau. The office was as crowded as a trolley but the people in line were short, mostly Asians who were here to work as maids and houseboys in our neighborhood. For a tall Greek there's always room before the trolley doors slam shut.

My declaration must have been reported in newspapers neither Ann nor I could read because after practice one day not long afterwards, Vassilis told me that two college students were waiting outside to meet the future "seeteezen." They were officers of an ecology organization that wanted me to appear in a public service spot against pollution. The Nefos made me puke during the suicides, and Ann complained about it obscuring our balcony view of the sea behind the Acropolis, but I didn't know anything about ecology. "Then milou Ellenikah," I told them, "I don't speak Greek." This self-contradictory phrase usually put off people who babbled at Mikhalis Kyvernos, but Dimitri and Jorgos weren't discouraged. "We will run Greek words below you, like the movies," Dimitri said.

"Subtitles, you mean?"

"Yes." Subtitles were another advantage of living in Greece. A guy I knew in the CBA left an Italian team because all the American movies were dubbed. "You are perfect for us," Jorgos added. "Because you are a new star here, people will watch our program. They will listen to what you say because you have the same problems over in America. We need a new way to persuade citizens that we all have the same home." The group didn't have any money, but I thought "Be Like Mike" and agreed to help them out.

The filming took a morning. I stood in my green sweatsuit in front of some trees turned brown by acid rain and read the cue cards: "Trees are the planet's nervous system. 'Dendri' are dendrites. When the Nefos kills forests here in Greece or in America, the sea rises in Salonika. Like Miami, Salonika is one of the ten cities in the world most threatened by the greenhouse effect." Whoever wrote the script knew about playing the point. "We need to anticipate," I read, "not just a second or a minute ahead but two or three generations, the continuing story. We should visualize the Nefos floating up, spreading out, combining with other toxic clouds, diffusing and trapping heat all over the globe. We must imagine the future, what will come to pass: forests dying and burning, temperature rising, lakes evaporating, farms drying up, temperature rising, ice caps melting, sea water rising, shipping disrupted, temperature rising, lowlands flooding, water tables salinized, animals dying, people starving, temperature rising, cities disappearing, whole countries like the Maldives covered by the rising sea."

After these lines, we moved to high ground, the Parthenon museum. I stood in front of a glass case holding statues of five gift-bearing maidens whose faces had been eaten away by auto exhaust. I had some trouble pronouncing "caryatids" but finally got it right: "These caryatids stood outside for twenty-five hundred years. Then only fifty years of pollution almost destroyed them. Now they can exist only in this greenhouse within this museum. To prevent the same thing from happening to us, it is not enough to fix our machines, consume less, conserve our resources, use our Greek sun. We must change our idea of the planet. We should remember our past, when we gave the world 'climate' and 'atmosphere' and the ancient word for home: 'eco.' In the future, we must think of the whole planet—the sea and air and earth—as our home."

For those last two words, I used the Greek: "Spiti Mas," the name of the group. Only after pronouncing the words did I realize that "spiti" was in "hospitality:" our home is your home. And it was only after Dimitri told me he'd send me a tape for my family that I thought about my own maiden, Sara, and her distant future. According to "Spiti Mas," it would be different, warmer, hot. Not even Ann, with her long-term plans, forecast this future, a time when people, like the statues, would exist in a glass house. That night I found a strange poorly edited tape running in my head. An elderly woman and a little girl were sitting on a bench. It might have been Dexameni, where I waited for Sara's school bus and watched her ride her bike, but the Acropolis wasn't in the background. The little old lady dressed in black was called Sara by the girl who was Sara. The tape was gray and slow. The background was fuzzy. The weather wasn't clear. I wasn't in the picture, yet I could see the old woman and little girl were sweating in this setting. They were just sitting there, but their faces were covered with sweat. The grandmother and girl looked stuck to the bench, unable to escape the heat. The tape was over before they could get up and leave.

The actual female Keevers liked the tape Dimitri sent for our preview. To Ann, I was protecting an ancient site Greeks had let deteriorate. "That was good on the caryatids," she said, "but the cameraman should have shot that black grime on all the under surfaces of the Parthenon." Sara congratulated me on my "spiti" and asked me to say "our milk," which had an impossible Greek "g" between "gala" and "y'all." But between the private viewing and the first showing on TV just before Christmas, the weather had changed.

"When do you expect global warming to reach Athens?" Ann asked, rubbing her hands together and then sticking them under my armpits. With her brown hair, hazel eyes, and dark complexion, Ann looked more like a native than I did, and she was better suited to the summer heat. I could feel her hands trembling under my arms. I pulled her up close for more warmth.

"I spoke to the concierge. He held up three fingers. Lou said it's the same in all apartments. Radiators come on three times a day. Maybe Santa will bring you something electric from far away."

"I'd like to go far away. After Christmas, let's use some of your bonus dollars and go somewhere hot. We could go to Kenya and get on one of those big game tours. I saw them on CNN. You can bring a rifle or a camcorder."

"They must be big games," I said, "if fans bring guns to the gyms."

"Not games. Game. Big animals. Sara would like that kind of trip."

"Can't do it, Ann. The bonus is deep in the basement of a Zurich bank. The money doesn't reach street level until June, when the Greeks pick their new national team."

"In June it will be hot and we can go to the islands," she said, snuggling back against me.

"What about my service to the nation?"

"I don't understand how you can play for Greece."

"I live here. Another four years and I can play in the Olympics."

"We'll be long gone by then, and you'll be long over the hill too."

"Twenty-two games and a month-long halftime could extend my career. You could still be walking up the hill with the plastic sacks."

I wanted to kid Ann out of an argument. But she pulled away again and put her hands in her pockets. Her nose was red.

"Do you think we could find a heated apartment that also has a phone next year?"

I opened my eyes wide, held my partially closed right hand at belt level, and twisted it to the right, the approximate motion of turning a key. It's Greek for "What's happening here?"

"I'm serious, Michael. I can't even enjoy the view when I know the little heat we get is leaking out the glass doors. I don't believe I'd want to spend another winter here. I've never been so cold in my life. What about you?"

"Eighteen years in Vermont."

"I mean would you want to stay another year?"

"It has crossed my mind. We're nine and two. I'm meeting all the escalators."

"I'm happy for you. I'm happy for us. But what is it you like outside the gym?"

"The short trips, sleeping in my own bed, an afternoon nap, hanging out at the café, watching people on the streets. I'll have to check my tape. Get back to me next year."

"It's not a long list, but with basketball it should last you six months."

I didn't say anything more. While I was counting up my stats, Ann was figuring her own numbers. Five years were out of the question. With Panathinaikos winning, I'd been thinking eighteen months but hadn't said anything. Now it sounded like Ann was counting down. Her glumness might be seasonal: we had to buy a plastic tree, the turkey came with instructions for boiling, Ann couldn't hum along with Greek carols, she missed her family. Ann also wasn't used to home life in immigrant housing. When I was in the CBA, she made the money and I worked part-time. She wrote the lists and I went to Kroger's. Even my travel confirmed her independence, her ability to organize and schedule, her capacity to live almost alone. I didn't like the travel, but a player's life gave me lots of hours with Sara. For us, quality time was play time. At first, I didn't let Sara out of my hands. I'd hold her on my lap and buzz bomb food into her mouth. I perfected a two-hand diaper change without bassinet. If she was cranky, I'd lie on my back and fly her through the air like Superman. When she was walking, she'd help make the beds, we'd steer the shopping cart together, and then check out the best sandboxes and swings. "Push hard, Daddy," Sara used to say, "run underneath." I taught Sara how to make peanut butter and jelly sandwiches with one knife. We did numbers and colors throwing the laundry into separate baskets. We spent hours looking through her *Waldo* books, finding the right guy in a crowd.

I believe the family that plays together stays together. Here Sara and I spend a lot of time with each other. So do Ann and Sara. But Ann and I have less to do now that Athens has moved indoors. The museums were too quiet the first time through, the copies of *Sports Illustrated* at the American Library are a month old, and Ann and I never have agreed on movies. There's body heat in our short Greek bed, but the rest of the apartment is uncomfortable. The electric radiator will help. Next year, with plenty of time to look, we should be able to find a better place. If it doesn't have a phone, I'll buy Ann a cellular with our extra money. Next Christmas we'd definitely afford Kenya. But conveniences alone won't persuade Ann. We'll have plenty in the bank for a down payment. When we talk again about next season, she will want a longer list, reasons why I want to stay lined up like items in a recipe.

The next afternoon, while I sat in the sun at Dexameni and watched Sara ride her bike, I thought I should remind Ann of how good Athens is for Sara, meeting kids from other countries at the American Community School, making friends in Greek, catching the Parthenon out of the corner of her eye. What difference does it make, I wondered, that Sara sees that stacked marble every day. It is old, very old. It is, according to Ann, precisely constructed and beautiful. Its sculptures tell a story. It's a wonder of the world. So was the Astrodome until the superdomes came along. But even I know the Parthenon is different. That is the difference. It's one of a kind, passed down from the past. Up on the Acropolis with "Spiti Mas," I realized the building is a gift, something to give. What other five-year-old in Memphis or Rockford has ridden her bike in Dexameni, churning her short legs, concentrating on her balance, glancing ahead for danger, taking a quick look at Dad, maybe telling herself what other kids are saying about her blue-and-white beauty but never thinking about the building in front of her, now off to her left, now behind her, now out to her right, a distant place of no interest, a building you can't walk into, though a place from which we could see our home. For Sara, the Parthenon is only briefly framed between rows of apartment houses as she rides back and forth on her training wheels, but it's permanent, will always be there on her brain tape, something special to be picked out from the crowds of memories at ten, at twenty, at forty and eighty as Sara's years double, a thin slice of difference that will last long after that other gift is being ridden by some Aleka or Nikos, even less aware of the building they first saw when their mothers or au pairs wheeled their strollers through Dexameni. Sara will have her fingerprints, voice print, genetic blueprint, all the prints. I want her to have pictures inside, stills of the Parthenon, tape of her bike rides.

It's the difference I like. It's Greece's gift: "diafora." I'm different to the players and fans. The difference makes a difference. I'm successful, the team's successful. The US is overrun with six-three white guards. In Greece I'm a rarity, a phenomenon, a Greek word I'd just read in the *Athens News*.

I'd like to keep giving Sara the Greek difference. It's something I've learned from the Greeks. They're always giving each other gifts—birthdays and name days, whenever they visit each other, when they eat together. Lou says a child is a gift. The Greeks don't like to give up the ball, but I think they love their children more than we do. Wherever you go in Athens, there's a toy store on every block. And two sweet shops. Mothers in Dexameni cajole their children to eat little cakes and pies before dinner. A thin child is a scandal. Koko is sending his eight-year-old to an Italian tutor so he can join the family business, rent paddleboats to summer tourists. I wonder if Sara feels the difference, sees kids her age being carressed and kissed and cooed over when they return from a thirty-second walk to the jungle gym. Nothing puts pleasure on a Greek face like the sight of a small child. A relative is best but any child lights up the grandmothers and grandfathers. Mothers and their teenage sons hold hands in public. The boys don't look embarrassed. Middle-aged men and women are routinely called "pedi-mou," my child. Greeks hug their children close. They gave me, a supposed grandchild, a chance to come home.

I feel safe in Athens, safer than in Rockford or Memphis, small as they are. Terrorism was our American friends' favorite theme before we left. They think the Mediterranean is like the Ohio River, that Beirut is a bridge south of Athens. If you stay alert in the crosswalks, there's nothing to fear in our neighborhood. Old ladies and young girls walk home alone from the cafes or movies at midnight. Ann likes this about Athens. An earthquake might destroy the city, but I won't be strangled, clubbed, stabbed, or shot for the drachmas in my pocket or the expensive Cons on my feet. Sara won't be molested, raped, or kidnapped if her uncertain steering takes her out of my sight or I drowse off in the sun. The *Athens News* reports such crimes in this huge city as if it was a small-town newspaper and the events were incredible, impossible here.

Athens is a place. That's what I'll have to make Ann feel to stay next year. I know: every place is someplace, even if it's called Quad Cities and has a franchise named the Thunder. My hometown is a place, a presidential preserve, all sharp white clapboards and maple trees. A house, a store, a church, a cheese factory, and a parking lot with cars from Massachusetts, Connecticut, and New York. Even in Vermont's one-month summer, Plymouth is hushed, as if tourists came to the birth-place from the graveyard, humbled and quieted by Cal's simple Vermont marble marker. After five in the afternoon, you might as well be in the cemetery. House, store, church, and cheese factory are the buildings in this place. Like the gravestones, they're all identified by signs. Nobody needs a map. During the four years I spent in Memphis, I never saw anyone walking with a map. Who would visit unless they had to?

Athens is a place with people, five million natives, map-readers from all over the world. They find their way here every season. On the coldest winter day, some Australians or South Africans will be looking at the compass in Syntagma Square, orienting themselves, using one day of their summer vacation to run cold fingers over their maps, the strange words and zigzag streets that will take them up to the Acropolis. It draws a crowd, every day, every hour. From my balcony, I watch the crowds through my zoom. They walk around and around the Parthenon. Then they stand at the retaining wall and look out over the rest of the world. On a December Tuesday night, every Plaka taverna has some tourists writing postcards, including one Japanese couple looking at their guidebooks written in characters even stranger than Greek. On winter Sunday afternoons, when all Athenians are asleep and I can cross any street without a light, I know that in two hours the Greeks will be back, rushing some-where, making noise. Ride through downtown Memphis on a summer Sunday afternoon and you might just as well be in Spring Grove cemetery. The wide streets and parking lots with-out cars make me feel hollow, empty, alone even if Ann and Sara are in the car. In Athens I never feel lonely, no matter how much time I spend by myself. For reasons I don't understand and will never be able to explain to Ann, in Athens—no matter how cold it is inside or outside—I feel at home.

Chapter 3

After New Year's, Ann spent mornings trying to keep warm at the American Library and I went to Valtadoros Cafe, my halftime home away from home, a five-minute walk from our apartment. Wait for Achilleas the waiter, order your orange juice and coffee, wait for your order, read the paper, wait for the grounds to settle, check out the people around you, sip the coffee, drink a little water, wait for the concentrated caffeine rush inside, watch the people passing by. Ann and I had often discussed the clothes of passersby, guessed at their occupations, and speculated about their relationships. Sitting by myself, I collect Greek heads—round ones with full cheeks and lips, faces with high cheekbones and jaws with complicated lines and angles. I'm a secret admirer of eyebrows—the wild gray brush roaming the foreheads of older men, magic marker slashes of black, thick natural arches on teenage girls before plucking and penciling, the eyelid-hugging growth of young Greek men who look like PLO agents.

In Rockford, I was just another tallish blonde guy, maybe all-American and all-CBA but rarely recognized on the sidewalk or at the mall. In the NBA, stars over six-two can't leave their hotel rooms without disguises. But in Greece fans treat players the way Americans respond to local TV personalities, people you can approach and talk to about something more than last night's game. One day a woman sitting next to me at Valtadoros asked why there were so many public clocks in the States; I couldn't answer but we talked it over. A café regular, a guy about fifty who looks a little like Telly Savalas, asks my opinion of movies, action flicks and spy stories that I'd seen in the States and that were just arriving in Greece. Sometimes kids and other fans ask for an autograph, so I was learning how to sign in Greek.

One morning in early January I noticed more people than usual in the café, as if it was a holiday. Greeks all around me were toasting each other with their water glasses. I was just finishing the sports section of the *Athens News* when a woman about my age walked up to my table, pointed at the paper, and said "Whussup at home?"

She looked Greek—short, the same dark skin as Kappa, large brown eyes under brows that almost met, a couple of moles on her left cheek, vertical crinkles next to her mouth that appeared to be permanent laugh lines—but her close-clipped black hair bristled like an American punk's and her first run-together words sounded like Henderson.

"Rockets in the West, Bullets in the East."

"How about the Pacers?"

"Reggie's hurt. They're at .500."

"We need a point, too."

"Tell me you're a scout," I said, "and you've come to take me to the League."

"I am a scout," she said, the crinkles becoming a grin, "a talent scout and basketball fan. I was told I might find you here. Do you have time to talk about making an ad for a camcorder?"

"T.V. Danny" Cater, I thought, my main man. Eleni Epimenidakis introduced herself, a Greek-American from Indianapolis who did freelance writing and production work in Athens. She'd just seen the "Spiti Mas" spot and wanted to use me in another television ad, which would feature Greek-American celebrities who had returned to the homeland, all praising the American-made camera. It wasn't my brand, but I could retrain Vassilis with the new model. Eleni said I wouldn't have to praise Greece, just the camera. I told her I hoped to stay another year, and we exchanged stories about living here. She thought the screaming, arm-waving fanatics in Greek gyms were amusing, but she, like Henderson and me, hated the fog of cigarette smoke that settled over the court in the second half. Eleni made fun of natives she'd worked for, their suspicion of MTV cutting. "Even car ads they want covered with tinkling folk music and solemn spokesmen," she said. The camcorder ad would be different: a team of young repatriates, lots of slash and flash. When she asked about personal details she might use in my segment, I told her that my grandfather had changed his name from Kyvernos to Keever when he first came over, that my father never spoke the language, and that I didn't know a single Greek when I was growing up in Vermont.

"The Green Mountain State," she said, "you must have had plenty of water there?"

"When it wasn't ice and snow. Why?"

"We're going to have a problem here. Do you see fine red sand on your balcony in the morning?"

"Some days," I said.

"It blows here from North Africa. Greece is turning into a desert."

It had drizzled only a couple of times since we'd arrived, but I thought this was a joke. Spiti Mas hadn't said anything about a drought. I told Eleni we'd both be in the ground before the dust piled up into dunes.

"I'm not kidding. The farms and villages flooded for Athens reservoirs are reappearing. I've seen film. The government keeps it a secret. No water to drink. It's the tourist nightmare, worse than diarrhea. That's the reason you don't read about it."

She nodded at my copy of the *Athens News*. "Don't frighten away the tourists. But soon officials will admit there'll be a water shortage during the summer. So tourists can shower after the beach, we'll have to buy bottled water. One American to another: I'm betting there'll be hoarding. I thought you'd want to know."

I thanked Eleni for the warning and turned the conversation back to the camcorder ad. More people knew Jordan from Nike ads than from NBA telecasts, and Shaq's commercial income is supplemented by his actual salary. With me in the fold, Eleni said, she'd start contacting other returnees she knew about. "Half the cabinet was educated in the States and came back here," she told me.

When Eleni got up to leave, she asked, "Do you know Dexameni?"

"It's on my way home."

"If we walk over there now, we can see a yearly Greek comedy." She grinned again and said "Yes, the traditional method of solving our water problem."

A thousand people were milling around in little Dexameni when we got there just before noon. Cameramen, photographers, men in suits and ties, Kolonaki matrons in their furs, plus the usual grandmothers, mothers, au pairs, and preschoolers. No soccer game, no bike riding today. The open space was jammed. Women stood on benches. Two men were sitting on the jungle gym. Kids were on tree limbs. We stood out on the sidewalk and looked in.

"Up there," Eleni pointed to a wall at the high end of the park, "is the central Athens pumping station."

Sara and I and Ann were in Dexameni almost every day, but the pumping station made no sound. The crowd pressed up toward the wall and began to quiet. A bald man in a suit made a short speech. "The mayor," Eleni said. Then an old bearded priest in a long black robe climbed up steps in the wall. When he reached the top, he faced the crowd and stood still. The people blessed themselves in unison, up, down, right, left. An altarboy handed the priest a container of incense on a chain. The priest turned and made some passes over the cement station. He turned back and swung the incense over the still, heads-down crowd. The incense floated out to us at the edge of the crowd, a sweet cloud. I was impressed. This was the quietest I'd ever seen a Greek crowd.

"To insure our future water supply," Eleni whispered to me out of the side of her mouth, "the mayor enlists the priest to mumble ancient prayers and pollute the air with incense. This is our Epiphany." She made a small mocking sound, like the English "pshaw" I'd heard in movies. "Greeks are priest-ridden," she went on whispering, "like those other island people, the Irish." Then Eleni turned toward me and spoke a little louder.

"But these things you must know from your Celtic background."

Eleni pronounced "Celtic" with two hard "c's." When I heard "Keltik," with the same "k" that begins Keever, I felt something in my face move but I didn't say anything about her pronunciation. Walking to the apartment, I thought "Keltik" could be Greek-influenced English for the Boston Celtics, except that Eleni's speech was perfect and she knew the NBA. Watching the news on TV that evening, I saw tape of the priest and people in Dexameni, tape of other priests around the country throwing crosses into the sea from island quais, the docks of Piraeus, the piers of Patras, the seawalk in Salonika. Into the water dove some healthy young man, who grabbed the cross, climbed out, and handed it back to the priest. Except for the shivering diver, everybody on the tape was smiling and laughing, crowding in on the priest and cross, packing the screen tight like a championship team huddling around the coach and trophy. Except for the swimming, I thought, they are doing the same thing in Ireland, blessing the seas they'll fish in, the water that will become stout, the rain that will keep their island green and the tourists coming. Eleni's "Keltik" could refer to the many Irish-Americans in Boston where I first went to college. Or perhaps, I tried to tell myself, the mispronunciation was a mockery of Greeks' English by a Greek-American, some kind of inside joke like her parody of "What's up?" Or "Keltik" might be what I couldn't avoid: a language test for citizen Kyvernos, University of Greece freshman recruit supposedly on vacation, the worst kind of test to not pass, the examination that determines second semester eligibility and threatens the scholar-athlete's full ride.

Eleni's "Keltik" was a single word with a crowd of meanings, mysterious intentions, unpredictable effects. I didn't know how much my face had revealed, how quick her eyes were, what she already knew about me, how much she could find out about my background. Figuring where I stood was like multiplying positives and negatives: no matter how I arranged possibilities, the answer was always negative. Trying to calculate future probabilities was as complicated as the inside basketball I'd never been able to explain to Ann. When she instructed me in painting, she'd say, while staring at an eight-foot square canvas that looked like a dropcloth, "You have to see the composition." I'd tell her not to watch me and the ball. Watch the composition, the patterns. But five greens and five reds or blues or yellows, plus two guys in grey, one or two blacks, and the Kyvernos towhead aren't composition to her, not even on the VCR. She watches the ball move from man to man, connecting the dots like Sara's pencil tip moving from one to two to three to four and on until a cartoon figure emerges from the numbers. I try to explain how to look with the example of biology and geography textbooks, their plastic transparencies, thin-cut slices of life adding up to a whole. "Think of the action as overlays you're looking at and through, overlays that change as fast as pages being riffled." Nope. For Ann, books are to read, not view.

Probably no fan sees the overlays from a seat outside and above the court. Coaches on the bench, players in the trenches—they don't see them either. Only the number one guard coming into the front court has to face the overlays head on, a series of receding panes that ends with the glass backboard. My four players and their five players are all moving in different planes and between planes, all at different speeds, all relative to each other, some toward me, some away from me. They all have different bodies—sizes, weights, strength, and spring. All have different skills and their own personal histories, taped and live. At the head of all these alls, my many brains all at once perceive the pattern and juggle conceivable combinations, possible competitions, probable deceptions, and plausible decisions. A tenth of a second later, I do it all over again, rearrange the balls in mental air, recompose the whole, recalculate the time passed, the time left, the new positions, the now places. But my brains are not through yet. They have to turn the fan's perception inside-out. My eyes follow objects but look for nothing, gaps and holes, the transparencies the ball must pass through, the open space to the open man. These connections, reconnections, and disconnections are too numerous and too fast for rules. A moving mainframe would be a second late. The best robot ever designed would never get off the bench. Inside my head, it's all filmy memory, fuzzy logic, informed estimation, exact guesswork, lightning brainwork, a million times faster than the sprinter's footwork. "Low lying and high flying, rooted in pure perception and able to cruise over the forest," my Athlete's Body professor said about the athlete's mind. I have to preserve some dumbness to see and feel the whole from inside. I have to trust my collaborating brains to make the future happen. In all this complexity, happening all the time and going to happen all the time, all I know for sure from tenth to tenth is that it's *my* guesswork, that my smallest decision will have huge effects, and that in the moving transparencies and in the crowd all are waiting and will be waiting for me to choose where and when and how the ball I possess will move and change all the composition.

"The game is like a whole gallery in motion," I used to tell Ann, only half kidding.

"It may be difficult," she'd say, "but it's not art."

"It's better than art. Twenty ballerinas tiptoeing across stage you call art. Some of them can get up. But they're following the script. They all know where they're going. There's no conflict. Half of them aren't trying to stop the other half from putting their noses in the air and taking off. The crowd isn't screaming 'Fall down, bitches.'"

Now I felt the overlays could be anywhere, nowhere, or everywhere, extended to whatever horizon stopped my eyes. So far there was only one probable opponent, but since Eleni could emerge from any plane at any time and make me take a fall she was like a crowd of threats, just as she was a crowd of different people—Greek and American, white and black, funny and serious—when she first walked up to my table. Avoid contact was my first inclination: stop going to Valtadoros, walk

45

alternate routes to the pit, rent another apartment. But avoiding Eleni was impossible: my movements were scheduled, fans dropped into the pit to watch us practice, strangers somehow got into the locker room after games. Besides, I quickly decided, I wanted her to think I was oblivious to her threat. How could she know my face didn't move out of embarrassment for her mispronunciation? I wondered if this strategy was really dumb, but I couldn't think of anything else to do except start scanning faces in the crowd, on the sidewalks, off to my left, out to my right, even behind me with those eyes players said I had in the back of my head. Looking into Kolonaki shop windows at clothes I couldn't afford even with my bonus, I used the glass like a giant screen of the street and sidewalk in back of me. When Eleni did pop out, I wanted to see her first and get my game face on.

Our first game back was against a Piraeus team I'd picked apart and we'd beaten by ten in October. In the pit we were tied after twenty minutes. In the second half, they played zone to slow our break, collapsed on Henderson inside, covered Lou and Pop, and left me alone at the top of the key, just above the three-point circle, a few inches farther out than the college arc and considerably inside the NBA line. OK, Kyvernos, let's see if you're really Greek. When I hit four in a row, three of them three-pointers, Olympiakos came out with token pressure. I missed one, hit two more from the same spot for sixteen points, and we won by five.

Nobody was celebrating in the locker. Z said Olympiakos should never have been that close, not in our building. Kappa looked through me as if I'd had fifteen turnovers. Dop told me "great game" in a sarcastic tone. "Good shooting," Lou said. He was the shooter's coach. If he'd been in charge of naming the sport, "basket" would be volleyball since that net game has the Greek word for "shoot" in it. Lou was a serious man, formal for an athlete. Although his wife was American, he never used contractions. I'd never talked to a thinking shooter in the States. What was there to think about: the hoop was always in the same place, ten feet above the floor, up there over the traffic, the moving picket fence of arms and legs I had to compute from one tenth of a second to the next. Lou was an absolutist. He believed in the immobile object, the static goal, the absolute hoop, the true shot, *the* shooter, himself.

"I don't get it," I told him. "I go nine for twelve, we win, and some of the guys are pissed. I had to take those shots. Olympiakos was daring me to. You must have seen that."

"If no one else is open, you have to shoot."

"Then why are Dop and Kappa pissed?"

"Perhaps they feel you did not try hard enough to find open men."

"The zone was shutting off everything but me. And I was wide open. Everybody can't shoot every game. Dop wants his twelve. Everybody wants twelve."

"Of course," Lou said. "In Greece everyone must shoot."

"Everybody wants to shoot."

"No. Everyone must shoot. In football, only a few players are close enough to shoot. In basketball, everyone can shoot, so everyone must shoot."

"Even if it means losing games?"

"Sometimes this happens," Lou said with a shrug. "We are paid to score points. Your job is to see the open man."

First I thought this was Greek shooter's logic reappearing from training camp after a month layoff: the open man should shoot as long as he's not one of the shooter's teammates. Then I wondered if I'd concentrated too much on the hoop, on myself, if Eleni's shadow in the point's peripheral vision had squeezed it, narrowed the lines of sight.

My job was to see everything and hold everybody together, but I felt the team was breaking up. The next game was another win, and I had fifteen assists, five of them alley-oops to Henderson. But afterwards Koko came over to my locker and bitched that he was getting fewer minutes because he couldn't handle my passes. I told Koko he was playing less because I couldn't hear Z's defensive instructions over the noise of Koko's creaking knees. "Yes, too much fast break." At least Henderson should be happy with the buckets. I tried again to break through the steroid stare that was his pregame, game, and postgame face.

"You're going to be the next 'Mailman,'" I said, referring to the Utah Jazz's Karl Malone, All-Star and Dream-Teamer.

"That mean you're the next Stockton? That skinny white dude more like a stockboy, bringing the goods to the big fella."

"That white boy leads the league in assists every year."

"And who is it that gets him the ball? The big brothers."

Henderson was as proud and remote as Lou, even if the brother was here alone and living in a hotel. Rebounder's attitude, shooter's pride: I was supposed to tolerate them, connect them, and use them. But my job was becoming more difficult, maybe because all this former "Keltik" really wanted was to be "in the zone," the shooter's term for a world without consciousness or conscience. I'd been there just a couple of times. It's like playing on a planet with an atmosphere of helium and laughing gas. In the zone you don't have a single worry. Eleni wouldn't exist. The man playing you is a "foo." Your brain is like the appendix, a vestigial organ not needed by eyes and hands. The Spalding feels as light as an office Nerf ball. The basket looks six feet wide, its center as large as a manhole. In fact, Matera's tape measures taught us, the hoop is eighteen inches across. The facts are irrelevant because all your shots are in, the ball finding the center over and over. When someone's in the zone, long shots are so perfectly arched and bullseyed that the net tries to turn itself inside out. Shorter shots settle delicately, hesitating before dropping to the floor. The nets tell the story. "Swish" is sissy, white. I learned the new sounds of shooting when I spent a summer in Boston doing remedial work, Black Basketball I. On a power move, the jammers cried "whomp" as they threw it down. The guards called "wick" as the ball left their hands, predicting the whispered descent through the net and the click of the afterbounce on the Roxbury cement.

Every game has its precisions. To wick from twenty-five feet—jump a foot or two in the air, see through the defender's hand, absorb the body brush below, throw a twenty-one-ounce ball ten feet above its target and have it drop through with four-and-a-half-inch clearance on every side—is a basketball mystery. Lou is right about that. I want him to appreciate that a point can never be "in" the same way. He can be as quick as Muggsy Bogues. He can be a dolphin with sonar, but at least one other player has to be in his zone simultaneously, getting position, timing the cuts, bouncing back the sonar, catching the ball, finishing the play. Lou's shot is ancient, Olympians throwing the javelin, heaving the discus, putting the shot. It's mechanical, all levers and pulleys. So is Henderson's rebounding, Greco-Roman tag-team wrestling. Passing is electronic, like bouncing a transatlantic call off a satellite. If the person on the other end isn't "in," the ball might as well be sent into outer space. One wrong digit and you've made an expensive mistake. Henderson should be able to admit that, even if, like

John Stockton, I am white. I've never heard the right name for this dual "in." Kellogg called it "execution;" it sounded like killing. Cater said "synergy," but couldn't explain it. More mysterious than the "wick," maybe passing should be called the "with."

Just when I needed some "with" at home, Ann wanted to have a conversation about conversation, a sure sign of unhappiness. In the States, Ann made her living by listening and talking. When we first met, she didn't understand how I could spend hours watching silent tape of myself. "An exhibit for the archives of narcissism," she called the iso. It wasn't personal, I used to tell her, and quoted Coach Cater: "Language is what people used before they invented videotape." In Rockford Ann worked as a consultant on women in the new workplace, former secretaries driving trucks, waitresses raking parks. She talked eight hours a day, then came home and yammered long-distance with her sisters. "Without talk," she'd tell me, "there's no understanding, no thinking." After years of watching me watch tape, Ann finally admitted video is a form of thinking, the sophisticated work of the chimpanzee mind. I told her someone has to remember our beginnings. What about our advances, she said, counting her fingers. I told her I can do two things at once: watch tape and listen to her. She said I need the tape to give me time to say something funny. I accused her of filling up airtime so I don't have an opening to say something funny. She said my jokes don't say anything anyway. "My point exactly," I told her.

That was not the kind of conversation Ann needed in Athens. In the evenings last fall, after Sara and her simple, silly questions—"Daddy, why do Greeks speak Greek? Why are the numbers the same but the number words different?"—were put to bed, Ann and I used to talk about how odd it was to be sitting out on our balcony, looking at the floodlighted Parthenon and listening to CNN from inside the apartment. Back then we discussed how strange Greeks were, their musical auto horns and cackled consonants, the way men tucked in their tee shirts like basketball players. We noticed that we noticed unusual things here—that the guy at the kiosk throws down change instead of handing it to us, that Greek men don't cross their legs when sitting, that Greek women wear higher heels than American women. But exchanged perceptions were no longer enough. Ann's mind and mouth needed different exercise, something more challenging. The expected conversation about next year would never take place. I wished I could ask Ann to analyze Eleni's "Keltik," but that word had to remain silent. If my secret reached Ann, I'd be the one talking to myself. As cold as Ann's hands and feet were, she'd take Sara back to Memphis if the real meaning of "Kyvernos" got out. Ann had almost no way of suspecting what Drink and I had done because we had no social life. For some reason, Lou was keeping his American wife hidden in a distant suburb. Henderson was no conversationalist.

"Why don't you solve both your problems by getting out and finding a job?" I suggested. "Something in a heated office."

She responded by picking up the newspaper and reading the want ads: "Filipina needed three days a week." "Beautiful English-speaking woman required for bar." "Secretary wanted speaking Greek and Arabic."

"How about the Library?"

"I checked there last week. They already have more employees than books."

"You could volunteer at Sara's school."

"They don't allow adults on the bus."

"Give English lessons at home. I've seen ads in the paper. 'Honors graduate of Memphis State University. Husband of Greek Key.' That should bring 'em to you."

"You don't understand, Michael. I don't want to teach someone how to speak. I want to find someone who knows how to speak. Someone to whom I can say 'Pillsbury dough-boy' and not have to explain both words."

"Check out the tourist shops in Monistiraki. You've seen the ropers they use to bring in customers. You might meet some interesting people. You might even get to use your French."

Shopowners wanted to hire her. Did she have an EEC passport? No. Did she have a work permit? No. She would then be willing to work under the table for a dollar an hour? No. After talking with three Greek men in leather jackets and tasseled loafers, Ann came back home and we had another conversation, this time about natives trying to take advantage of an American.

"Tourists can walk in and walk out," Ann said, "but those assholes thought I was desperate. Tourists get cheated once. It was going to happen to me every day."

I sympathized with Ann but couldn't think of a job she might get. I asked her to come with the team to Salonika. No thanks. Since it was in the north, it was sure to be colder than Athens. The GBA didn't have a team in Crete. Like a benched player, Ann would just have to pull on her sweats and wait for the sun she knew was coming. My problem was more pressing, the solution less certain: at any moment I might be stripped of my uniform, thrown off the team, and tossed out of the country, if we had enough money to leave.

We won the game in Salonika and another one in Piraeus, but I couldn't catch a break in Athens. As Eleni had predicted, the front page of the *Athens News* started carrying a large box with remaining days of water in the city's up-country reservoirs. The numbers were like a pre-Christmas countdown: drinking days left before death, playing days before Eleni showed up. When the stats appeared we were at thirty-five, and I wondered why "Spiti Mas" was against acid rain, why they hadn't warned us about this drought. "Dehydration," Vassilis said, was a Greek word, bad for the muscles and nerves. At home we started flushing less, taking fewer showers, wearing clothes longer, and watering the plants with rinse water. Water bills tripled as a disincentive. Although a law was passed against hosing sidewalks and washing cars, Greeks ran their hoses late at night. Officials were talking about desalinization, but the islands had plenty of water. Other cities also had drinking water. Athens was the exception, a cement-covered desert.

Ann was stockpiling bottled water, but nobody could do anything about the power lines. Covered with dust that rain usually washed off, the lines couldn't carry enough electricity. Neighborhoods around the city were experiencing random brownouts and cutoffs. Computers and cash-registers went down. Banks and offices had to close. Kolonaki's jewelers couldn't shine their high-intensity spots on the gems. Traffic lights were out and electric trolleys died in the street, creating massive jams, forcing people out of cars and buses onto the sidewalks, adding to the crowds already there. Ann and Sara were afraid to use the elevator, so it was five flights up. Some evenings Sara couldn't watch "The Brady Bunch," and Ann couldn't read. Even the lights illuminating the Parthenon went out one night. Ann sat in our candlelight, pointed out at the darkened Acropolis, and said, "Welcome to the Third World."

I think this comment was supposed to initiate a conversation. I didn't respond because of another secret I couldn't tell Ann. Athletes insist on staying warm, but these new conditions had a strange appeal. Walking back and forth to the pit, strolling around the city center, watching downtown businesses empty out Greeks, I felt safe inside the new masses of people, somehow hidden from Eleni's view. Like basketball action, the city's surprises kept my mind off the threat of exposure. When Drinkman was selling me, he'd called Athens "the center of the world." With water and electricity running low, with crowds jostling in the streets, Athens seemed like the end of the world, and I felt like an athlete outside, as well as inside, the gym.

Chapter 4

Traveling is almost never called in the GBA. You're up taking away the three and the man you're guarding does a little two-foot hop to get the shot away. Or he goes to the hoop, you time his release, and he takes a third step away from you to put up an ugly wrong-foot kiss. A double or triple-feature of tape didn't help anticipate the international runway, the extra step needed for white flight. Henderson enforced American rules by leveling any Greek who came skipping into his neighborhood. "Stand off my kitchen," he growled while the "GR," as he called Greeks, checked his limbs.

About most of the distances Panathinaikos traveled Drinkman had been right: a short bus ride to our games in Athens and Piraeus, an hour's flight up to Salonika. Our one trip this year to Patras would get me out of Eleni's range and give me a break from Ann's irritation, but I didn't know it was going to be a six-hour train ride in seats made for people without legs. Lou and Pop were sitting together when I got on. I kept hearing "balla," so it must have been a shooter's discussion. Koko and Henderson had their backgammon board. "I fuck you now," I heard Koko say. Henderson was doing him some good. Dop was reading. I sat with Kappa. The two kids, T and Jorgos, walked up and down the aisle. Kappa was flicking his worry beads in a pattern I recognized as excitement. I asked Kappa if he was looking forward to Patras.

"Yes. We have fun there. Many sailors come to Patras. Many women."

"Piraeus has sailors. What's the difference?"

"Patras is—how do you say—a 'road trip.'"

"You don't like Athens?"

"Athens is good. I do not like my house."

"What's wrong with it?"

"You do not believe this. I know how life is in America. I am twenty-seven and still live in the house of my parents with my sisters."

"Run away from home."

Kappa didn't catch this. "Why can't you leave?" I asked. His parents could be old or in ill health.

"Houses cost too many money."

"It's the same in the United States right now. Why don't you rent an apartment?"

"'Apartment'?"

"A flat."

"My parents' house is a flat. Greek boys do not have their own flats. My parents think a boy who lives by himself is a 'pousti.'"

"Pousti" was a word I knew: "faggot." It was up there in frequency with "malaka," which meant "masturbator," "fuck off." The use of "boy" for young man was also characteristic of Greek English.

"So you like road trips?" I said.

"Yes. We stay at a hotel. I do what I want. Sometimes I go on road trip without team."

"How's that?"

"My parents think basketball is no good. They never go to games. Sometimes I tell them 'road trip' and go to hotel in Plaka. Maybe I meet tourist girl or make company with Greek girl."

"Make company" was somewhere between "make love" and "have company." Kappa had the looks to do both, hooded eyes and active lips. He had the smell too, cologne strong enough to run a chain saw. When he wasn't flipping his worry beads, he was fiddling with his hair like Sam Malone on "Cheers." I asked him what he told his parents when he got back home.

"We win again."

Patras, across from Italy, is the Gary of Greece, cement factories and oil tanks along the coast, just like Indiana. The country's third largest city, Patras crowds on top of itself, trapped between the sea and the mountain behind it. The seafront is all shipping companies, so even downtown streets are congested with idling tractor trailers waiting to offload their produce. Other trucks grind out of town with their Fiats and Italian shoes for Athenians. Not even the Lightning would have stayed at our hotel, an old high-ceilinged building with drafty windows, hanging bulbs, and no TVs. Kappa must be ponderously unhappy. Looking out my window into the gray streets, I wondered if tourists taking the ferry from Italy ever make a U-turn, drive their cars back on the boat, and give up on this outhouse of Greek civilization.

That afternoon we didn't go out for our usual shootaround. Z had a new lineup practicing zone in the hotel dining room. Petros was going to start up front with Koko and Henderson.

Lou and I were in the backcourt. Z said Apollonos had added an "overweight" player since we beat them in the pit: Sam Sam-heels. Z overused "over," but if this was Jug Samuels, he might be right. When Jug was at Mississippi State he had close to three-hundred pounds rolled around his six-eleven frame. The last time I saw Jug he was using two chairs on the Albany Patroons sideline and getting about three minutes a game. Now, as a rookie, he was fifth in the GBA in rebounding. I hoped we'd get a chance to talk. Reminiscing about the CBA had to be better than watching TV with Lou in the lobby while Kappa and the kids went out to practice what Kappa called "sure sex."

That evening, we rode to the Apollonos building in an old school bus. The visitors' locker room was cold and damp. It was a trick teams said the Celtics used to make guests uncomfortable and irritable. But the Celts dressed in the same dingy conditions. Red Auerbach wanted his players out on the floor, not answering fan mail or soaking in the whirlpool. The Apollonos locker was cold. The gym was freezing. Windows high above the bleachers were all open and the wind was blowing in off the port. Vassilis went looking for a janitor. When I tried to dribble the floor to get warm, the ball wouldn't come up. It was dead and so was the floor, a synthetic surface that felt like a gymnastics mat. One foul line was raised up like a frost heave in a Vermont road. The surface also needed sweeping and mopping. I spit on my hand and wiped my sneakers. Two steps and I was sliding again. "Fazbreaks" and changes of direction were going to be impossible if Vassilis didn't find a janitor or a dust mop.

The baskets were in the right place and the right height. But the rims were stiff and the nets were new. This I'd seen in the CBA. Power teams tighten up the bolts attaching the hoop to the backboard to take away shooters' slop. Control teams use tight nets to slow down their opponents. The gym sounded like brick-layers were still building it. The wind was blowing shots off the rim: whang, clang, thud. Dribbles made a sick thump instead of the usual splat. I'd played in some bad places—a gym in Poultney, Vermont, that had radiators all along one sideline; an ancient Iowa fieldhouse where sand from the jumping pits somehow got on the floor; Jug's old court in Albany, what they called an armory but smelling more like a morgue—but this was the worst building I'd ever been in as a pro. Even the lighting was bad, bulbs burned out or not turned on. There were TV cameras under the baskets, but without more light the viewers at home might as well be peering through the cigarette smoke we ran through in the pit. After the shootaround, we went back out to the bus and crowded up near the heater. Vassilis was now looking for the Apollonos GM.

When we came back in, the windows were closed but the temperature was the same. About four-hundred fans sat in parkas and ski hats. Watching Apollonos running layups, I understood why Petros was in the lineup. Their players all looked like they had spent the morning unloading ships. Jug had to be over three-fifty now. Their forwards were almost as heavy. The guards were short and thick. Tyrone Poulos was a white John Bagley. I shook hands with Jug at midcourt. "I'll come get you after the game," he said. Nothing else. He was trying to get a sweat. During the introductions, we got a few jeers and whistles but Apollonos got no applause. The fans didn't want to take off their gloves. I looked into the near future, saw no change in the weather, and forecast a very ugly game. Just before the tip, Z took me aside and said that against Apollonos it was important "to avoiding injury."

Apollonos plays zone as anticipated and takes the full thirty seconds on offense before missing. It's too cold to latch onto an outlet pass. If Lou and I try to break with the ball, we look like the coyote in old Roadrunner cartoons, spinning and sliding. Our shooters, what there are of them, can't get a grip on the ball. It feels like a real rock. All the action is in the paint. We shoot, they shoot, we miss, they miss. Their grizzlies battle our kodiaks for rebounds. With their cold and slippery paws they put up follow shots. These miss and they scrap again. The referees give up calling everything but knockdown fouls. None of the big guys can make the free throws. Petros throws up two air balls, the second one three feet short. He hustles after it and kicks it into the stands. Poulos misses the technical at his end. If the game starts to move, Apollonos calls time out. Henderson is the only player sweating. He must have fifteen rebounds at the half. I can't remember getting an assist. I'm two for six shooting and have fallen on my ass twice. The score is 23-20. The grizzlies are ahead.

Z seems pleased in the locker room. No concussions or broken bones. Henderson catches his breath and says, "Vohethia, motherfuckers, I need some help." So Henderson has been learning Greek. "Vohethia," Z tells Petros and Koko. Dop has been in the toilet since the half ended. He'll give up his twelve shots to stay out of this game.

With five minutes left, we're down by six. Z calls time and puts in the zone press team: Dop and Kappa to go with Henderson, Lou, and me. "Make the guards pass and suddenly foul others," Z tells Henderson and me. When we swarm the ball, the floor looks like an ice-skating rink on Saturday afternoon. After missing three foul shots, Poulos doesn't want to shoot any more. He gives it up to the big guys and we hack them. Jug blows the front ends of two one-and-ones. We get a couple of steals and a slow-motion break. Lou takes time to set his feet and hits his first three to put us ahead by four. Now Apollonos has to chase us, try to foul. I slip by Poulos, he tackles me from behind, and we slide ten feet on the dusty floor. After that foul, my teammates are happy to give me the ball and let the heavies knock me down. A few foul shots wouldn't do much for the shooters' averages. I'm the point. It's my job to hold the rock and sink foul shots at the end. Standing still at the line, blowing on my hands, and licking my fingers, I manage five of six to put us up seven with twenty seconds left. Then I pick off a Poulos pass, and he tackles me again, with seven seconds to go, a totally unnecessary foul by an American who should know better. I don't talk any trash and I don't throw the ball at him. I just step up to the line, give the cameraman plenty of time to get me in focus, and tell Tyrone, "These are for you." Then I make both ends of the one-and-one with my left, my off hand.

In the locker room Henderson shouts at Z: "Why the fuck didn't you use the press earlier?" I'd never heard Henderson say anything to Z.

Z wasn't upset. "This is like the NBA, no? Physical game. Small players could catch injury in this game."

"NBA, shit," Henderson said. "This was like a fucking tractor pull. In the States they'd forfeit the game for lack of talent. Plus wind chill."

Henderson didn't even take a shower. He put his clothes on over his sweats and went out to the bus. Vassilis couldn't get the whirlpool to work. The showers were lukewarm and the towels had been stolen from a D-class hotel fifteen years ago.

"Bad basketball," I told Jug when he came by to pick me up.

"But just once a week," he said and gave me that jug-eared grin that got him his name down at Mississippi State.

"What about the fans? This looked like a high school crowd."

"My man Tyrone says we get more people with the windows open."

"But they're all sitting on their hands."

"That don't bother me none. Fans don't help my J. It still clanging."

"Could be the fucking cold, Jug."

"You may be right about that, Key. But check out them rebounds."

"How'd you get up here anyway?"

Jug said that after a season wiping up for Albany, Apollonos gave him a tryout on a New York City playground. They didn't have the money clubs in Athens and Salonika had. He was their kind of player, big and cheap. They still needed one more player to close the windows, mop the floor, and enter civilization. I told him Patras looked like a shithole to me.

"You got that just right, Key," Jug said, "I be fifth in rebounds and be last in hitting my nut."

"My boy Kappa says Patras is full of foxes."

"Maybe so, Key, but ever one of them is white."

"Just a matter of time," I said. "Your shot will start to fall. Greeks love the shooters."

"Greeks ain't goin' to love no black man. They always talkin about the Greek family and the Greek nation and the Greek religion. It just like the Klan. I can deal with they language and food. I even like the music. That bouzouki sound like the ukelele my granpop used to play. But shit, man, I can't keep rebounding if I can't hit my nut."

Patras must be tough for Jug. I went to Boston to get some experience against the "blood speed" Kellogg had warned us about: "Green Mountain state, my ass. This is the White Mountain state, all stationary white boys. Cross the border and you'll see." I was living in Brighton, a mixed neighborhood, and taking the bus or MTA to Roxbury, Jamaica Plain, wherever the action was fast and high. I was usually the only white guy on the court. The brothers treated me like the Indians acted toward crazy whites in the old Westerns they still showed during the day on Greek TV: as a harmless curiosity. It was a lot easier for me to get into the pick-up games than for Jug to get into a Greek girl.

Jug told me Panathinaikos should win the championship. He wanted to know what happened to Henderson. I asked him what he meant.

"James done changed his game. That boy can hurt you now."

"You knew Henderson in the States?"

"Mississippi State was up at the Alaska Shootout with Michigan when James was a freshman. We got to talk some. He said the game was going to be six-nine guards. He sure did play like a center today."

"We talking about the same Henderson, Jug?"

"Shit, Key, James could be a coach. Something must have made him go bad. He didn't even speak to me tonight."

Motherfucker Henderson a coach. He did some talking to Z in the locker. I'd have to speak to James.

On the train ride back, I listened to Koko beat Henderson five out of six. When Koko went looking for another victim, I slipped in next to Henderson and told him I'd been talking to Jug.

"Samuels should give up his passport. His game ain't shit. Him and those other clumsy motherfuckers. He should have to live here the rest of his fat, fucking life."

"Jug says he's got some personal problems. He also says you didn't used to be so tough."

"I get you the rock, don't I?"

"Sure enough, but if you didn't notice, we're the only native speakers of English on this team. I rode up with Kappa. Have you talked with him lately? You had something to say to Z last night. I'd like to hear your ideas about six-nine guards. I'd have to shoot a lot of tape to handle them."

"Anybody can play guard. Guards can't do nothing else."

"Why did you want to be one then?"

"In high school I did it all. Rebound, dribble, pass, shoot the J. I wasn't Magic but I was a lot closer to him than to Jug. That little dickhead coach at Michigan told me I could play the one or two spot when he recruited me. Then he signed two bluechip guards, and I went on the weights."

"So it was all that rebounding that made you bad. Jug said it might be living in Greece."

Henderson looked out the window for a long time. I thought he was ignoring me again, as he had all season.

"Look, Michael, you know the story over here. The

59

Atholes want a banger, a black banger. What that means is they want a mean nigger. That's what the fans expect. It's what some Greeks fear. It works. Check my stats. The Greeks give me room. But they don't get the joke. The self-made banger. Bangers like Jug are born, not made. More racist shit. I'll do it for a year. If I don't make the league next year, I'll use my deferred admission and go to U of M Law School on my bonus."

"Law School?" I was amazed, then embarrassed by the way it had come out. How was I supposed to know Henderson was passing here east of the color line? The best I could do was keep going. "You'll be one bitch of a prosecutor. `Judge, we going to fry this weak-ass motherfucker.'" I imitated the banger's pronunciation: "mothafuckah."

Henderson chuckled, something I hadn't heard before. Then he put on his glare, lowered his voice to the familiar growl, and said, "Listen up, Keever. You tell anybody about Law School and I'll crush yo ass, hear? Now go fetch the board from big fella and I'll show you how to think."

In backgammon, I found out, the white pieces move one way, the black pieces the other, careful not to intersect on their way home. Inside the backgammon rectangle, weather doesn't slow down the action, the throwing of dice, the jumping of men, the crowd off the board. Henderson was ahead four-zip when I gave up for this trip. Koko must be cheating. I knew damn well he was too slow to beat Henderson straight up. And Henderson was still too remote to hear about my problem. He wouldn't be sympathetic to a blackmail victim, not if he thought about the word or knew about the difference in our bonuses. I could imagine what he'd say: "Anybody can pretend to be Greek. Blacks can't do nothing else but be black." As the train passed through the industrial sections of Athens, I thought maybe I should teach Ann how to play backgammon. If I can't beat her, there's always Sara.

Chapter 5

In March the windows of Kolonaki's designer boutiques were covered with newspapers for a couple of days. When they were removed, the usual leather-dressed manequins were replaced by freakish displays, Gorbachev's wine-stained head on Batman's body, a Bill Cosby mask on a mermaid. Greeks were getting ready for carnival. Men and women set up stands on street corners and sold fat plastic baseball bats in unnatural purple and pink. I'd never seen a baseball field in Greece. The Greeks are buying the bats, so I assume they're for carnival. Mask and weapon: just what a fake Greek needs.

I'm sitting out taking the sun at Valtadoros Cafe when a man leading a bear on a chain comes walking up the aisle, passing three feet from me. It walks like a bear and smells like a bear but must be a man in a bear's suit. There's no reason for a man to bring a real bear through Kolonaki Square. "Giftos," Achilleas, the day waiter, says. Gypsy. A gypsy bear? A gypsy leading the bear? A gypsy in a bear suit? This has to be for carnival, but I'm not getting down on all fours to hide from Eleni.

Sara wanted to wear a costume like the Tsoliathes, the tallest Greeks not playing ball—the ceremonial guards who stand in Syntagma and in front of the presidential mansion near the National Garden. They wear heavy clogs (with lifts, I suspect), leotards, pleated miniskirts, fancy embroidered blouses, and soft hats with graduation tassels. They carry an antique wooden rifle that looks more like a club than a gun.

"No gun," Ann said.

"But Mom, all the Tsoliathes carry guns. They're not real."

"I know they're not real, Sara, but I don't want you pretending to be a Greek man with a gun."

"Athena has a spear and shield. Sara will look pretty funny carrying one of those plastic bats they're selling in the streets," I put in for shooters. For Sara and realism, Ann relented. On Fat Tuesday night, Sara marched to the Plaka. I don't know why, but seeing Sara in that uniform, goose-stepping like the national guards, really pleased me. Nobody could have told she wasn't Greek. I dressed as an incognito athlete, and Ann wore her spy's belted raincoat. She'd had to use it once last week, so the lights were all on in Syntagma Square. We saw businessmen and space invaders, students going to night classes and heavy metal idols, women with shopping bags waiting for trolleys and a girl with false breasts hanging out of her dress. "Cicolina," Ann said, "the Italian porn star and member of parliament." The little kids in clown suits and cartoon character masks were definitely part of carnival too. The Arab sheiks and women in saris could be tourists. The young men with swishing black capes, charcoal eye shadow, and pointed shoes could be macho Greeks making fun of "poustes," gays, or Romanian visitors.

The Plaka lanes are a wall-to-wall pedestrian parade, more jammed with Greeks than I'd ever seen them with tourists. The Greeks are tourists now, people wearing new clothes for a special occasion. Couples and families are wandering back and forth in the alleys. They're moving slowly, as if they'd spent too much time in the summer sun. They look left and right, trying to recognize buildings made unfamiliar by the crowd. Carnival is better than tourism. Now the Greeks can stare even longer than usual. They are also free to laugh at each other without fear of injuring pride. Unlike tourists, who have to hide their amusement at local comedy, the Greeks are pointing at the natives' costumes and making loud jokes about this carnival country they're in for the night. "Xeni, xeni," I hear all around me, "strange, strange."

At midnight we find out why so many people are carrying plastic bats. The Greeks start knocking heads. Teenagers push through the crowd, chasing other teenagers and taking home-run swings in the cramped space. Friends walk side by side, throwing confetti up over their heads, laughing, whacking each other, and yelling "chronia polla," many years. A couple is holding hands and taking turns rapping each other on top of the head. Strangers going in opposite directions nod, smile, toss confetti, bop each other, and deliver their wish: "chronia polla." To the Greeks, I'm either too tall or, in this light, too obviously a true stranger. Ann, with her brown hair, and Sara, with her costume, are the natives in the family. Ann takes a few whacks on the head and shoulders. I think she's secretly pleased, but she doesn't want me to find her a bat. People smile down and tap the Tsolias on her hat. Even teenagers give Sara special treatment, sprinkling confetti, touching her lightly, wishing her "chronia polla," and bending over so she can tap them back with her plastic gun and tell them "chronia polla."

"Crazy with a car, gentle with a plastic bat," Ann says, shaking her head. "I'll never understand these people."

"Maybe you're trying too hard to understand them. Why not accept them and enjoy what you like here?"

"You don't accept all of them shooting in the pit, do you?"

"That's different. That's selfishness. These people are just having a good time."

"They look to me like they're pretending to have a good time."

"That's because you don't like crowds. The Greeks out tonight are like fans celebrating a championship."

"By hitting each other?"

"Yelling 'many years' and jostling each other aren't enough. High-fives, chest bumps, and sweaty hugs wouldn't be enough, not for these people. They want to hammer each other, drive home their point, their wish for a long and healthy life. Family and friends are not enough. The Greeks nail strangers in strange costumes to fasten themselves together in glee."

"And why, coach, do they act like this?"

"The Greeks want these things," I tell Ann, "because they are Greeks, 'Ellenes' and 'Ellenithes' in 'Ellatha.'"

Ann seems surprised at the three Greek words coming out of my mouth.

"I have another Greek word," she says, "one that covers the Greeks much better: 'hyper.' Hyperactive and hyperbolic."

"What's that mean, Mom?" Sara asks.

"In Greek, it means 'overshoot.' In English, it's 'exaggerate.'"

"Your Mom must be Greek," I tell Sara, "because she's exaggerating."

"Not me," Ann tells Sara and me, "never, never, never."

It was a nice warm night, a family occasion with something new to see in a country that was buying us a home in Memphis, and yet Ann was pounding on the Greeks. Greece, I realized, was not the problem. What Ann thought about Greeks might be true but was mostly irrelevant. Although too proud to admit it, Ann was homesick, an illness as simple as she used to say I was. Even in Rockford, she'd been anxious to get back to Memphis. Now she couldn't call her family without walking a half hour to the phone office and standing in line. Although I could recognize homesickness, it was a disease I'd never had.

I understood it in general, but not Ann's specific strain. Working in a world capital, I could not comprehend how anyone could be homesick for a town in Tennessee. While we were walking back to the apartment, I suggested that Ann go home for a couple of weeks. When she got angry and yelled at me for treating her like a helpless American housewife, I asked if she might be more Greek than she wanted to admit.

"That's what worries me, Michael. I don't like being jumpy and combative. I wasn't like this when we first came. I feel Greeks are getting under my skin, changing me."

She was right, of course, but I didn't want to admit it. Now I knew why Ann was spending at least one morning a week gazing at the statues of archaic goddesses in the Cycladic museum. When I saw their serene faces, simple shapes, and unchanging forms, I didn't understand their attraction. A half hour into Lent, I realized those white marble women reminded Ann of herself at home.

The Saturday after Carnival, Panathinaikos had an open date in the league. At the last minute, the owner scheduled an exhibition game against a Turkish team in Istanbul. Ann refused to take Sara to a city where she couldn't drink the water. That was fortunate for me, because on Thursday Eleni came back to Valtadoros. As she walked toward my table, she was grinning and I thought all the Keevers are going home now. Sitting down, Eleni spoke some gibberish words. They could have been Greek, though I didn't think so.

"You're going to Turkey," she said then.

"That was Turkish?"

"That was bar-bar. When ancient Greek sailors heard other tongues, they'd go 'bar, bar, bar.' From that came the word 'barbarian,' a secret name."

Eleni wanted to surprise me with this pop quiz, but my face was ready and didn't move.

"Language is to keep secrets in," she went on. "But you know how this works. Basketball teams do the same. They make up names for their plays and players."

Eleni stopped, raised her eyebrows, and grinned again, as if we were buddies sharing a little secret joke. My features didn't move. Maybe she thought I'd be easy this time, but my face was either stone stupid or innocent. Let her be uncertain. I wasn't confessing anything. She'd have to say the magic word "McKeever" to make me move.

"Not Panathinaikos," I told her. "They don't even have a name for the team or the stadium."

Eleni didn't say any more about names. Maybe she really believed language was to keep secrets in. Or to play games with. Perhaps she wanted to keep me as uncertain as I wanted her to be.

"I came in to ask you a favor," she said. "Would you take some money to Istanbul for me?"

"My wife asked me the same thing," I said, "but I'm not going there to shop."

"You don't have to bring anything back. Just take the money and give it to a man at your hotel."

Drugs were my immediate thought. Then some kind of money laundering. Keep it dumb and light.

"Is this favor like a casting couch, something I need to do to get in the camcorder ad?"

"No, no," she laughed. "Just a convenience that will save me a trip."

"Why don't you write a check?"

"Turks don't accept Greek checks."

"You could send it UPS."

"It's too much to send. Forty thousand dollars."

"Isn't that a lot of cash to give someone you barely know?"

"You're an American. I can trust you with dollars."

"What if I run off with the money?"

"Then you wouldn't be in the commercial, would you?"

I looked out the window to stall for time. Panathinaikos and I were on track for what was now $70,000 in Switzerland, but I had to finish the season. If I didn't do the favor, Eleni could expose me and the bonus would be gone. If I did the favor, she could expose me afterwards. The favor didn't sound that risky. If I did it, though, Eleni could ask me other, more dangerous favors. Future problems didn't matter. Right now I didn't have a choice. "Dumb boards," Ann used to call my teammates when she first met me. I just hoped Eleni wouldn't see through the knothole.

"OK," I said, "no problem, just as long as I get in the camcorder ad."

Eleni handed me a taped packet, the size and weight of money. Greek words were written all over the tape. Walking back to the apartment with the packet, I had more time to think about my options. I could take the money, Sara, and Ann to

Istanbul and not come back to Greece. $40,000 was almost two-thirds of $70,000. Cut my probable loss. Then I realized the packet was probably another test, a follow-up to the quiz I'd passed. That's why Eleni told me the amount and let me fence with her. If I opened up the packet and found no money, I'd lose everything. If I delivered it, Eleni would figure my name was fake. But, then again, how could she know if I was guilty or just a dumb American willing to do a favor for a pretty American. I thought it was unlikely she was asking me to smuggle drugs *into* Turkey. It was no use trying to imagine, like Ann would, what Eleni might ask me in a month or two. I still didn't have any choice. Instead of picking up a pile of cash like a stupid bone on his visit to an outlaw school, I'd be the one delivering the money.

In Istanbul I handed the packet to a man who knew the password: "barbarian." The next day I committed eleven turnovers and we lost to the Turks. Before the flight back, I went to a shop next to our hotel to get a rug. I'd never be back to Istanbul. I might not be long in Greece.

"You must learn about carpets before you buy," the sales-man insisted, a rug coach. He had his boy throw four carpets on the floor. He tossed them with flair, making them sail and land flat. I understood tales of flying carpets. "A handmade carpet will last longer than we will," the salesman said, and winked, "but many fakes are in the market. Only one of these four is real. The others are machine-made. Can you pick?" One looked new and artificial, bright colors alternating in a very busy design. The other three were older and quieter. Not so showy, more authentic. I pointed at one of them. "No," the man said, "you have chosen what you were prepared to choose. The manufacturers do market research. Their computers design carpets that look like tourists think they should, run down like Istanbul." He scraped fibers off my choice and burned them with his lighter. Polyester. He dug into the pile of another with his car keys. The color wasn't the same all the way down. He turned over the third. The colors didn't stain through to the back. The one that looked artificial passed all his tests. It was hand-made by a woman in Hakkari. He could give me her name, he said. I could take a bus to the village, talk to the woman, check her loom, feel her sheep. I bought the bright and active carpet because it was the one I thought Ann and Sara would like, the one Sara could lie on and imagine herself flying.

At the Athens airport, customs officers didn't ask me to unroll the carpet or look at the bill of sale. But this time, with almost no one in the terminal, I noticed a sign in several languages hanging above the agents: "Any foreign national bringing more than $1,000 in currency into Greece must declare the sum if he wishes to take it from the country." We'd entered with travelers checks. I'd calmly walked out with, possibly, $39,000 over the limit, even an American basketball player's limit. Watching the agents run their hands through a few off-season tourists' suitcases and peer into businessmen's briefcases, remembering the policemen standing around the X-ray machine when I left, I understood why Eleni gave me the packet and realized it wasn't going to be easy getting away with the $70,000 we'd come to Greece for. On the floor, violations produce an immediate whistle. On tape, you can see the turn-overs just before they occur. Now I knew why the first move in Drinkman's office was the guard's quick two-foot shuffle as he starts to the hoop: traveling. Rerun, the move begins "Keever's Travels," a long run of turn-overs. When a bunch of mistakes turn into a crowd, the coach keeps the point after practice and makes him run the suicides by himself, traveling up and down the floor, racing back and forth, panting and staggering, punishment for fucking up.

Three days later I was sitting in Dexameni, watching Sara ride her bike, when Eleni walked up the stairs into the park. This time I saw her from twenty feet away and wondered if she was really Greek-American. The dark complexion might be makeup; the thick eyebrows and black kinky hair might be dyed and permed. She could be Henderson's half sister or Lebanese or just about anything. I didn't know Indianapolis well enough to quiz her on it, and since I couldn't test out her Greek, I had to be content with my suspicion. It even crossed my mind that her come-on was carefully rehearsed American English.

"Thanks for delivering the money," she said, cheerful as a cheerleader. "Can we talk about making money?"

"I never pass up a chance to make money, but I was just getting ready to leave for practice."

I didn't want to seem like I was avoiding her, but I also didn't want Sara yelling "Daddy" to me or riding over to the bench and asking who Eleni was.

"This won't take long."

"OK," I said, and asked about the camcorder commercial. What the hell, I thought, some people believe athletes are all subnormal. Maybe Eleni figured I couldn't read the airport signs. Play dumb, stay dumb.

"Unfortunately for both of us, the ad's on hold for now. The agency needs more name recognition. They'd like to see you on the national team."

"I have to be selected first."

"Trust a Hoosier. You'll make the team."

"I'm glad you think so. I'd like to suit up for Greece."

"The national team is most important, but my people also want to make a commercial they can show for more than three months. They'd really like it if you played for Panathinaikos next year." Eleni's "really" sounded like Sara's "rilly," which she was picking up from old American sitcoms.

What a fucking turnaround, I thought. Eleni turns out to be a recruiter with a future. Now she's trying to force me to do exactly what I wanted to do before she gave me my ethnic test.

"I'd love to stay, but the club won't negotiate until the end of this season."

"So we'll just have to wait and see?"

"Right, but now I really need to get to practice."

I wanted Eleni to leave so I could take Sara home. As Eleni got up to go, she nodded toward the center of the square, where Sara was pedaling around in circles.

"Is that your little girl with the long blonde hair?" she asked.

"That's right," I said. I didn't dare lie about Sara.

"Does she like it here?"

"When she can be outside, she does."

"It's a great chance for her. I didn't come over until my junior year in college. I could read two-thousand-year-old inscriptions at Olympia but couldn't ask for a glass of water in my father's village. My ten-year-old cousins called me 'Amerikanakee,' little American. I spent most of my time in Athens, but it's no place for a child. Too many people, not enough air. Next year you should live in a suburb, someplace outside the basin. You don't want the pollution to stunt your daughter's growth."

Now Eleni was beginning to sound like Ann: move to Idra and take the hydrofoil to practice. Maybe I should have followed up what Eleni said about herself, but she was leaving and talking about Sara with her was creepy. Eleni made me feel that Sara was in danger, not from the air but from someone I couldn't see.

"A pretty girl," Eleni said as she walked away, "but she doesn't 'rilly' look half Greek."

There were other light-haired kids in Dexameni. Vassilis had told me people with my coloring and blue eyes were mountain Greeks from the north. Eleni must have been observing us from hiding or had someone watching us, listening to us.

"Xeni," I thought the next couple of days in Dexameni, doesn't come close to describing what's going on here. "Strange shit," Henderson mutters when a Panathole does something completely unpredictable, like standing at the offensive end bitching at a referee while his man is running free down at the other end. Waiting to be suddenly cut off like the electricity, I have the national team and next season handed to me like gifts. Maybe. With the commercial talk, Eleni treated me as if she believed I was dumb, but identifying Sara also threatened me in case I was playing dumb. Either Eleni still wasn't sure about my background or she was trying to bring down my guard. If Eleni does want me here next year, she'll be happy that I seem oblivious to her threat. It was impossible to figure what Eleni really wanted, say nothing about what she really was. Perhaps it was short-term thinking, but I assumed the national team was her priority. When Greek All-Stars play other countries, lots of money must be wagered—drachmas, liras, francs, pesos, pounds. But it was also possible Eleni was serious about next year. She was straightforward this time: no jokes, no word games. She seemed genuinely worried that Sara would become a "little American." But even if Ann agreed to come back, I'd be crazy to risk a second year. Sooner or later, I think, Eleni will try to collect on my secret, and when she does Ann will know it. I'd concealed Drink's name change from her, but I was taking responsibility now. Still, if Eleni really does want me in the country next year, that should relieve some pressure on this season. And if she really thinks I'd risk staying, her mistake might give me an advantage somewhere down the line. Besides the foot difference in height and eighty pounds in weight, that mistake was about all I had on Eleni. Thinking about her small body, I realized trying to avoid her and hustling her off were mistakes. What I need to do is bring her to me, invite her in close, then plant other mistakes, prepare new deceptions.

At practice that week my family's future was interfering with the next second. When I missed Henderson with an easy dish, he said I could be traded to Apollonos for Tyrone Poulos, Jug's gutless playmaker. Z even had me run the second team one day until the subs complained about getting hit in the face by my passes. The next two games at home I started off slow, but the fans' "lefkos magos" got me going and we won both. "Cain't let those cocksuckers take one in our building," Larry Bird had told me in the Garden, the only words he ever spoke to me. We were still undefeated in the pit.

Between games I couldn't keep my mind on basketball. I took home tape of Peristeri but didn't watch it. I remember Z telling us they'd be trouble in their place, but I also remembered we'd killed them early in the season. On the bus ride to their building, I did wonder if we might be playing outdoors like some of the Greek youth teams. The sections we passed through were poorer than any parts of Athens I'd seen. Peristeri looked like Patras. Every third building was an auto-repair shop. One rundown square was full of men in head-dresses and women in veils.

When our bus pulled up in front of the Peristeri gym, five hundred people were waiting to greet us. Tomatoes and other fruit splattered against the blackened windows. A kid ran up to the front of the bus and slung a melon grenade-style against the windshield. After softening up their target, the people moved in and started rocking the bus from side to side. "Motherfuckers," Henderson screamed through the glass. The driver wailed on his horn. All of us jumped out of our seats and stood in the aisles. We didn't want to be trapped in our seats if the people managed to turn over the bus. Then a band of policemen who had been standing out of produce range charged in. The people nearest the bus couldn't run in time and were beaten with rubber sticks that didn't look that flexible. "This is going to be another physical game," I told Henderson as the police formed a corridor from the bus to the gym door. "Wait for now," Z told Henderson and me. The other players left the bus first, heads down, jackets pulled up over their faces like mafiosi going to court. The people started throwing again, an awkward heaving motion, a cross between a shot and a ten-nis serve, the throw of a country without baseball. Oranges and tomatoes hit the Greeks and the police. A soda can caught Kappa on his left hand. When the players were inside, Z,

Vassilis, Henderson, and I came out running, heads up. Something just missed my face. An eggplant got Henderson on the shoulder.

"What the fuck was that all about?" I asked Z now that Peristeri had my attention.

"They hate Panathinaikos. Last year our American destroyed their best player's knee."

"Was it an accident?" Henderson asked.

Z just gave him the Greek shrug, eyes cast to the heavens, arms stretched down toward the ground.

Vassilis filled in more of the background: "It isn't just the injury. Peristeri can't afford any foreign players. The fans here think we have everything in Kolonaki."

"They should come to the fucking pit," Henderson said.

In the locker room, we changed into our uniforms and stretched. Z said we'd go out, run our layup line, shoot, and come back in. On the floor, I could hear the fans outside. Although the gym was smaller than the pit, it seemed larger. It was certainly odd running layups in full uniform with no one in the stands. I asked Lou if we'd play this one without fans. They'd be allowed in just before the game started, he said.

Back in the locker room for our final instructions, Z told Henderson and me we weren't starting. "Too dangerous," he said, "Peristeri is overangry." This was, I thought, just the kind of game we needed to be in: Henderson to intimidate and me to control the crowd, put them in their seats. "Perhaps after ten minutes," Z said. "Do not sit together on the bench." Now we could hear the fans. They were stomping the wooden bleachers, blowing air horns and whistles, singing and chanting. "Iste malakes, iste poustes." You are masturbators, you are faggots, over and over.

At the end of the tunnel to the floor, we found policemen forming a double line like cheerleaders in the States. "Run," Z said. We came out full speed, but it wasn't fast enough. The fans were prepared. Tomatoes and eggs came raining down on us from the nearest bleachers. Petros got a tomato in the back of the neck. Koko had egg all over one sneaker. We covered up our faces with our hands and stumbled to the bench. Juicy, overripe tomatoes splattered on the floor in front of us. From behind we were shielded by a double line of policemen. The stands looked like all the fans were doing the wave at the same time, waves and waves of outthrust palms directed down at us,

71

tidal waves of motion and sound: "iste malakes, iste poustes." So this is why Panathinaikos has the metal chute from the locker to the floor. I'd seen fans angry, but what I'd never seen and couldn't understand was hometown fans throwing garbage on the floor. This was their home court they were fucking up with overripe produce and rotten eggs. Not even in the CBA did shit like this go down.

The PA man was screaming. Two janitors with mops tried to clean up the floor, but the referees were in a hurry to get this one underway. They ran to the center circle, Peristeri broke their huddle, and our starting five sprinted out for the tip. This was no place for introductions. Nobody shook hands. This evening, even without the American point guard, all the Panathinaikos players were going up and down full speed. Nobody wanted to be an easy target. Everyone was moving without the ball, running the patterns. In the first couple of minutes, even Ann could have seen the patterns on the floor, red tomato tracks like footprints in a dance studio. I could tell our guys were nervous. They were passing the ball around. The delay made the fans scream louder, which made the Peristeri players frantic. They were firing quick threes, gambling on defense, and fouling. Dop stepped to the line and watched a peach bounce off the floor next to him and roll the length of the court. Our other players tried to stand as close as possible to Peristeri players. Although we were playing eggshell defense, not wanting to offend, we still ran out to a quick ten-point lead.

Their coach calls time to settle down his team. After their huddle they try to take the ball at Koko, who's running like he has splints. He's standing in the pivot when a driving forward crashes into him. Both he and the forward go down, but no foul is called. The forward wasn't shooting. Before Koko and the Peristeri man can get untangled, coins come flying down on the floor, heavy Greek coins, as big as and thicker than American half-dollars. Koko takes one on the shoulder. The other player gets hit at least twice. The fans don't care. They're willing to hit the home team to get the enemy. Our starters run over to the bench and make all of us a target. Enraged, the fans are throwing wildly from all over the building. The coins are gliding in like Frisbees, tumbling end-over-end like dumdums. The air looks like metal confetti. The policemen can't stop the fans, can't rush into the thousands with their batons. Lou's chin is cut open. That's when I pull my warmup jacket over my head. I can hear Z screaming at the referees. They won't come near our bench. The PA man is screaming but the fans aren't listening. What sounds like a cherry bomb explodes out on the floor. I can't believe it. I feel the policemen press back against us. I smell the eggs and tomatoes on their coats. A coin gets me on the left knee. Inside my warmup jacket, I'm sweating like the suicides. No Low Key now.

The coins stop clicking off the floor, but the noise is rising. The crowd is no longer chanting. It's howling, a single surrounding noise. I open up my jacket to take a look. No more waves. The crowd is a tide of black-haired men down out of their seats and pressing against the single line of policemen surrounding the court. The crowd is in a frenzy. I'm afraid they'll break through the dike and come washing across the floor. We're inside this crowd, inside its building. Pandemonium. They'll cut off the exits, knock us over, and kick the shit out of all of us, Americans and Greeks, even Henderson and Petros. The crowd directly across from us pushes the police back a few steps onto the floor, our little island. I can see their faces between and over the heads of the policemen who are bending forward against the fans. This crowd isn't a force of nature. Their mouths are all different shapes. They're all screaming something different but the same. Every one of them, the big ones and small ones, the old ones and young ones, everyone wants to run. The Greeks have thrown down their cigarettes, dumped their beer, left their coats in the stands, and emptied their hands so they can jump through the police barrier and overrun the floor. The fans want to break the law, run the court, pull us off the bench. They'll trample each other and asphyxiate themselves to impersonate players, take the floor together, stampede to an easy victory, fuck us up, fill their building with themselves, fake athletes.

A Peristeri player saves us. He grabs the microphone from the PA announcer and screams, "kalma, kalma." With his free hand he's repeating the message, softly patting the air in front of him like a slow-motion dribble without a ball. He wants to play, to keep playing. The howling dies a little. The player cuts the volume a little. The police push the fans back off the floor. The player gives a short speech. I have no idea what he's saying. Afterwards the fans applaud and climb back to their seats.

The janitors sweep the coins off the floor, a bonus they should give the player at the mike. Vassilis puts some tape on Lou's chin. The refs give Peristeri the ball on the side. We let them shoot, and they play even worse than before the delay. We're up by twenty-two with thirty seconds left in the half. While Pop prepares to shoot a foul at the other end of the court, Z tells Henderson and me to run for the locker room. "Now." While the fans are watching Pop release his second free throw, we bolt across the floor to the tunnel and catch the Greeks with their hands out of their pockets. We do get showered with beer, soda, and something that is either retsina or cat piss.

When the rest of the team comes in, Z tells the Americans, "Good game. Now you can leave."

"Leave?" I ask, "at the half?"

"Yes," Z says, "Vassilis will show you a back door. Take a taxi home. It will be more better for the team and for you."

"You're fucking right about that last," Henderson says.

"Go ahead," Lou tells me, "maybe we will be here a long time waiting for the fans to leave the area."

Walking away from the gym, I hoped no fans were coming late to the game. Sometimes taxis were hard to find, and even hunched over in the dark I'd be recognized with a six-nine black man. Riding back toward the pit, Henderson said this was the "more badder yet." Why didn't Z pull the team off and protest? Get a forfeit and get the fuck out of there. Maybe there were no forfeits in Greece, I told him. Maybe the Mailman had to get through no matter what. Besides, how would the whole team have gotten out of there? The two of us had caught the crowd off guard. The Greeks were in until the end. That's the Greeks, Henderson said. We bitched some more and then I asked Henderson what he thought Z meant by "good game."

"You and I were the bait. We're expensive Kolonaki imports. Z shows us off, makes the fans over-hysterical, and switches lineups. Peristeri plays hyper and we win easy. Z was using us."

"Everybody was getting knicked. Lou will need stitches."

"That's just because those motherfuckers couldn't throw straight. Why do you think Z told us not to sit together? Fuck this place and that motherfucker Z. That's what I say." Henderson wasn't putting on his ghetto growl. The "motherfuckers" had new weight.

Henderson could be right. If he was, Z probably knew the fans wouldn't cross over the line. He could have at least told us what he was up to. Henderson would never have run out on the floor for the sake of Greek strategy. I guess I might have. There was the risk of losing an eye, but how else can the coach on the floor control a game without leaving the bench? Like they say in the NBA, "no blood, no foul." It's not just shooters who practice positive imaging, concentrating on the "wick." The point has to turn negatives into positives or he'll fold under the pressure of seventy or eighty possessions a game. The best shooter misses more than half his shots. With the same percentage of turnovers, the point would sit before he got a sweat. You have to make the "more better" of any situation. This kind of positive thinking was not, though, a method that worked with Henderson. Just before he got out of the cab, he asked me if I knew where fans came from. The question confused me until I realized Henderson meant the word "fans." "From fanatic," he said, "Greek."

Chapter 6

Greece is a place all right. Here you're not competing against just the other players and coaches. First there are your teammates and your own coach. Then there's the crowd that wants into the action. Behind the crowd are the owners of the buildings, men who open up the windows and let the cold air in. The "gym" the ancient Greeks invented is now short for school. In this second semester I was learning that the athlete's inside story couldn't be separated from the outside. The sports books I'd read in the States were about people, the stars. Over here you have to keep your eyes on both the backcourt men and the background, the setting as well as the set shots and setups. It's not enough to be a hero, another Greek word. You have to talk the talk, the "lexes."

Our fourth guard, one of the new kids up from the junior team, told me his "uncle would be very pleased if I showed the passing to his team of boys at their new ground." What the hell, I thought, a clinic might push Eleni into the back of my head. "Passing of the guard," I also thought. Coaching could be a way to stay in Greece if Eleni exposed my secret. There were no rules against foreign coaches. And what would Keever's keyhole be? The whole.

T, whose full name was, I think, Themistocles, took me on a half-hour trolley ride to Kypseli, a section of Athens far from our apartment in Kolonaki. Row after row of new apartment buildings, but project standardized. The balconies were narrow, skimpy. Kypseli Square was ringed by trolleys and buses. We got out and walked to a school surrounded on all sides by apartment buildings. The court was, in fact, a ground, a playground that had just been resurfaced. Two full courts and new fiberglass backboards. In Kypseli I could see why basketball was so popular in Greece: thousands of people would have to lose their homes for the school to have a soccer field.

The playground was crowded. A pack of kids were shooting at one basket, teenagers were playing five on five at two others, and men between twenty and forty were standing around arguing on the fourth. There were too many players to waste a hoop running full court. T and I watched the pickup games while waiting for his uncle. Nobody played any defense, nobody hustled, and everybody took turns shooting, true of bad games everywhere. In Greece, though, when the game is over whoever is waiting gets to play. The winners sit with the losers. T's uncle showed up, thanked me for coming, and explained that youth teams often do not have gyms. This was his home court. He introduced me to his players, a man in a suit made a short speech, and T's uncle introduced me to the small crowd. I used T and a couple of his uncle's players to demonstrate defensive positioning and to walk through some basic pass plays. We ran a few full-court figure eights. I kept it simple. I didn't have anything to say, and I didn't have any tape. I ended up by showing the kids Lou's shooting stroke: back arched, shoulders square, elbow tucked, wrist cocked, fingers curled, eyes fastened on the front of the rim. The audience gave me a nice hand, and the team began their practice.

As I was signing autographs, a man with a camera and a notebook asked me some questions. What did I think of the ground? What advice would I give to Greek children? I told him the country needed to build more gyms. The kids should drink lots of milk, learn to hustle, and play less socialist basketball.

"I do not understand," he said.

"Milk for their bones. You know, make them tall."

"I see. And the other, the 'socialist basketball'?"

"If the winning team stayed on the court in pickup games, the kids would work harder, play stronger defense. And to win, everybody can't share the shooting."

"This is how basket is played in America?"

"Pick-up games should have the incentive of keeping the court. That's how skills and will are developed."

On the trolley ride home, I recalled my first organized games, how disappointed I was. When the buzzer sounded, you had to head for the locker. You went home whether you had won or lost, whether you were tired or not. The full court, uniforms, and referees couldn't match the all-afternoon Saturday tournaments in Jim Cummins' barn. One hoop, three or four three-man teams. We played to keep playing and to keep warm in the sub-zero cold. Every third game we'd take the rubber ball down to the milk room and run steaming water over it to make it bounce. In city schoolyards and recreation centers, playing well and beating the other team are only means. Winners own the space. Even in college and the CBA, no reward was ever quite like continuing to play, holding the court, keeping it, not passing it on.

The next day Dop was waiting for me with a newspaper opened to a picture of me in defensive position. I could pick out Kyvernos in the headline. He slapped the page and said "Why do you say these things?"

"What things?"

"This headline says 'Kyvernos Advises Capitalist Basketball.'"

"I knew a player who owned the bank shot. We called him 'Money.' Money in the bank. That's capitalist ball."

"Kyvernos criticizes Greek socialism, stresses competition, powerful defense, and monopoly of winners. To young players, he recommends cheating."

"What is this shit about cheating? I never used the word."

Dop looked back at the article. "'Drink more milk and learn to cheat' it says here."

"'Learn to hustle,' I said. The asshole didn't try very hard to find the right meaning in his dictionary."

"What about these other comments on socialism?"

"Look, Dop, I was talking basketball and the reporter turned it into a political statement."

Dop asked me if I'd ever studied politics. I told him it was part of my military education in General Studies. His English was good but not good enough to get that. He asked me why I attacked socialism. He told me Americans did not understand what socialism meant. I suppose he was right. I'd seen Dop coming to the pit, riding on his big Suzuki, wearing an expensive leather jacket, pleated pants, and Timberland deck shoes without socks. I didn't picture Dop as a socialist. He combed his curly hair straight back. He didn't even wear glasses. But he was heated up about this article. He wouldn't let it go. In the locker room the next day Dop sounded like a party historian, going on about the great change the socialist party, PASOK, had brought to Greece, the redistribution of money and power, large public works projects, a spirit of national cooperation. Koko said something to Dop in Greek, something short and quick accompanied by a hand motion I'd never seen: palm held belt high and turned down to the floor, fingers rolled over and up one by one. Dop broke into a loud flurry of Greek. He put his thumb and first two fingers together and waved them in Koko's face. This I understood. It was the lecture gesture: "Let me tell you." Koko yelled back, more animated than I'd ever seen him, on or off the floor. His hands were going too fast for me to figure. Kappa came into it. He held his left palm in front of him and turned his right index finger into it: "I have something for you." The three of them were screaming all at once. Kappa jumped up onto the bench to raise his voice to frontcourt level. The other players began rumbling at each other. T rested his elbows on his stomach, put his forearms together, and held his palms flat, as if he were carrying some blessed offering. It meant, "Can I speak?" Petros pointed his elbow at T and gave him a condescending "bah:" "fuck off." Henderson and I went out to the floor where Lou was shooting threes. I asked him what Koko's fingers meant. "Thieves," Lou said. From the floor we could hear the players in the locker room discussing politics. CBA players yelled at each other about poaching on the very small group of groupies waiting in their idling cars out in the winter nights. How, I wondered, will these Atholes ever work together in the playoffs if they're screaming at each other about politics. That's when I realized Z's genius, another Greek word I'd just read in "Word for the Day." By speeding up play, he got the shooters plenty of points and made it easier for them to pass. Forcing the break, Z forced the Greeks to forget themselves.

I asked Vassilis about the article.

"These things happen when we are running up to an election. Even forest fires are political. Did you read about them in September?"

"No, I don't think so," I said, and wondered if the *Athens News* covered them.

"The New Democracy opposition blamed PASOK for not putting out fires caused by the drought. PASOK accused New Democracy and the Communists of setting the fires to embarrass the government. The Communists accused PASOK of setting them in order to blame the Communists for setting them. All the parties had something to gain from the forest fires."

"What about the heat on me?" I asked. "When does that die down?"

"It will take a while for things to calm," Vassilis said.

I checked with him the next few days. I wanted to avoid any more exposure than I already had. Eleni must read the paper, follow her boy's stats. If she thinks some investigative reporter will be looking further into my background, she might want to use her information before someone else makes it worthless. The newspapers might just as well have uniforms and home courts. A New Democracy paper said it took an out-sider to recognize PASOK's poor youth programs and inade-quate sports facilities. A far-right paper that supported return-ing the king and queen quoted me and railed against the failure of excellence in contemporary Greek life. A Communist paper asked what right a player from abroad had to criticize the homeland. My name wouldn't disappear. The first reporter's translation was like a tape that couldn't be reversed, only copied, added to, and spread around through the crowd of read-ers like some pirated movie. Players hustle, prostitutes hustle, con men hustle. Why did the reporter have to choose the worst meaning? Because, I realized, Greece is the country that gave us that other synonym for cheating: "politics."

Henderson wasn't involved. He came by my stall before a Wednesday practice and said, "I heard from my agent this morning. The Bucks are interested."

"That's great, James. When do they want to sign you?"

"I'm leaving tomorrow morning."

"Tomorrow? What about the Atholes? What the fuck are we going to do without you in the playoffs?"

"I'm sorry about that. Maybe Koko's knees will come around with the warmer weather."

"Did you tell him?"

"Yeah."

"What did he say?"

"'You fuck them now.'"

We're the ones who'll get fucked, I thought. Without Henderson in the middle, we'll get it rammed down our throats and jammed up our asses. Like me, Henderson had been recruited. Maybe he'd change his mind.

"What about your bonus?" I asked him.

"If I stick with the Bucks, I'll make a lot more than the bonus."

"You don't mean you're going for a ten-day, James."

"Technically yes, but my agent says I should finish out this year. With the experience, I'll have a better shot next year. This is my break, Michael."

What was I doing trying to piss on Henderson's parade? I knew the CBA code: you get the call and you go, no matter what and where your team is. I stuck out my hand.

"Congratulations, James. Crush 'em for the GBA."

Henderson had Vassilis translate a little farewell speech to the team. Henderson told the Greeks he'd enjoyed playing with them and living in their country. He apologized for leaving so suddenly and wished us luck. He hoped we'd understand and told us an anecdote from his childhood. He was about ten when he first saw Dr. J. on TV. "The man was beautiful, powerful, and smart. I told myself then if I could be only one of the three and play in the NBA, that's what I wanted to do."

That night I lay awake like after a loss. Right up to the end Henderson played part of his role. He had two out of his three covered. Maybe they wouldn't be enough for the League. Henderson might be back on the eleventh day. No, he'd stick. He was too good for the GBA or CBA. He was bigger now, had more confidence in his shot. We had to get someone else. An enforcer but someone who wouldn't stick me every chance he got. Someone I could beat at backgammon. Henderson did take care of business. A big risk, going six thousand miles for a ten and an agent's assurance. Henderson was big enough to do it. The motherfucker was a force. He'd done it here his way and alone—no family, no squeeze, no group, no friends I ever saw. Malone and Stockton. I wondered if they spoke to each other off the court. We'd never been out together, yet I felt I'd lost a friend. The shooter owes you. You and the center owe each other. You exchange gifts. James and I exchanged shots. We were mixed weight sparring partners. Why else would James take my parting shots? Because the proud, selfish motherfucker felt sorry for the desperate delivery boy without a Mailman.

James had Law School and the bonus in his pocket. Why would he take the ten-day risk? Getting out early and quick could be his way of fucking up white-man land, all of us "foo's." He wasn't going for the money. Where did the obsession with the NBA begin? Henderson could have seen Dr. J. and decided to become a physician. Had Henderson at ten wanted to be a beauty, a crowd-pleaser? Did he understand that the other kids called him spider-man because of his long fingers? Did he remember his mother's comment to her friends when she bought James his first pair of sneakers? "That James is going to be big." If you're black and tall at ten, the pressures must be powerful, even if you're middle class. Even if you're a homeboy like Jug. I'm tall in a Greek trolley. In the States, I pass for normal. "You never played basketball?"—that's what James would have heard from the bailiffs and clients until he was gray. He liked to stick me. James was stuck with his body. He'd made himself a banger but he'd just stretched his skin. Even sadder were the millions of black kids on the playgrounds, the five-ten's and six-footers who have the skin and the Jones but not the size. No chance for them. I kidded him about taking Koko along to carry his bags. Maybe James was following around his body, bulking it up to be what others thought it should be. He bitched about being used, yet he was in the weight room everyday. Body by whites. Now they were giving him his break and he was going home. He had the Jones. He couldn't just say no. He probably couldn't say just how he got it. The Dr. J. story was a story. Henderson had the need. And if some Sun Belt team called Valtadoros? If Houston wanted me to dish for Hakeem? Would I have deserted the Atholes? Was I still awake or not? I'd had my ten-day. My NBA future was in the past. Henderson was moving up. I was trying to stay put. I rolled and thrashed. We needed a brother. When I got to sleep, I dreamed it was snowing on the motherfucker when he got to Milwaukee.

At practice the next day, Z told us the GM was trying to sign another American. He should be here after the two-week Easter break, but against PAOK, a team we'd beaten by seventeen in November, we'd have to play three forwards (Dop, Pop, and young Jorgos), keep the floor open, keep moving, use the passing game, and everybody hit the boards. Our shots were falling in the first half, but the size and weight mismatches caught up with us after intermission. Koko's knees wouldn't let him play. Petros couldn't help. Our fans didn't help because we couldn't put together a run to raise them from their seats, not without some rebounds. We lost by seven, our first defeat this half and first all year in the pit. Dop had ten rebounds, his career high. He was too beat to take his twelve shots. The other shooters were difficult to control without Henderson's stability in the middle. Lou, Pop, and even young Jorgos were taking stupid, September shots. I'd pass, the ball would go up, and I'd go after it. I had four rebounds, double my season high and two more than I wanted. We had to replace Henderson.

Chapter 7

During our Easter break, Ann wanted to get out of Athens. I was glad to oblige. Since Eleni had told me to stay next year, I'd been coined in Peristeri, mistranslated in Kypseli, and deprived of the ball in the pit. Ann was interested in historic sites on the Peloponnese. I suggested we take a bus tour, as we had to Delphi. Ann went to the tourist office and reported back that "Every week of the year" in their brochure did not include Easter weekend. We decided to rent a car, and Ann planned our itinerary: we'd leave early Good Friday, before the traffic, and sneak back into Athens the afternoon after Easter. Getting out was easy. At 4 A.M. all we had to worry about were taxis cruising with their headlights off. We were in Corinth by six for breakfast and, after dodging a few sleepy farmers on tractors, in Epidauros an hour before the ticket seller. Ann told Sara and me about the amazing acoustics in the amphitheater, which held twice as many ancient Greeks as the pit. On Good Friday it was empty. Ann sent me up to the top row; Sara stayed on stage and said "akous me" in a normal voice. "What?" I yelled down. "Can you hear me?" Sara said. "No," I yelled back, "can you hear me?" "No," Ann said, "can you see us without the camera?" I came down and taped them clowning on stage. Watching Ann fool around with Sara, I felt as if we were at home, on our home court. Then we walked around the spa, where I learned old Greeks soaked their aching bones and muscles in hot water. That night we stayed in Nafplion on the coast and watched the traditional Friday evening procession. The villagers removed a model of Christ's tomb from the church, put it on poles like an ancient king, and carried it up and down the streets and alleys. "We'd never have known about this if we were in Athens," Ann whispered as the box and pack of villagers passed by. Nafplion she liked: its Greeks were quiet, slowly pacing folk.

Reading her Blue Guide aloud the next day at the ruined palace of Mycenae, Ann was in her elements: information and outdoors. Sara and I tired of all the names and dates, but the sun was warm, water was plentiful, and Ann enjoyed having the site almost to ourselves. Easter we had to climb over a low wire fence to get into the Stone-Age fortress of Tiryns. Gesturing at yellow wild flowers and high green grass that filled the courtyard, Ann said, "It's a good time to visit Greece." I suppose she was right, but I liked the September crowds at Delphi and the Greek weekenders on Idra. The piled stone walls of Tiryns reminded me of Vermont and my reasons for getting out: the long, lonely winters I left for a full-ride in Memphis, what I thought was the south. Ann insisted that she and Sara find the secret tunnel under the back wall, an exit rulers could use if enemies were battering the gate or water and food were running low. Pacing off the distances written in her guide and directing Sara to look for clues, Ann didn't look or sound homesick. I wondered if I'd made too easy an excuse for her unhappiness at Carnival. Here at Tiryns, as in the States, Ann was the one with knowledge and control. In Athens I was speaking on television and directing Greeks on the floor. Perhaps Ann was dissatisfied with the way our roles had switched. If she only knew how Eleni's bait and switch had made Athens feel threatening to me, Ann wouldn't resent the celebrity I couldn't avoid.

Monday morning Ann timed our departure from Nafplion so we'd reach Athens while Greeks were napping. On the two-lane, winding road to Corinth, we came up behind two trailer trucks going about thirty-five miles an hour. As soon as we slowed down, cars behind us began passing. They passed us by pictorial no passing signs and signs that read "No Overtaking," Greek English for no passing. They crossed the solid line and the double solid line. They swerved around us on curves and went by the trucks on brows of hills. They passed going through villages, coming upon flashing lights at junctions, and while crossing railroad tracks. The bump of the tracks caused the guy who tried that to fly up in the air and slam back down on his muffler, but he kept going, dragging it up the highway, throwing sparks as he went by the trucks. Men passed us, women passed us, families jammed into the front seats of pickups passed us. The passengers looked over at me with expressions that suggested I had insulted them. Athenians drove small foreign models for quick cutting and easy parking on sidewalks. The country Greeks in old American models lumbered out into the no-passing lane, engine revving over their wailing horns, and took forever to get back on their own side of the road. I realized why I'd never seen a junkyard in Greece. The Greeks ran their vehicles until they were totaled, mashed into metal lumps in head-on collisions. Not even the goofiest, Millered-up high school kid in Vermont would have taken the chances on country roads these Greeks did. I wondered if there was an earthquake or tidal wave behind us. I couldn't imagine a reason short of natural disaster why the Greeks were in such a hurry to get to Corinth, to get anywhere. After observing for a few miles, Ann wouldn't let me pass the trucks when we came to a straight stretch. They were our protection against Greeks coming the other way. We and our blockers got to Corinth in four rather than two hours.

On the Corinth-Athens highway, we were on our own, exposed, and we learned how to drive in a crowd. Although Greeks from all over the Peloponnese funnel into this route to the capital, most of the road is two-lane with wide, paved shoulders. When a Greek wants to pass you, he flicks his lights on and off. You're supposed to pull over and drive the shoulder, even if you're going around a curve at the time, even if you're already going eighty kilometers an hour. It's a wide shoulder but a narrow lane for any car bigger than a Honda Civic. I didn't understand the first time a car flashed behind me. He pulled up to within ten feet of my bumper and flashed again. Then he laid on the horn, threw me an open palm, and waved me over. I was in his lane. About the fourth time I had to pull over, we were going around a curve. There was a bridge. No shoulder. I slammed on the brakes and then had to floor the Ford to get back out into the traffic coming around the curve.

What made Ann climb into the back seat with Sara was a move we'd not seen on the way up to Corinth in the dark. If an oncoming Greek wants to pass both the car in his lane and the car or truck on the shoulder, he puts on his lights and shoots out into *your* lane. Now it's his lane. You're supposed to give way and get onto the shoulder—if there is one, if there's no truck already there, if you see the car coming at you, if you understand Greek right of way. The Peloponnesians going to Corinth were taking suicidal chances. The Athenians heading our way could kill us *and* themselves. The cars with lights on kept coming at us, crowding us onto the shoulder.

"Eetheeotees, fucking eetheeotees," Ann said, giving "idiots" its Greek pronunciation. I had to agree with her. "Proud, selfish, crazy idiots. Just pull over, slow down, and drive on the shoulder."

"I can't," I tell her. "When I come to a bridge, I'll have to stop, and the cars in the fast lane will never let me back on the road or we'll get nailed from behind."

"Then stop at the next gas station, and we'll wait for the traffic to thin."

"Do you want to do this at night?"

We had to keep going. Ordinary defensive driving was impossible. I had to run by Greek rules: exceed the speed limit, hog the fast lane, blink cars in front onto the shoulder, be ready to duck oncoming lights, figure the inches between lanes, and avoid thinking about the hundreds of feet between the shoulder and the Saronic Gulf below.

As fast as traffic was moving, the delay from Nafplion to Corinth still brought us into Athens at rush hour. For some reason traffic entering the city was thicker than traffic leaving. We were bumper to bumper and backed up at toll booths. I decided not to retrace our early morning route through city streets. We swung around the city on the Piraeus road so we could come up Syngrou Avenue, the four-lane highway that runs from the sea to the Plaka and the car rental agency. Traffic was also thick on Syngrou, a lot of squealing stops and starts at lights, honking horns and waving arms where four lanes merged into three, but the possible fender-bender or bumper-cruncher, even the grinding buses and diesel fumes, were a relief from high-speed chicken out on the highway. Some cars had flags flying from their aerials or flapping out their windows. The drivers were beeping in rhythmic code: beep beep, beep beep beep. Closer in, the drivers were pulling up onto sidewalks, parking at bus stops, double-parking on side streets. We dropped off our car and walked to Amalias, one of the wide avenues that converges in Syntagma. The police had set up a barricade: pedestrian traffic only. It was only a few blocks to Syntagma and then home. We'd been sitting in the car and standing at the sites for four days. We didn't mind the walk. A couple of blocks up Amalias, music was coming out of loud-speakers hung up on telephone poles. All six lanes of Amalias were flowing with people, all heading toward the center. Many had flags. Some carried banners. Families walked together, the kids blowing whistles. Middle-aged women strolled two by two, arm in arm. This was something to tape. I got out my camera and panned the crowd, the banners and the set faces of the men who carried them.

Sara picked up a plastic flag from the street. "Is it a

parade?" she asked. We didn't know. I thought it might be a soccer celebration. I'd heard the Greeks went crazy over soccer. Whatever it was, it was on the way home. Entrepreneurs had set up portable souvlaki stands in the street. We bought some sodas out of an oil drum cooled with blocks of ice and walked along with the crowd. As we moved toward Syntagma, more people emptied into Amalias from side streets. Our pace slowed as the crowd became more dense. Older people and families leaned in doorways or sat on steps and ledges. We kept going, single file now, bumping shoulders and hips. I'd never been in a crowd this size.

A block from Syntagma, huge floodlights on three-story stagings shone toward us and into the square. On one a TV crew was shooting the crowd. Loudspeakers were closer together here. I could barely hear Ann when she said, "What do you think it is?" I didn't know. The cameras reminded me of outdoor rock concerts in muddy fields or state funerals. I did know we needed to keep going forward, toward the square. The gates to the National Garden on the right of Amalias were chained. The side streets back to the left were filled with people heading this way. Our only choice was Amalias. It was a six-lane rush-hour trolley, standing room only and nobody getting off. One man had climbed a small tree. He was waving a flag twice as big as he was. It was too crowded to tape him.

Only we and the young men blasting air horns now wanted to get into the square. As we burrowed through the crowd toward the Parliament building on the high side of the square, fireworks shot off from the stagings and exploded just above the crowd. A single voice now shouted through the loudspeakers. More fireworks went off, a powerful synchronized blast leaving an acrid cloud in the air. The voice shouted and the crowd roared, again and again. Then the voice firing up the crowd began a chant the people repeated. They were swaying now, chanting and rocking on their toes and heels.

The crowd was a moving wall of bodies. There wasn't enough room to put one foot in front of the other. I turned and wedged sideways between bodies, stepping on their feet, scraping them with the bag on my back. Sara came behind me, holding onto my left hand and Ann's right. I knew Sara was crying. I couldn't pick her up. The crowd was too dense. I needed my right hand free to steer and nudge through the bodies. There were thousands of people between us and the other side of the square, and each person required a new decision: pass in front or in back, which would be in another person's face. I didn't know these people, which ones might give a few inches and let us through, who might hold their little piece of ground. I pushed in front of the shorter ones, in back of the larger ones. Slowly, very slowly, sidestep by sidestep, Greek by Greek, we snaked through the moving mass.

When we're halfway through the square, the chanting ends, the crowd grows still. The loudspeakers play music I'd heard somewhere before, not Greek, maybe some kind of French anthem. Then a woman's voice screams through the loudspeakers. The people all stretch up on their tiptoes to look down to the left. I stop and use my height advantage to look over the Greeks' heads, the ones I am wedged against, the tens of thousands jamming together in the square below, sitting in the trees, standing in the fountain, trampling the grass.

On a staging that rises high above the cafes and the familiar American Express sign, a man stands in front of a huge red flag. He's throwing his arms up like Coach Jacobs begging for crowd support in overtime. I feel a hand on my elbow and look down. It's a thick, tanned hand that reminds me of my father's, a farmer's hand. I turn and see a short man. I'm blocking his view. "You. . . go. . . home," he shouts slowly, one word at a time, the simple English of a non-native speaker. "I. . . know," I holler back and think of Eleni. We can't stay here. I don't know how long this will last. We can't go back. I have to get Sara home. I'm afraid she will pass out breathing belt-high air. More fireworks go shooting off from the stagings. Another male voice begins, shriller than the last. The crowd is still, listening, intent on a voice many can't see. It's more difficult to move now than when the Greeks were moving. It's harder to leave the crowd than to get into it. I feel trapped by these thousands of short bodies. I'm sweating in my down jacket. Edging sideways is like running suicides inside a closet. The heat and pressure of the crowd make it hard to breathe. Sara's hand is sweaty. I'm sure she will faint. I've got to get her out of here. The voice screams and then shrieks as the sound feeds back. I can't make out a single word except "Ellatha." I've got to move. I let go of Sara's hand and spread out my elbows, making space for myself to reach down and hoist Sara up out of the crowd onto my shoulders. I hold my bag with my left hand and hold her hands next to my head with my right. My elbow is pointed straight out, as if I were about to shoot. I scream "Passing through" as loud as I can and lead with my elbow. The Greeks hear me or they see the elbow coming at eye level or they see Sara on my shoulders. They surrender a little space. Ann comes behind, holding onto my belt. I keep screaming "Passing through" and keep my elbow out. The Greeks give us some room and we squeeze through the standing crowd, slowly but directly making our way toward the Grand Bretagne Hotel on the other side of the square. There, where the view of the man on the staging is obstructed, the crowd thins just a little and I drop my elbow. We push along down Panepistemiou, heading toward a side street that will take us up the hill to Kolonaki. Families are standing together or sitting on the curbs, looking up at the loudspeakers. A little further on, scooters, motorcycles, and cars are parked every which way on the sidewalks. It'll be a long time before the Greeks get this untangled. We stop and I put Sara down.

"Daddy, I was scared."

"I know you were. You were brave too. Nothing is going to happen to you when you're with Mommy and Daddy."

"Why are all the people here?"

"I think it's a rally, a political rally."

"What's that?"

"When lots of people get together to cheer for the person they want to be president."

Ann was frightened too. I knew because she hadn't said anything. Her face was blank, as if she couldn't say anything. When we were close to our apartment, she asked what the man in the square told me.

"That we should leave," I said.

"Excellent advice. After today, can you tell me why we shouldn't take it?"

"Don't forget the bonus, Ann. You don't want to leave without the money, do you?"

Ann was silent for a couple of minutes.

"OK, then, just one more question: Who are these people, anyway?"

"Greeks, I'd guess," was the best I could do.

The next morning the *Athens News* has the story. Two hundred fifty thousand people had gathered for the kickoff rally of Synaspismos, the parties of the left—Communists, Euro-communists, and other splinter groups. This crowd was only half the number of people who had been in the square the night before for the conservatives and were expected tonight by the ruling socialists.

From our balcony we have an overview as PASOK, Dop's party, brings its half million into Syntagma. Standing at the railing, we can hear the car horns, loudspeakers, and fireworks. On our TV, we watch people moving toward Syntagma, long shots down the avenues, close-ups from the stagings we'd passed under. I'd never seen so many people, not live, not this close. From all over the country, Greeks had left their gyms and churches, parks and tavernas, towns and cities to gather in their capital. Viewed from above, the crowd seems more dangerous than when we were inside it. We were able to leave, but the crowd looks trapped by its numbers down in the square. Safe on our balcony, we're as speechless as we were in the noise. Sara and Ann and I are all agog. We stand on our overlook and silently watch the unmoving mass beneath us. The fireworks launched from the stagings sound like bombs. Above this huge pit of people, smoke rises up through the floodlight glaze, obscuring the Acropolis and collecting into a fuzzy dome over the city center.

Chapter 8

Henderson's replacement was a kid named Lester Howard from West Carolina Community College in North Carolina. West Carolina had just finished fourth in the national Junior College tournament; Lester had led the club in scoring and was named to the all-tournament team. Lester was six-eleven but only twenty. He reminded me of the Cavaliers' Brad Daugherty, light-skinned, a widow's peak in his close-cropped hair, and a quizzical expression. Unlike Daugherty, who graduated from UNC at twenty-one, Lester was no genius. He left West Carolina early for Athens because his grades would never get him into a four-year school. Lester also lacked Daugherty's linebacker thighs. Lester was, however, available. We were desperate. Welcome to the GBA.

Z made Lester my project. I got him a room at the hotel where Henderson had lived, picked him up for practice, walked him back, took him out for dinner, taught him how to order souvlaki, potatoes, and tomatoes ("patates" and "domates" in Greek). Lester didn't ask many questions; he just looked puzzled most of the time. Walking with him, I got more than my usual sideways glances, but I also thought of Lester as a bodyguard. Not an intimidator but a buddy, someone to head off intimate conversations. Z wanted to break in Lester fast. Although JC ball is usually hurry-scurry, an educational CBA, West Carolina played a deliberate game. Lester wasn't ready to run in the pit. He played ten and sat down for ten. Drinkman would have called Lester a "Coaster," a West Coast player, "all touch and no thump." Lester didn't body up and stop you from shooting. He'd give you the shot and then wipe it off. Lester loved the international rule that allows a defender to flick away a shot if it hits the rim and bounces above it. "The rock just sitting up there waiting for me to slap it," Lester told me. While he was watching the ball bounce on the rim, the other rebounders were bouncing him under the backboard. On offense, I hit Lester in the chest, face, back of the head, and, finally, in the hands with passes. Lester was a slow learner but a nice kid. With some practices and a couple of games, he'd definitely contribute in the playoffs. Lester was very young. Maybe he was only playing dumb. I hoped I wasn't kidding myself about our great light hope.

With two games left, the top of the standings was tight:

Panathinaikos	17-3
Grigora	16-4
Olympiakos	16-4
Aris	15-5

Only four teams make the GBA playoffs. We all had an easy finish, so this was the crucial weekend. After beating us in Salonika the first half, Aris had to come to the pit. If we won, we'd have the home-court advantage through the playoffs and play Aris in the first round. Aris had won the championship the last two years and had the league-leading scorer, Nikos Kallis. Now thirty-five, Kallis coasted during most of the season, putting up points when it counted. I took home tape of our first game. On the small screen this Greek hero looks more like a Puerto Rican welterweight than the white marble busts in Plaka tourist shops. He has long thin calves, powerful round shoulders, and thick hairy arms. His skin is stretched tight on his sharp face. He has a thin pinched mouth and thick eyebrows knit in a constant frown. Against Kappa and Lou, Kallis had scored thirty-four in Salonika. Now that I had tape to study, Z wanted me covering him.

Like so many basketball terms, point included, "cover" is misleading. You don't drape yourself over your man like a net dropped on an animal from a helicopter. You don't pull yourself over him like the plastic sheathes Athenians without garages put on their cars. Your man isn't inside you. You have to get inside him, inside his head, fuck up his primary desire, take him out of his rhythm, piss him off. To D down, I reverse the point guard's gallery of possibilities, reduce probabilities, cast off irrelevant information, simplify the pro I'm facing into a prototype, and attack that stick figure. "Stick with him," your coach hollers. When the man you're guarding tries to take you one-on-one, your teammates shout "stick him, stick him," like corner men reminding a backpedaler to jab. Your man's teammates are screaming "Light him up," "Burn him down," "Smoke him out." Fear sharpens strategy to the sticking point. If you don't get inside the match-up, you will be the match that's burned.

Kallis shot face-up threes on Kappa and scored some points with bursts to the hoop on Lou, but Kallis's favorite move was to dribble into the key, turn his back on the defender, bob up and down, back and forth with a high dribble, waiting for the defender to overcommit. Then he'd elevate and shoot the fade-away. Bobs and hops were a tough combination. The way to give Kallis trouble was to get below him, go down into an exaggerated low defensive stance, and take away the space the six-foot Kallis usually owned. Get inside and under him.

I was the player I couldn't defend. Three days before the Aris game, I found a note from Eleni in my mailbox at the pit. She wanted to talk with me after practice. Alone. She'd be waiting in a cafe down the street from the pit. Of course, I thought, this is the biggest game of the year. But Lester had worked. Receiving the note was like watching tape: it gave me time to compose myself. I just hoped Lester wouldn't get lost walking back to his hotel.

"I've got a big problem," Eleni said when I sat down. Not, "You've got a big problem," as I expected.

"What's that?"

"Money. I need money to replace the cash you took to Istanbul. Some friends and I are trying to do something to solve the water problem, but it's expensive. We need some quick cash."

"Lottery tickets. Greeks all buy them. I get five a week from that one-legged guy in Kolonaki."

"We need a sure thing. We want to bet on Aris and be certain they're going to win."

Eleni sounded almost apologetic. She didn't use "fix" or "throw" or "lock," but not even a Prop 48 freshman could miss the point now. Turn on Keever number two, preempt, get out in front. I gave Eleni what Ann used to call my "game smirk."

"So you believe I'm not really Greek, huh?"

She smiled back. "We know you're not."

"I've been wondering about that since you mentioned my daughter," I said, preserving the illusion—if she wanted it— that I was dumb before the comment on Sara, projecting the illusion that I wasn't worried, just curious.

"I had someone in the States check into your family background."

"What did this person find?"

"You'll find that out in the newspapers."

"I'd be the one with a problem then. But what you're asking makes no sense, Eleni."

I stopped and made her ask what I meant.

93

"A month ago you tell me you want me to play for the national team and stay next year, so I work on that. Now you want me to throw the most important game of the season. How does that help me make the Greek squad? If I screw up now, what makes you think Panathinaikos will offer me a contract next year? You know I want to be here next year. You've got to make up your mind what you want."

Keever is no moralist, just a guy trying to figure the angles, keep himself playing, keep himself talking and watching. Half-way through my little speech, Eleni's hands started to fidget under the table. I could see her elbows shiver.

"We need the money now," she said. "This summer the water shortage could be catastrophic."

"I understand. So here's what I can do for you. Even without Henderson, we're favored by seven points because of the pit. You bet on Aris and I'll make sure we don't cover the spread. We get the home-court advantage in the playoffs, you get your money, I protect my reputation, and we all have enough to drink."

Point-shaving, I thought. Yes, I was being slowly cut down to Greek size by this small woman. Eleni didn't like the idea. She came back quickly and insistently.

"You have to lose. Otherwise, you could make us lose."

"I can see what you're afraid of. But either way, Eleni, you have to trust me. If I was the kind of guy who'd kiss off my life here to protect the game's integrity and prove a point, I could easily do that. Since I'm here, you know I'm no idealist. So let's work together. I've got money riding on the playoffs. Without Henderson, we're going to need the pit."

Eleni looked surprised. Her face was much too mobile.

"Do you have that kind of control over the game?"

Eleni must have figured this meeting was going to be quick and simple. Now she was asking the questions. She looked into my eyes to see if I was lying. If she'd played basketball, she'd have known better. All coaches agree: never look at the eyes. It's a tough instinct to decondition, the reason the look-off pass works year after year. I let her look.

"I'm the point, Eleni. That's my job. Lay down your money, but this is the last time I can do this for a while. Nobody would take a bet on the cupcake game next week. And during the playoffs, anything can happen. You might lose money."

"You'll be out of a job and lose your bonus if Panathinaikos wins by seven or more."

So Eleni knew about my bonus. No problem. I had this covered.

"That will never happen," I said, remembering Drinkman's assurance, "because I'll have money invested myself. I've got about a half-million drachmas in the bank, but I can't be walking the streets asking around for a bookie. I want to give you the drachs to get down with your money."

Trust me. I trust you. Think of the future, I beamed at Eleni, all that money to be made through mutual trust.

"Do you also want my address and phone number? Do you think I'd let you set up a meeting with me?"

Eleni's voice had risen just a little, and she looked around the café. I was either a stupid jock or a dumb joker. I insisted on being a greedy cheat, recruiting myself, selling myself, keeping her in my game, joining Eleni in hers.

"You decide, but with me controlling the action and you laying the bets, Eleni, we can make a lot of money working together next year."

"I want to see what happens with Aris. Then you'll hear from me."

"Fine, but don't forget: I can't help you in the playoffs."

She reached down for her bag, and I stood up. If our discussion was over, I wanted to beat her out, leave her thinking.

"No," Eleni said, "you sit here and pay for the beers I ordered."

Then she got up and walked quickly out the door. Waiting for an old bald guy to bring the drinks, I thought either Eleni doesn't have proof or she doesn't know the value of what she has. If she had the goods on me, would she have opened up by asking for my sympathy? Would she be so skittish? The police weren't going to come busting in and arrest her for fixing a game. Vassilis wasn't taping her from across the street. Lester wouldn't beat her up. Perhaps the shift from losing to shaving points spooked her. Or maybe real money was at stake this time. She might really be betting. One sure thing: I couldn't afford to bet that she lacked the evidence. She rushed out, but I was still in the bind, even if she bought the idea of working together. I could use both those beers. I motioned the waiter over.

"Beeras," I said.

"Ti beeras?" he said. What beers?

So Eleni thought she was slick, keeping me here waiting to pay so I couldn't follow her. I'd been waiting for months and was prepared to wait some more to get that fucking bonus. In fact, I'd been waiting for years, all except those ten days with the Celtics, for which I was paid the league's rookie minimum of $1,150, about $200 a minute for the time I played. I calculated how I'd hold down both Kallis and the score. Apply the pressure early, get out to a lead, and let Aris back in slowly. Behind my eyes I ran some more tape of Kallis bobbing and hopping, using up Kappa and Lou. I ejected that and loaded tape of Eleni's eyes, her back when she rushed out. Walking home I realized what I was going to do was for the good of all—not just Ann and Sara, who would profit from the bonus, but also the team. If I let Eleni expose me now, Panathinaikos would get killed in the playoffs and everybody would suffer— players, management, fans, even the cafes and tavernas around the pit. If I shaved the points, Eleni could help solve the water shortage for all Athenians. This I knew was self-deception, but I couldn't prove it wrong.

On game night fans were already standing in the aisles when we came out for the shootaround. When we ran the layup line, they were hanging from the girders at the top of the aisles. Twice as many policemen as usual lined up under the baskets, probably to see the game for free. The chants insulting Aris came fast and loud. While we were practicing our foul shots, Lester kept glancing around the gym, more bewildered than quizzical. "The court's the same all over the world," I told him.

Lester outjumped Lekos, the Aris center, by six inches. In the first three minutes, Lester erased a Lekos shot and on a missed free throw rose up way above the rim and batted the ball off the board. I was squatting on Kallis, dragging my knuckles on the floor like a gibbon, flicking at his dribble, making him work, but Aris was hurting us on their offensive boards. Dop and Lester were getting ridden under the rim, where all they could do was take the ball out of bounds after Duvnik, their Slav, and Lekos got through tipping it around and in. On defense Aris was pressing us man to man full-court, running in young subs to wear us down. I wasn't turning over the ball, but either the big-game pressure or the pressure defense was getting to the shooters. Pop was firing too fast.

For every one he or Lou hit, Dop missed two. Duvnik was jamming Lester out of the paint. We were one and done. The Aris guards were leaving early, and Kallis was beating us out in the open floor. We were down by fourteen at the half. Walking into the locker, I thought Eleni's bet and my integrity were safe.

We weren't playing that badly, just without Henderson. Kallis had ten. Duvnik had fifteen. Z said that Aris really wanted this one, that their momentum would slow if we could keep them off the boards, that we were still in the game. I'd heard Z scream plenty in Greek. I hadn't seen him this emotional in English. He was afraid we'd quit on him. He was thinking get it close. He told us to be patient, chip away at the spread, make the extra pass. I doubted Z really believed we could come back, but he wanted to avoid getting humiliated in the pit and on national TV. He told me to keep the ball in my hands, penetrate, draw some fouls, score with the clock off.

Lester outjumps Lekos by a foot, and off the tip I hit Lou for a three. I get down on Kallis and he's called for palming. Aris drops back to a half-court man to man. We run our motion offense. I find Pop on a back-door cut and the next time I see Lou behind a screen on the baseline for two. It's a seven-point run. I'm inside the iso tape and inside Kallis's skin, making him take extra bobs and hops. Z may have been talking the usual blowout shit at halftime, but we are playing together and closing the gap. Kallis seems listless, one less bob and hop. He bobs, backs away at the foul line. I stay down. When he shoots, I come out of my stance, explode up to my real height, and get a little of the ball, a little of his hand, and a foul. Kallis holds his hand as if Henderson had crushed it. What a pussy. He flexes his fingers and calls out the trainer, who sprays his hand. Kallis misses the first foul shot. He's holding his hand again and walking over to the bench. He's taking himself out. In comes a replacement. No guts, no pride. I wish Henderson could be here to see the show. The sub misses the second foul shot. Lester cuffs the ball above the rim and we're out on a three-on-two break.

I've been saving something for a time like this. At the top of the key, I look off one defender on Pop in the left lane. I turn a little right and look off the other defender on Lou in the right lane. I pick up my dribble in my right hand and start the ball around my back to freeze the defenders where they are. Behind my back, I pass the ball from my right hand to my left hand, bring it out, and this time keep the ball for myself, splitting the defenders and dropping it in, the uncontested layup the byproduct of a season's high-li, the third option fucking up the first- and second-guessers. We're ahead for the first time all night. The crowd chants "lefkos magos." I come up the floor pumping my fist and glance at Kallis. He'll be pissed. He's sitting on the bench smiling. What the fuck? Finakis shoots an air ball. We come down and Lester hits a turnaround over Duvnik. Bounding back up the floor, Lester looks like one of the saved. I glance again at the Aris bench. Kallis and the other players are laughing. I take a quick look at our bench. We're up by three and Z looks as if we're losing by ten. Lester and Keever, American slow learners. We haven't just staged a great comeback. Aris is giving away this one, dumping it. They want us in the first round. They've seen Lester, kicked our ass for a half in our building, and prefer us to Grigora or Olympiakos even if we will have the home-court advantage.

Now I have a serious problem. I call time out, go over to the bench, and ask Z what the fuck is going on. "They want to lose," he says and shrugs as if it's something that happens frequently. "Who they?" Lester asks. "The other team," I tell him. Lester can't take that in. Henderson, I think, and start screaming. "This fucking shit makes me fucking sick," I yell into our huddle. "We'll show these motherfuckers," I scream. "Two teams can play this fucking game." I wave my arms like a Greek for the fans, hoping they'll understand what is going to happen.

The next five minutes were uglier than the game up in Patras. Aris was missing shots. I was throwing the ball away. They stood in the lane for ten seconds. I took four steps without dribbling. We went ahead by seven. Then I started fouling and told Lester to do the same. The Aris players were too proud of their Greek shooting to put up air balls or clangers at the foul line, so a few dropped in. I kept the ball in my hands and forced them to foul me. I was a "xenos." I didn't mind blowing off some foul shots. My final stats were ten points, two for eleven from the foul line, seven assists (all in the first thirty minutes), and sixteen turnovers, twice as many as I'd ever committed in a game. We won by four, but some fans were booing and throwing palms at the end. It was hard to tell who the palms were aimed at, but just before the final buzzer the janitors folded out the metal chutes we'd never needed before. Filing in to the dressing room, we could hear objects hit the metal ceiling. It was definitely different in Greece: after the biggest win of the season, I could feel all my endorphins turning to cat piss.

While I was getting my rubdown from Vassilis, Lester came into the trainer's room and asked why Aris quit.

"They want to fuck us at home in the playoffs."

"I just played j-c, but I know this shit ain't professional ball."

"Forget professional, Les. Remember drachmas and dollars. Just make sure you get your money."

After Lester left, I asked Vassilis why a championship team like Aris was willing to dump a game.

"There's not as much money to go around as in the US. There professional codes can be honored. Here people and organizations scramble for any advantage. You know there's no credit here, don't you?"

"What do you mean?"

"No bank loans for cars and houses. Barely any credit cards. You have to have cash up front. That's why people flock to the seeties and the islands. How do you say: the fast buck. It's also why many seeteezens have second jobs like most of the team."

Now I was the slow learner. I'd never added up what I knew about individual Greeks: Koko's paddleboat business, Dop's job in a Kolonaki boutique, Kappa's little souvlaki shop, Pop's returning to his village to help out when we had time off. Lou didn't have another job. From what I could tell, he also didn't have a car or house of his own. I wondered if Ann and I had never been invited to my teammates' homes because, like Kappa, they lived with their parents or were ashamed to show an American their apartments. If players in the GBA have to take second jobs, everybody must. A few Kolonakians can afford au pairs to chase their kids, but the crowds of Greeks speeding in the streets and rushing on the sidewalks aren't athletes for the fun of it. The men are double-timing to put cash in the little leather handbags they carry. Women are pushing ahead for bargains and hoarding change because here change matters. No wonder Ann couldn't find work. Even I had a second job, smuggling money out of the country, shaving points. I was too busy protecting my investment to add up the places along with the people: the freezing gym in Patras, the poor neighborhoods around the gym in Peristeri, the dense, standardized buildings in Kypseli where kids didn't have a gym, our very own pit, just a twenty-minute walk from the boutiques and embassies of Kolonaki. Even our cramped, cold apartment was part of the big picture. Greece wasn't the Third World, as Ann had said, but the capital of a Second World country would have enough water to drink and to wash dust off electric lines.

"Money I know about," I said, "but I still don't get Aris. Without Henderson, we're no match for them, at least not until Lester understands the game here. Why would they humiliate themselves in front of six thousand fans?"

"It helps to understand a little heestory," Vassilis told me. "For hundreds of years, we were like African-Americans. We had to take Turkish names. You know, 'pseudonyms.' 'Greece,' for example, is a Turkish word for slave. To survive our eenvaders, we needed to be clever. Cleverness was something to be proud of. Our strategy was scheming. These are both Greek words. Aris fans would be proud of their team."

"Why were our fans throwing stuff, then?"

"Perhaps we were too obvious trying to throw the game back to Aris."

"Not throwing. Showing. Giving those motherfuckers some of their own ugly shit and still winning."

"Yes, I understand, but I'm the one who has to clean up this sheet on metal and on the floor."

It wasn't enough that Eleni had made me turn the fans against me. Now, I thought, she has even my man Vassilis "peesed" at me. As he worked on my shoulders, I reran what he'd said. Was he accusing me of trying to throw the game and failing? Or was he upset about the obvious turnovers and air balls? And what was this stuff about fake names. Then I put one and one together: the two people who talked to me about false names might know each other. Vassilis and Eleni were the only people who congratulated me on the Spiti Mas feature. Maybe it was Vassilis who'd tipped off Eleni about me. That would account for all her appealing poses in January. Then I'd tried to assume her "Keltik" was an accident. It was safer to assume that Vassilis's "pseudonym" was significant. Vassilis was as proud of those sneaky "s" words as he was of "muscle" and "hygiene." People taught me the Greek that was important to them, as if the words preceded events, controlled them. "Strategy" and "scheming" made me suspect Vassilis' historical explanation was sophistry. The Greeks had invented athletic competition. That was the history they were responsible to. What if the guy at Marathon had quit early? I felt terrible about what I'd done and how the fans had reacted, but at least I wasn't deceiving myself. I'd turned the ball over for the cash, not for the culture.

Vassilis did some light chopping on my hamstrings, and I thought let's see what else the trainer has to say about the country I'm trapped inside. If he's in with Eleni, I'd like to know just what I'm up against.

"OK," I said, "so Aris was clever to fuck up themselves. What about craziness? Why do Greeks take suicidal chances on the highway? Why did the fans go ballistic at Peristeri?"

"Since moving off farms and leaving their flocks, our people feel powerless. We no longer steer boats so we do foolish things in cars to assert ourselves. In seeties we band together. Crowds give us the power we used to feel with all our cousins around us in veellages and towns."

"Even if the crowds don't have enough water to drink?" I asked, wondering how Vassilis would respond to the problem Eleni said would soon be a crisis.

"Not enough water is Athens' problem. The rest of Greece has too much water. Soon tourists will be visiting our beaches, and we will run to serve that crowd."

An inside job, I thought: this guy with the magic hands had set me up with Eleni. She and Vassilis were the only people I'd ever heard complain about tourists. Maybe they'd even known each other in the States. Expert on my body, he probably told her that my blonde hair, blue eyes, and freckled skin couldn't be Greek. Or maybe he and the other Panathinaikos officials knew all along I wasn't Greek-American and planned to renege on the bonus. Greek "paranoia," I knew, was something to be avoided. But I was pretty sure now it was at least two-on-one, more if Eleni had an accomplice in Istanbul and someone observing me in Dexameni. Who was running whom? It might not matter. If Vassilis was the one with the knowledge, he still needed someone I didn't know to control me while he, like me, was a Panathole with a secret. He knew mine but didn't know I knew his. I hoped I'd get the chance some day to get my hands on Vassilis and even the score.

Chapter 9

"Forget play," Muray Jacobs used to say this time of year, "now we off them." He wasn't exaggerating his usual hate and loathing when he compared the playoffs to war. The regular season is guerilla action: you make contact in Grand Rapids, fire away, and fly to Pensacola. By the time you see the Grand Rapids Hoops again, half their roster will be elsewhere and you'll have forgotten the cheap fouls, the steals, and the woofing you talked about on the flight to Pensacola. In the playoffs the same guys go after each other night after night. The year the Lightning won the championship in seven games with Albany, I had a solid black and blue line across my chest where my opposite number liked to jam the heel of his hand after I passed the ball. The games are more physical because more is at stake and because the defense tightens up, but mostly because in the second season the match-ups stay the same, pride suffers, anger builds, and "get-back" rules.

In the pit, the season was summer. We were back to shirts and skins and Z still had to interrupt scrimmages to mop up sweat in the paint. At the end of practices, he put us through the suicides to remind us the year was beginning again. Air was hard to find. Vassilis was around with ice and bottled water, but I didn't think about him or Eleni. The playoffs are microscope time. Lester needed work. Panathinaikos and I had business to settle with Aris.

The NBA stretches out its second season half-way through the baseball season. The Greek playoffs are more compressed and dramatic. The games would begin May 7 with two best-of-three series: Olympiakos versus Grigora, Panathinaikos versus Aris. The championship best-of-five series would begin on the 15th with a game every other day. We'd be finished by May 25 at the latest. When the playoffs were done, the national team would announce its selections, the Greek way of making peace among the clans, reconciling the cousins for the third season, which would end in Cairo at the Mediterranean Games in late June. Lou and Vassilis both told me I'd be selected: despite the Ice Bowl in Patras and the giveaway with Aris, I was leading the league in assists and close to the thunder jammers in high-li. It would be two more months before we could leave, but now the microscope was aimed at Aris.

The GBA has a screwy way of awarding the home-court advantage. Our series would begin in Salonika and return to the pit for the next two games, if a third was necessary. The scheduling saves on travel but the team with the supposed advantage can start in the hole if it loses the first one away from home. When we left for Salonika Friday morning, the schedule seemed a happy accident. Athens was unseasonably hot, ninety degrees and windless. The Palais de Sport in Salonika is climate-controlled, maybe seventy-two degrees for our shootaround in this best of all Greek gyms. Saturday night, when Aris fans fill the seats and aisles, stomping and chanting, blowing their air horns and throwing their palms, the temperature in the Palais will seem to rise, the noise and motion bringing in a high pressure system. Panathinaikos street clothes will be damp in the armpits, a fine sweat will bead up as soon as the stretching begins, and the players will put on their wrist bands before warming up. Back in the locker, the Greeks will line up at the urinals, someone will vomit his pregame meal, and the water bottles will get sucked dry as the players try to lubricate Adam's apples that feel like tennis balls. Pressure squeezes the liquids out of you, compresses your lungs, tightens your chest.

Koko was the only Greek playoff veteran. It was hard to tell who might forget the body's conditioning, allow the mind to send its static, choke. In the second season, some guys don't want the ball. They'll sky to grab it and dive to deflect it but they don't really want it, not on the offensive end. Shooters let defenders prevent cuts or look away from the ball. Point guards give up the ball too soon or narrow their vision, see only the most probable holes in the arms and hands. Sure, the defense is closer, tougher. You have to know the defender's playoff nerves, exploit his sweaty mind, use his desire and fear for deception, fuck him up, fuck him off.

I'd spent three years in the CBA practicing pressure. For fan interest, the league awards points in the standings for quarters won. The end of most quarters is like the last two minutes of a close game. The crowd is screaming, the players trying to be quarter heroes, more out of control than the CBA norm. I'd also been through two seasons of playoffs with the Lightning. In game seven against Albany, Jacobs went over the top on hate and drew a blank in the fourth quarter. It was up to the coach on the floor. In international ball, there are fewer timeouts. The last two minutes don't become fifteen. The coach can scream from the sideline but the instructions may be noise. The point has to have it all inside him. That's what I was here for: see the floor, handle the pressure, hold the Greeks together, and take charge at the end. Now winning is the only entertainment the Greek Key has to provide. This is what I'd been playing for and waiting for: testing time, mystery time.

At the end of a game, I will myself to stay low. I don't know how. Tape helps. Years and years of repetition help. Brothers call clutch shooters "ice." It's not just temperature. I feel concentrated but transparent, dense, hard and perfectly pointed like a 2 A.M. Vermont icicle, slightly dangerous, a possible projectile. At this point, I believe the crowd is out of my mind. I'm probably out of my mind or my mind is out of me. My opponent is barely there. I'm barely there and all there. Winning and losing are gone. I doubt that I fear or want. If my brain or spinal cord is mumbling anything to itself, I'd guess it's one word: "mine." In the last possession, the rock is mine. I own the rock, nobody rips me off, I decide how it leaves my hands. The last seconds take me all the way back to the freezing shed that gave me that icy sense of possession. While other boys were standing in their haylofts practicing the long slow arc of their shots, I was bouncing the ball off the floor and walls of the low-roofed room in our tractor shed. Right hand to left hand, left to right, between my legs, behind my back, spin left, spin right, double reverse, eyes closed or lights off I'd dribble the ball and then whip it behind my back left or right, throw it between my legs front or back, flick it over my shoulder, send it flying at the spots I'd painted on the walls, spots thigh low for bounce passes, hoop high for alley oops. The ball would carom around the room, a different bounce every time, and I hustled to be there, cut if off, keep it bouncing, right, left, keep it moving, whip, flick, keep myself moving, running, dribbling, making the ball part of my body, mine. The shed was basketball without the basket, preparation for the high-li, training in possession, the point's purity, his only certainty: "mine."

An hour before game time I start forgetting senses, disconnecting unneeded elements from the connectionist network, flushing useless information down the hole in the bottom of the athlete's mind. Gatorade or cat piss in the bottles. It won't make a difference. Athletes' heads jerk to smelling salts because they've cancelled the idea of odor for two hours.

Jackson on the Lightning used to stick plugs in his ears. I have to hear the coach, so I imagine quiet, reversing the days in the shed when I invented the crowd roaring behind the walls. A face slap won't register in the playoffs. It takes an elbow in the mouth, a knee in the nuts, or a broken ankle to break the circuit between eyes and hands. I clear the pathway. Hand-eye coordination is the camera, the hand-held tool aiding the eye, magnifying private and secret space, holding still a body's blink or flipping it backward and forward, planning deception of the other's eye, the camera's opaque lens preparing the future no-look, the sleight-of-hand. Now it's time to become transparent eyeballs, trust the two little brains' memory and prediction. Thirty seconds before the tip, nature's zoom kicks in and I see the beads of sweat trapped in the oil of Lester's hair, the crease between Pop's eyebrows that nearly knits them, the enlarged whites of the Aris center's eyes as we slap palms.

If your eyes are ready, your throat won't choke. In the second season, your tongue exists to breathe and swallow. Yes, it modulates the lungs' grunts and gasps, sounds the simple codes, repeats the repeated exhortations and warnings. I've seen the tape of game one plenty of times, have watched the players' mouths move, studied my own lips curl and twitch, yet nothing the tongue does is remembered. The tape is silent. Some rapid-fire Greek was doing play-by-play, the players answered questions in the locker room, and sportswriters filed their stories, yet speaking about a playoff game is like shouting in a library, a violation of basketball's essential silence. All athletes have secrets, consciousness and action they can't tell anyone, not another athlete, not their spouse, not the guy in the corridor waiting for the story. We're a secret even to ourselves. The Greek word for "secret" expresses the feeling best: "mystico." At the end of a game or a season, the secrets are deeper, more difficult to recover, mysterious, the ultimate inside basketball. Just when the fan is most curious, the athlete is least capable of saying what happened in the minutes of living between eye and hand, hand and eye. Finally, of course, there are the numbers, no secret to anyone.

Aris plays a one-three-one zone: double-team the point, force the ball out of my hands, double up again, make all the other players passers, two-on-one, take away our control, force us to adapt to their power, turn up the heat, wear down our five, bring in the crowd, run in their reserves, increase the pressure, squeeze a green between two yellows, literal pressure, body pressure, four arms and legs enveloping man and ball, pressing out panic, squirting out the ball for an easy hoop at the other end. To break the trap, players should be spread out on the floor, equally spaced. You have to know where all your team-mates are and you have to swing the ball, see the trap coming and keep your head up, looking over and through the arms, or use your head as a butt to split the trap, then raise your head and decide a place to send the ball, the obvious place an illusion, what the defense wants to give you, the easy pass the wrong pass, playing into the turnover or the next trap, so you hold the ball two tenths to let the defense rotate to the obvious, you look at the obvious and find the next open man, the place the defense just left, perhaps the original passer, and now the process repeats, the trap closing a few tenths late, the passer with a little more time to use his knowledge and the trappers' rush, to refuse the quick shot and the predictable pass, to look at the man nearby and send the ball diagonally across the floor where it's now almost time to shoot, the trappers slow to cover the diagonal distance, perhaps lagging because the turnover or rushed shot has not come, the receiver now a shooter or a passer depending on the score, passing off if protecting a lead or, if behind, deciding between the open twelve-foot jumper or the up-fake and penetration, the trap numbers suddenly reversed: two greens on one yellow, the Aris safety man, now the player with pressure and a decision: come to the ball with his long arms and strong hands trying for a block or fake coming to the ball and stay home to protect against the dish and jam, the ending that puts the crowd back in their seats and helps deflate the pressure next time.

Action moves like water in a kinked hose, by spurts and sprays in their traps, the floor a chaos, large still spaces and small clusters of intensity, the ball like some high-powered electromagnet or sacred object, pulling to it arms waving, swinging, blotting out sight lines, reaching, chopping, hands out of control, cutting air, poking eyes, hacking wrists, whacking hands and ball, slapping it loose, tipping passes, grabbing, holding, pushing off the man who no longer has the ball to pick up speed downcourt or to the next rotation. Despite the flying and flailing bodies, the hacks and strips, whistles and lucky bounces, the tape is like a story, like a war story with men in action, characters doing things to each other, contact and conflict for the crowd to watch with easy attention, absorbed in the struggle, rooting on their heroes, no longer needing binoculars or zoom or knowledge to cheer breakaway slams, the rehearsed high-li. The crowd cries at the blunders of overplay and laughs at the stupid turnovers, feels the collisions and exhaustion. With its lead changes and plot turns, run-outs and recoveries, the game is like a twenty-minute overtime, a fan's game, the floor halved, the differences obvious, Aris shooters firing away on one end, forcing Panathinaikos shooters to become passers on the other end, the outcome in doubt until the last seconds, the game's second season, the fan's delight, the clean climax: in or out, winner or loser, hero or chump. The tape runs and runs and runs and stops.

Time: 00.17

Home: 76   Visitor: 75

The camera, like a fan's eye, follows the ball.

17: Aris doubles me at the center circle, forcing the ball out of my hands. I look at Kappa right and pass to Lou left.

15: Lou dribbles toward the key. Finakis leaves me to trap with Kallis.

13: Lou looks at me and passes to Kappa on the right wing.

11: Kallis leaves Lou to trap with Aris' third guard. Kappa takes one dribble and passes across to me on the left wing. The ball is mine.

9: Finakis rotates back to me. Lekos comes up from Lester to trap. I look at Lester on the baseline, fake right, and slip between Lekos and Finakis toward the foul line.

The camera angle opens up and sees the floor. The page becomes a blackboard:

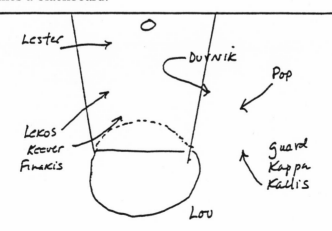

8: Duvnik starts toward me. Kallis won't be able to help. The third guard will be late getting to Pop. Lekos scrambles back toward Lester, who's moving toward the hoop.

7: Duvnik comes to me. Pop will step up to his spot for the bank. Money in the bank. This is the shot we want.

6: I turn toward the hoop, look straight at Duvnik, and deliver a bounce pass under his left hand to Pop.

5: Duvnik reverses. As Pop catches the ball, his knees bend for the jumper. Bringing the ball up, Pop sees Lester under the basket. With the ball at shoulder level, Pop changes his mind. He releases the pass at ear level.

4: Duvnik's desperate outstretched right hand tips the ball. The force of the pass and Duvnik's hand sends the ball straight up in the air, high into the lights, the players converging where it will come down, the big men coiling to tear at the ball, the ball descending, the clock ticking down, time running out in super-slow motion.

Time: 00.00

Home: 76   Visitor: 75

We'd overpassed. I couldn't remember Pop ever trying to throw a pass before. The only words I know to say to him are "Then peirazi," it doesn't matter, and "spiti," home, we'll get them at home.

The only things I can say to myself lying in bed after the game all seem to begin with "I might have." I might have pulled up for the foul-line jumper; it would have gone in or missed. I might have taken the ball strong at Duvnik; the shot would have gone in, missed, or been blocked. I might have been fouled by Duvnik, made or missed the shot, made both free throws, made one, or missed both. I might have looked at Pop and passed to Lester, who might have caught it, might have made the shot, might have been fouled by Lekos, who also might have deflected the pass. I might have looked at Lester, switched the ball to my left hand, and passed to Pop, either behind my back with my left hand or behind my head with the two-hand wraparound, either of which Duvnik might have deflected or Pop might have mishandled. I might have looped a pass over Kallis to Kappa, flipped the ball back deep to Lou, traveled or charged, slipped on a wet spot or collapsed with a leg cramp. I might have been blinded by a flash camera or struck between the eyes by a coin. I might have choked. Another secret I'll never know. I did know that, under the microscope, I didn't have Eleni as an excuse.

Athens was still ninety degrees when we got back Sunday morning. We went from the airport to the pit for practice, shooting and working against the Aris traps. After forty minutes, Z sent us home and told us to get some rest, more time for some players to turn over in their mind what they had done or hadn't done in the Palais.

Monday it was ninety degrees again. Monday night it was more than that in the pit and nothing that we had done or thought—Saturday in Salonika or the rest of the season either home or away—made any difference. Nothing that we had planned made any difference. A season's tape was useless. In front of maybe three thousand sweating, silent fans, both teams slogged the floor like retreating foot soldiers, sucking in the pit's overheated air, sweating out the chemicals required for coordination, Aris power against our control, the home team's strategy and teamwork and subtlety melted by the heat, the contest cut down to sub-primal elements: rebounding, walking, and shooting. Nothing Vassilis could put in our bodies and nothing Z could put in our heads at the half could help us in the pit. In the second half, players on both teams turned into athletes without skills and then turned into nameless men finishing the suicides, struggling, staggering, colliding, falling, gasping, choking. In the pit, on our home court, there were no secrets. Everything was obvious and too fucking ugly to bear describing. We lost by ten. One and done. Two and through. Halfway into the second season, we were out.

Chapter 10

"Since you lost to Aris, maybe you won't be named to the national team," Ann said, converting failure into wish.

"Maybe not," I answered, "but I have to be around to see. If I am picked, I think I need to play. I'm worried that Panathinaikos might try to renege on the bonus if I don't."

"It's covered in your contract, isn't it?"

"It's supposed to be, but I don't trust the GM. I also can't picture Drinkman flying over here to enforce my contract."

My argument, possibly true, was persuasive. I'd told Ann about the reporter who had turned "hustle" into "cheat" and about the cleverness of Aris, the way they'd used the pit against us. We agreed to take a ten-day tour and return to Athens. These might be our last days in Greece. To remember them, I shot the tape I didn't need for the championship series. Much of the film was like highlights of our early months in Greece, the first half rerun. Segments remind me of what was said off-camera.

Under a blue morning sky at Knossos, a brightly colored, low-level Acropolis, I tape the sophisticated sewage system the Minoans built for their queen. While I'm recording the sub-floor tiles and drains reconstructed by the archaeologists, Ann tells Sara about Ariadne and Cretan men jumping over the horns of bulls. Sara listens carefully, as she did in front of the Parthenon when Ann told her about Athena the woman warrior.

The twilight deepens the yellows, reds, and oranges of the restored neoclassical buildings fronting the inner harbor of Chania. From our table on the quai, I pan across this Plaka with water, the newly painted hotels and tavernas and shops seen through masts and furled sails. When the clear Christmas lights strung above the tables come on and our waiter brings the cala-mari, Sara, Ann, and I try to remember all the places we've eaten calamari, recalling not by taverna but by location, not by street name but by the route walked, stone alleys or narrow sidewalks, the shapes and colors of buildings. Some places we identify by certain waiters, their physical eccentricities or funny English.

Like the steep slopes of Delphi, the end of the Samarian gorge resists the camera. Standing inside the walls, narrowed to ten feet, I shoot almost straight up and the camera is dizzied by 150 feet of sheer stone and the sun. Outside the walls, the camera gets the height and mass but not the tightness of this mountain keyhole we've passed through to the beach where the gorge's stream reaches the sea. After a swim, Ann and Sara sit in the cool fresh water, with their feet in the warm salt water, their hands examining one by one the grape-sized marble pebbles that compose the beach, black rocks with etched white lines, rounded by the roll down the gorge. Sitting in the blue sea and blue sky, Ann tells Sara stories about collecting shells on summer vacations at the Gulf. Sara throws her rejects out into the sea for another thousand years of polishing. Watching her toss the stones away makes me feel blue. We'll never be back. Once, only once.

On Santorini, we stay in Ia, a small whitewashed village like the one on Idra. From our terrace, I film the earthquake ruins of the older village just below us, the donkeys bringing tourists up the path from the boat, the red and gold cliffs far below, the town of Thera off on its own cliffs to our left, and the volcanic island in the blue before us, but again the camera is displeased by the long vertical perspective as I try to focus six or eight hundred feet almost straight down on a little blue-domed chapel by the sea. From the terrace wall, I turn and shoot our lodging, a blue door in the stucco-covered cliff, a blue-framed window on each side, the primary sources of light for our two-room cave hollowed out of rock. In the left window, Sara makes a face at the camera. Under the right window, Ann sits finishing her breakfast.

Ann takes over the camera on the volcanic island across from our cave. The island is where Greece began: smoking, flowing, fiery rock, now still and black, rock covered by piles of black rock, a few dusty black paths, and a sprinkle of inch-high plants growing in sea gull shit. This is the world before life decided to move. "Incredible," Ann says as the camera pans over and noses into the rock formations, fifteen-foot high boulders sheared into glassy curved lines like black butter cut by a hot knife, mounds of smaller rocks fractured and splintered as if they'd collided with another, larger island. "This is black on black Ad Reinhardt never imagined. Why have I never seen pictures of this place?" No blue or white here, no Greek colors, I tell her. "This is the perfect antithesis," she says, "but we need a still camera and tripod. We could spend three months here and put out a series of alternative postcards," one of the ideas she had for work last February.

"What can I do now?" Sara asks, walking back and forth on the small quai at Naoussa, a tiny fishing village on Naxos. We'd spent the day swimming and walking and lying around the beautiful beach Ann had found. We'd taken a shower and nap. There were still two hours before the tavernas would open. "I know the word for 'help,'" I tell her. "'Vohethia.' Ask the fisherman and his wife if they need help with their nets." Sara walks over and speaks to the woman kneeling on a mat, pulling seaweed and sticks from the delicate yellow nets. Surprised, the woman rises up on her knees, smiles, and asks Sara what she said. Sara, her back to the camera, points to the nets. The woman nods right to left, waves to us or the camera, and motions Sara to sit down. The woman speaks slowly, her heavy, dark hands showing the way. Sara's head nods and dips as she, the woman, and the man pick debris from the nets, preparing for the next day's work.

"How do they do it?" Ann says. "How do they still manage to make a living this way?"

"The man's filling up the net with fish here."

"When he can't do it any longer, I hope they're not forced to live in Athens."

In Mykonos I had to be careful taping. Shooting Sara with the island's pet pelican or Sara and Ann standing together, four arms angled out, pretending to be a windmill in front of the island's scenic landmark, I might catch in the frame men holding hands or women embracing, activities the accidentally taped might think we wanted to show our curious friends at home. At Paradise Beach, both sexes—all sexes—were nude. In the toy town's crowded alleys, boutiques, and tea rooms, they were cross-dressed. Except for the old fishermen displaying their authentic britches and the white-shirted waiters running from table to table, it was difficult to separate tourists from the natives. At dinnertime we all walked back and forth through the alleys, pushing and shoving and competing for tables. Our first night the waiter tried to charge us extra for retsina from the barrel, as if we'd just stepped off the plane. Although we had saved Mykonos for last because it was the island Ann had heard most about from her touring friends, it was a disappointment, overcrowded even at the beginning of the season.

Back at our hotel, looking out at the lighted cruise ships in the harbor, I tried to prepare Ann for my selection to the national team. "I want to play. I can make back some of the bonus money Aris cost us. You and Sara could come to Cairo for the Mediterranean Games. Egypt is all beach."

"Now that Sara's out of school, what are we going to do while you're practicing?"

"Go back to the beaches south of Athens."

"They're an hour by bus, and I read some of them were polluted during the drought. Maybe you won't be selected. We can collect the bonus, take a trip to the Ionians or Dodecanese, go back home, and start looking for a house."

"We'll have the rest of our lives back there. This is my only chance to represent a country. The NBA is monopolizing the Olympics."

"There's always the special Olympics."

"You can put up with Athens for three more weeks can't you?"

"It was three years in Rockford."

"You know you enjoyed that arrangement. You had a house husband to run your errands. You liked it that way, Ms. Logan."

"And you love it this way, Kyvernos."

I was going to give Ann the final word. It made no sense to argue before the national team had chosen its players. I was surprised to hear Ann keep talking.

"I've been waiting for years."

"Waiting for what?"

"Waiting for you to want something beyond basketball."

"You should have said something. You didn't need to keep it a secret."

"Yes I did. I wanted you to decide yourself. If I'd told you I was waiting, you'd have asked me for what. You'd have tried to fit my expectations. Now you've found something you really love, but I can't live here another year."

"I'm not asking you to."

"You don't need to. I know how important living here is to you. If you play for the national team and stay through July, you'll want to come back in September."

"No I won't, Ann."

"I want to believe you, Michael, but I just can't be sure. Too many unexpected things have happened. Living here has made me suspicious. Of everything: the weather, Greeks, you. Your playing on the national team still sounds fishy to me. Maybe I'm wrong. That's what I dislike about living away from home, the constant feeling of suspicion. It filters in and comes between us. I'm even suspicious of myself. Maybe I could make it through another year for you, but I just don't trust my own strength."

"Forget next year. I'll trade it off. I play for the national team, we do some more islands after the Mediterranean Games, and we go home for good. I promise."

To close off further discussion, I agreed with what Ann said earlier: "Besides, I may not be selected."

If I'm not, I sign on with Panathinaikos for next year, let Vassilis tell that to Eleni, get my bonus, renege on the contract, and visualize her in September waiting for me at the airport with a sign that says "Key Money."

Flying into Athens, we can see from miles away a yellow dome overhanging the city. Under the dome we're in a blizzard of light. Dust and smoke and other particles trapped by the Nefos are suspended in the air, reflecting and diffusing the sun, changing it into a soft solid, whiting out the white city. From the runway, neither Mt. Imitos nor the sea can be seen, purple and blue covered by white fuzz. On the tarmac, the heat is like August in Memphis. Even jet whine seems muffled by the white. I wonder if the islands have changed my perceptions or if Athens always felt like this and I just didn't notice.

Only a few tourists are in the domestic arrivals building. Tourists and Greeks are crowded around the entrances of the departure building next door. The little parking lot is jammed with tourist coaches and with taxis and cars dropping off passengers and then blaring their horns to get out. At the cab stand, thirty taxis are lined up in the sun waiting for in-town fares. Our driver must have been here a long time. Even with all the windows down, it's sweltering in the car, the windshield and back window acting like magnifying glass. In the outbound lanes, weekend drivers heading down the coast to the beaches are standing still in the heat, wailing on their horns. Only a few taxis are going toward Athens, but the driver seems afraid of the open road and snowy visibility. At thirty miles an hour, the wind coming in the windows isn't cooling us. It seems hotter than when we left for Crete.

On this Saturday morning, the city looks and sounds like a

Sunday afternoon, shuttered and still. Except for taxis and an occasional bus, the streets are clear. The sidewalks are empty. Why aren't the crowds out for their fresh bread and milk for the weekend? In Syntagma Square, no tourists are taking pictures of the Tsoliathes standing guard at the tomb of the unknown soldier. The square looks like a war zone, abandoned by civilians. I knew Athenians leave on summer weekends, but this emptiness at the center of the city is strange, disturbing. On the street up to Kolonaki a woman is walking under an umbrella. Can this be some kind of reverse magic, an attempt to bring rain? Dexameni is empty, no kids playing, no women screaming, the café tables and chairs piled and chained. I look out to the right. The Parthenon is gone, erased by the white air. Apartment buildings three blocks away mark the end of our visible world. Dissolving in this otherworldly air, the buildings look like this century's haunted houses, residences for the ghosts of nuclear winter. Turkey crosses my mind. If we were at war, planes wouldn't be landing.

The cabbie drops us in Kolonaki Square so we can get an *Athens News*. At Valtadoros no people are sitting out under the canopy drinking frappes, talking and waving their arms. A middle-aged man is inside up against the window. He's wearing one of those surgical masks and reading his paper. Now I get it: there must be a pollution alert. The weather in the pit during our final game has spread out and covered Athens. My regular kiosk is shuttered and locked, the wooden and metal box too hot for the owner. One kiosk near the British Consul is open. I give a quick look at the Greek papers hanging up. Huge headlines, all with the same Greek word and the same statistic: 120. You don't have to be a necrophiliac to recognize the Greek. I'd seen it on signs outside cemeteries: "nekropolis."

"Thermal Inversion Holds Over City" was the headline on the *Athens News*. With no wind from any direction, the Nefos was trapped in the basin and was trapping pollutants. The temperature had been over 100 Thursday and Friday. One hundred twenty people had died, thousands were in hospitals. The forecast was more of the same. While we were off lying on island beaches without newspapers and television, Athenians were dying in the heat.

Walking home, I feel lightheaded. I don't know if it's the news or all the diffused light, saturated heat, and dense air, but

I feel like vomiting. When we get to the apartment, we wedge the door open. The wind tunnel sucks in white air from the balcony. Sara gets on her bathing suit and climbs into the tub. We sit down in the living room, turn on our fan, and switch on the television. CNN International from Atlanta is recycling at the half hour. American TV is covering the story in our living room. First, a helicopter shot of the Parthenon, taken on a clearer day and shown now for the insomniac American viewer watching with the sound off at 4:30 A.M., the picture a lure to listen. A middle-American voice recites updated statistics: three days of 100-plus temperature, pollution index 50 points over the emergency 300, 155 Athenians now dead, more thought dead in their homes, the elderly who could not get out or get help, people in low-lying areas of the city. As if reading a local winter storm advisory, the voice from America sounds its global warning: Athenians with pulmonary and respiratory problems should stay inside, out of the sun, off the streets. Factories, businesses, and government offices will be closed, buses and trolleys on a reduced schedule, private cars forbidden from entering the city center. CNN then shows tape from yesterday afternoon, low-season tourists arriving at the airport, mopping their faces in the arrivals lobby, lying under shrubs and bushes near the terminal. Over the tape the voice advises travelers going through Athens to expect delays in connections to the islands.

We switch to Greek TV. The usual Saturday morning folk-dancing shows have been replaced by live crowd scenes. We see the people outside the departures building we just left. Inside, tourists in their bright clothes outnumber Greeks. Large groups with advance reservations are gathered around guides and transfer agents handing out boarding passes. Individual tourists and Greeks are mixed together, all standing in long, snaking lines for flights to the islands and other Greek cities. The waiting room for Rhodes is overfilled, tourists and Greeks sitting on the floor. Some Greeks sleeping on the plastic chairs in the Patras waiting room look like they'd been there overnight. The men are unshaven, the women and children wrung out. The announcer's voice drones over the clips, but something seems wrong with the relay. No noise comes in from the airport crowds. They're packed tight in the lines and on the chairs but there's only a murmur of sound.

A helicopter shot in Piraeus shows a row of twenty tourist

coaches parked along one of the quais. A group comes out of one bus and walks up the ramp to a ferry, the advantage of package travel. Thousands of dark-haired people, presumably Greek, are massed in front of the ticket stands on the quai. From above, the crowds waiting for different boats look like a single crowd motionless in the sun. A ground camera finds women and children sitting in the corridors of shade the ferries cast or lying on their bamboo mats under beach umbrellas they have to hold in their hands. High above them are the lucky ones, squeezed together on benches or draped over the railings like refugees from a Middle-East war, already looking seasick from the ticket ordeal in the sun, waiting for sea spray to cool their faces, looking forward to island air, always a breeze curling around the land like the draft between our doors.

Outside the train station, police have set up barricades and are turning away people dragging luggage toward the station. Except for a few backpackers with Eurail cards, the crowd is Greek. The people allowed inside the barricades are standing in the sun, craning their necks, trying to see into the ticket office, where the police are funneling a line through the door. The camera cuts inside, shows people sitting crammed together on benches or lying on the cement platform, heads resting on their bags.

The Greeks are all leaving the city.

At the toll plaza on the Athens-Corinth road, cars are jammed and jumbled, angled between lanes, wedging slowly forward, their drivers holding up left-handed pleas, some riders walking ahead as if herding goats into a pen. The little cars are full, five and six bodies in seats built for four small Greeks. The line must be a mile long. From above, the heat is rippling off the metal roofs, the light is reflecting up from the windshields and rear windows. Beside the road, middle-aged men in old-fashioned shoulder-strap tee shirts lean into steaming engines, passengers crouch in the shade of their cars, grandmothers still dressed in black sit in backseats and press wet cloths to the faces of children lying in their laps.

It's a good thing we don't want to leave.

The camera now shifts to a hospital, ranges through standing-room-only waiting areas and filled wards, holds on individuals, zooming into the intimacy of illness. Two young men carry an unconscious gray-haired woman, her mouth gaping open, her body sagging in the bedspread they use as a stretcher.

A man sweating through bulging suspenders slumps in a waiting-room chair while a younger woman standing next to him trickles bottled water on his bald spot and down the back of his neck. A man who looks too old and thin to sweat lolls his head, and the camera catches sweat on his neck beneath his oxygen mask. A woman about sixty-five, fat enough to look pregnant, lies hacking and choking on a gurney in the corridor. She is taking intravenous fluids in her left arm and with her right is making a feeble open-palm gesture: what's going on here? why is there no room?

Through the gurgle of an interview with a doctor come some Greek words I recognize—epidemic, toxic, asphyxia— and then the English words "air conditioning." The doctor raises his eyes. No. The Greeks don't have a word for air conditioning. The hospital is not air-conditioned. Only American Express, hotels, and Kolonaki boutiques have air conditioning. Athens is like LA without climate control. The camera shows the wall units in an operating room and then drops down to sheeted bodies lying on the floor. They must be overflow from the morgue. Again the camera zooms in as it passes over the line of corpses. In our living room we can see Greek noses beneath the white cotton, the toes of two tall Greeks hanging out below the six-foot sheets. The short, tucked sheets must be covering children, some Sara's size, some even smaller. The camera moves slowly, as if allowing the viewer to count the bodies in a foreign language.

The camera shifts outside to a large white tent pitched among some trees next to the hospital. Children are sitting or lying on military cots, mothers putting glasses to their mouths, fathers stripped to the waist fanning with their shirts. The pale, liquid-eyed children with sunken cheeks look dehydrated. The round-faced and wide-eyed seem exhausted by their lungs' every-second task. Many of the kids have casts on their arms or legs, bandages on their feet or heads. A couple are bald. The young are outside. Maybe it's cooler here under the white tent than inside the hospital, but the scene looks like a gypsy encampment, the tent and crowded clan, adults now caring for the children whose limbs they have broken and whose faces they have scarred to make the children better beggars and sadder sellers of wilted flowers in the outdoor cafes.

All Athenians couldn't leave the city, *the* place, *the* center. Too many had crowded in. They were all together inside the pressure cooker now. Not all of them were athletes. The quickest out would have been the motorcycle jockeys. Then the rich with travel agents. The people dying were the Athenians who walked the sidewalks and packed trolleys coming to our games. They couldn't do anything about the cloud over their heads. They were in over their heads. Breathing yellow air, they were under the weather. Without telephones in their homes, the elderly were cut off from families and help. Poor kids in basement apartments we'd seen were sucking down the heavy air. Greeks were choking on their crowded air and couldn't get out. They had to wait for the weather to change. Nobody could predict when that would happen. It wasn't a heat wave. It was "thermo stasis:" heat still. What could be worse, I wondered. To this hyper people, what could be more unnatural than stillness: no motion, no noise. Greeks were dying silently, not in the roar of an earthquake, tidal wave, or volcano, but in their own dead air. Spiti Mas would never need to rebroadcast a costumed athlete. Every station was carrying overviews of the yellow cloud, studio statistics like vote counts, tape of the sick adults, the poisoned children. For them, "spiti" was now a hospital. Greeks didn't need to know English or read subtitles to understand this phenomenon, see the city turning itself inside out, recognize what they were doing to themselves, why they were abandoning their homes.

High on Likavitos, high in our building, three healthy Americans had a cooling draft, fans, and plenty of bottled water.

We didn't have to leave.

Two days later the Nefos blew off to sea. The total dead from the Nefos was 179. Athenians rushing back to the city killed another forty-two of themselves in auto and motorcycle accidents.

I walked to the pit. Aris had beaten Olympiakos in five games for the championship. The national team had already announced its selections. I was on. Training camp would begin in four days, but it would be in Salonika. This news might be good for me. Ann had the inversion now to add to other Athens negatives. Salonika was smaller, close to the sea. When I had days off, we could take trips to the islands up there. Sara and Ann were evidence for Eleni that we'd be returning next year. With Henderson gone, Vassilis a suspect, and none of my teammates on the national club, Ann was also the only friend I had.

Ann seemed surprised when I told her the news, surprised and angry.

"We lived for a week in a hotel here," Ann said. "I don't want to spend three weeks in a hotel in Salonika."

"You've never been there. It's right on the sea."

"It's a Greek city, isn't it?"

"You could stay here and I'll fly down on weekends."

An occupied apartment would also be evidence that the Keevers were coming back.

"Michael, what are you saying? Where have you been the last few days? People were dying in their homes. You can't expect Sara and me to stay here by ourselves."

"Then come up to Salonika. I told you before: I'm afraid of losing the bonus if I don't play."

We argued about Salonika and switched back to Athens. I told Ann nothing like the inversion had ever happened before. What were the chances of it happening again in three weeks? I played off the huge benefits against the small risk. She said I was selfish and crazy to take any risks with Sara. I said Sara's life was in more danger on the streets of Memphis. We went round and round again: Memphis, Athens, Salonika, past, present, future.

Suddenly Ann said, "You knew you'd have to train in Salonika all along, didn't you?"

"No," I told her. "You know how the Greeks are about organization and communication."

"You're lying, Michael."

"I'm not lying," I said.

"You are lying. Sara and I are leaving. You decide what you want to do."

"Just like that? You're leaving?"

"That's right."

"You can't do that, Ann. I have to play on the national team."

"You'll have to do it alone. We're going home."

Ann and I repeated our arguments. I accused her of being hyperbolic. She said I was an idiot. Although it was the inversion that frightened Ann out of the country, she was too proud to admit that. Since there were pros and cons in both the Athens and Salonika columns, she kept coming back to my lying. She felt it was an absolute, her easy way out. I was lying and she was leaving. I was Greek and she was going, taking Sara with her. I wasn't lying, but I couldn't prove it. Ann distrusted me. At this point, she was wrong. Months ago I'd concealed the name change, but it was much too late to tell Ann about that.

"To fuck 'em up," Coach Jacobs told us, "you got to suck it up." I arranged Ann's and Sara's tickets, helped Ann pack, and saw them off at the airport. I came home, cleaned out the refrigerator, doused the plants on the balcony, and sat under the awning. When I went in for a beer, the refrigerator was off, the door was propped open, and the beer was warm. I went to Valtadoros for an Amstel. Maybe this is for the best, I thought. Once I get my bonus, I may have to leave in a rush. I don't want to be dragging along a wife and kid. Later I walked up to the Plaka and had dinner with the other tourists.

Chapter 11

Except for the Palais, Salonika was like September in Athens: living in a room, eating restaurant food, trying to train one-on-one Greeks to pass and catch. The national team's players had more talent than the Panatholes, but the Pangreeks' big heads kept them from moving without the ball and accepting assistance from an American-trained, English-speaking Greek. Coach Kotopoulos couldn't do much with them. Kallis refused to run the suicides. Most of my teammates refused to pass me the ball. Elias, a young forward from Olympiakos, told me that the veterans were making it tough on us because he and I were the only rookies. Elias didn't get many shots, but he was more interested in women than basketball. When we rode the bus to the Palais, Elias waved to all the girls. He also tried to teach me more Greek. I need action words, Elias said, so I started a list: "kano," I make; "thelo," I want. Elias tells me he wants to make many children. "Krima," he said, it's a pity, when I told him about Sara going back to the States. "Krima" I knew: "katalaveno." I'd heard "krima" said of tough shots that rim out. I remembered it by associating it with crime. It's a crime. Mine was changing my name to give Sara a home.

Some evenings Elias and I go to Aristotelous Square, a huge courtyard bordered on two sides by cafes under stately old buildings. On one open end is the bay. Aristotelous is the whole package, city life with sea view. Up and down the football-field pavement Salonikans pace invisible lines, turning and returning in the same lanes. This, Elias tells me, is the "volta." Dolled-up daughters are on their mothers' arms. Young men in expensive shirts link elbows with their fathers. The "volta" is courtship the old way, in motion on a court, in a crowd, face to face with hundreds of other faces. Can she walk straight, avoid collisions, link another's arm, keep the line going? It's the parade of desire, replaying as the walkers pass each other over and over. Everyone is nodding, gesturing, greeting, talking. They'll replay tomorrow night and after that until the eyes light up, the match is made, the vows said, the gifts exchanged. Then the couple will be lying together in a parent's apartment or house, making a future walker to cover and recover this reserved space. Elias saunters back and forth, while I sit by myself, a single traveler. Maybe this is the test to pass. Live it alone like Henderson did. How do you know how much pressure you can take when others insulate you? The unexamined life is not worth living. So Ann said the ancient Greeks said. Maybe the untraveled life is more like it.

I'd been in Salonika ten days and was getting used to being a second-stringer, a no-pressure job, when Eleni knocked on my hotel door. I assumed she'd turn up before I went to Egypt, but I was still a little surprised to find her on my doorstep like an NBA groupie.

"Where have you been?" I asked her.

She seemed surprised to be questioned.

"Visiting my family in Crete."

"Come on in," I said. As in Athens, her clothes revealed little about her: a loose denim shirt, jeans, black canvas Converse sneakers. At five-three and about ninety-five pounds, she could be an American teenager or just wearing American clothes like half the Greeks under thirty. I tried to smell her as she passed by. She looked out the window, looked in the bathroom, and then sat on the bed. I leaned against the low desk across from the bed.

"Did your bookie pay off?" I asked.

"Two of them did. A third refused. He said the game looked fixed."

"Those fuckers from Aris were dumping it."

"I understand."

"It doesn't look good here."

"What do you mean?"

"I'm not getting enough minutes. I doubt I can do anything more for you until next year."

"So you are planning to stay?"

"If Panathinaikos offers me a contract."

"Why didn't your wife and daughter come to Salonika with you?"

"They're off touring some islands with friends. They really love the beaches."

This was a lie I'd rehearsed. I also hadn't completely vacated the apartment. Keep Eleni's eyes on next year. But the story sent her in another direction.

"We have too many tourists," Eleni said. "Ten million tourists every year. One for each of us. Dutch seeking mountains, Germans searching warm water, English investigating the possibility of sun. They are the north-south drift, our summer Nefos."

Eleni's "we" and "our" were new, not the plural of associates but of natives, not persons of Greek descent but Greeks, people like Vassilis.

"Tourists bring money."

Eleni laughed this off with the Greek "pshaw" she'd used in Athens to dismiss priests and politicians. "We move in a vicious circle in Ellatha. We see imported media and want the things people have, the freezers and driers and cathedral-ceiling houses to put them in. To buy these imported goods, we import people—tourists. To please them, we improve our facilities with imported products. On the islands we build huge hotels with German air conditioning and American swimming pools. The whole country has become a seasonal service industry. We still have the worst national debt and balance of payments deficit in the EEC."

"From what I saw in the islands, entertaining strangers is a whole lot easier than crushing rocks or olives."

"Easier, yes, but the tourist industry creates impossible desires and expectations. It is our Hollywood. The government encourages these delusions. You've seen the ads on CNN: Greece is 'Paradise on Earth.' On holidays and tourism all parties agree. That is why we are overbuilt, overcommitted to tourism. The Middle East will erupt. Or the world economy will go bad. The crowds will disappear. The hotels and time-shares built on olive groves will be empty, the building industry will crumble, banks will fail, money will disappear."

"Then there'll be enough water for Greeks."

But Eleni was no longer satisfied with water.

"Water, yes, but otherwise the population is beyond the bioregion's carrying capacity. We used to know how to exist in our hot island space. By carrying tourists six months a year, Ellatha lives beyond its actual means. You saw what happened in Athens. A hundred more years of migration and we'll be like Egypt. It's so far over its carrying capacity it has to import people or starve."

Hunched forward on the bed, urgently speaking her specialized vocabulary, Eleni reminded me of coaches in the half-time locker room. From their front row seats, they always knew every player's weakness. Cater used to be sorrowful, disappointed that we hadn't followed film. Jacobs would get rabid. Instead of shouting his usual "Fuck 'em up" when we went out for the second half, he'd forget the "'em" and scream

"Fuck up, fuck up," the perfect slogan for the CBA. Eleni quoted the stat sheet: tourism is now the second largest item in world trade. In the year 2000 it will be the largest source of employment.

I had no idea if what she was telling me was true, but her vision of the future took me back fifteen years and six thousand miles to Round Top, a ski resort in Plymouth just south of the Killington empire. The lifts were still, chairs rusting high in the air. The base lodge windows were covered with plywood, discolored and warped by the weather. Two winters of light snow brought financial reverses. When the Massachusetts development company went under, Round Top started reversing itself. Pine was growing in the trails, the gravel parking lot was filling up with dandelions and condoms. The sugar-house craft shops were abandoned and the country inns were turning back into farmhouses, the wooden sleighs and buggies in their front yards replaced by junk cars. Where the multicolored tourism flags flew on porches, ripped plastic weatherproofing now flaps in the wind.

Some local people had put money into Round Top, hoping to get a piece of the down-country entertainment dollar. Not Dad. Not that he had anything to invest. He said there weren't enough flatlanders to support every Vermonter. He resented the skiers because they drove up his property taxes with their demand for building lots. I resented them for the big bills they flashed at the Grand Union on Saturday morning. For the skiers, the store began stocking varieties of lettuce I still can't name, tourist greens.

"We must learn how to live without tourists," Eleni said, as if ending discussion. But in a second she asked "Do you know the word 'kosmos'"?

"You mean 'universe'"?

"In Greek, it means 'world.' 'Kosmos' also is the word for 'crowd.' The world-crowd is turning Ellatha into ruins."

She was silent for a few seconds, and I thought of Vassilis. Words were driving them, old words and new words, all Greek. Eleni looked down at the bed as if meditating on the irony of delivering her prophecy in an A-class hotel. I wondered what this prediction had to do with next year. She looked back up at me.

"I'm sorry for everything I've put you through. I knew that first day we talked in Valtadoros that you loved this country.

My friends and I are trying to preserve what's left of it. You've helped. I wanted you to know that because Ellatha may need your assistance again."

Eleni was using my language against me: from assist to assistance.

"You're right. I do love this place, but I don't see what I can do for it."

"You know how crowds respond. You understand the power of television. I think you can help us keep off the 'kosmos.'"

Key to Keever: do not forget who Keever is.

"That would be OK with me," I said, "as long as my money here is assured."

"We haven't forgotten the money," Eleni said. "You've helped us with money and you'll get yours."

She got up off the bed and crossed to where I was standing. Like real Greeks, Eleni came close to speak, closer than Americans get, a foot away. She tilted her head back to look up at my face. Then she stuck out her right hand. She wanted to shake hands, as if we were sealing a deal. Her small hand was rough and strong, like a rock-climber's I knew in Memphis. Like smooth-fingered Vassilis, Eleni was doing something with her hands besides holding books about tourism.

"I'll be seeing you again," she said, making it sound more like a promise than a threat. Following her to the door, I wondered how Eleni—with long hair, lipstick, and a dress—would look in the "volta." Now that I'd made her some money, she was treating me like a long-range project again. She wasn't upset that I couldn't fix a national game. Her anger was directed at tourists. Maybe she and her friends were going to make an alternative commercial: a sweating and panting, dehydrated and exhausted athlete saying "Stay away from Greece." Even if Eleni roughed up her hand doing martial arts, it was hard to be afraid of someone so small and earnest about her nation's welfare. I had to remind myself that this woman could still cost me sixty thousand, in dollars.

The night Croatia came down to the Palais for an exhibition game I got a small dose of national pride. My stats weren't that great—ten minutes, three assists, four points, one steal—but it felt good running out in that blue and white warmup with ELLAS on the back, the full house chanting the word before they took up "Kallis, Kallis, Kallis." During garbage time, Elias and I hooked up for a back-door alley-oop that the big screen above the floor replayed for fans who had little else to cheer in a seventeen-point loss.

I called Memphis the next day, talked to a still irritated Ann, told Sara that I missed her. We'd go to Egypt in a few days. Drinking a beer under the bright canopy in Aristotelous Square, looking toward the Mediterranean Olympics and into the late afternoon light off the sea, I imagined staying alone in Athens next year. Maybe Eleni was grooming me for the real Olympics and would stay out of my face. I could arrange visits from Ann and Sara, fly back to the States for holidays. After everything that has happened, Athens still feels like home to me, the place you want to be, the space you fit. I wonder what brought me to this point. Point's turning point. Breaking up a family? Turning away from love? I'm still pissed at Ann for running off. Sara I do miss. What would a long-distance father be like for her? Temporary separation. Half the kids in America are permanently divorced. We could do it for nine months. Daddy's season-long turnover. Am I turning against myself? To prove I can do it? It's not me. It's the place. But how, then, can a city substitute for a family? When an international sub comes in, he stands at the scorer's table and holds his arms up in an X. It looks like a curse on the starter. He's now an O, a zero. The three of us started together and now I'm thinking about making two into part-timers. Greece is more than playing for pay. Its hold is different than a bunch of likes and betters, deeper than the love Eleni mentioned. Something atmospheric, as if there are nutrients in the air. I know the opposite is true, the Nefos toxins. They can be counted. The nutrients are more mysterious, like digestion, a process you have to trust. Not even Vassilis could explain my body's need for Athens.

I've decided I must be one of those people who suffer from seasonal disorder, a fucked-up body clock. It's an illness like Ann's homesickness, but one that can be cured here. Americans and northern Europeans walk around with light visors on or sit in front of huge light boxes to rouse themselves, recover their spirits. I saw them on TV. The light boxes look like projection TVs with white screens, electric doses of summer. In Greece the high light is always on, all four seasons. I take it in. It gives me ideas. Spiti Mas had me say that we must all imagine the future. Living in Greek light has taught me "phantasy," the root of the NBA's one-word motto: "fantastic." Sun and high pressure focus my imagination, like that keyhole-size beam of light from the projection booth, the secret room in every cinema.

Now the light is bouncing like the ball off the walls, reflecting from the calm sea and the white metal table. Despite being separated from my daughter, six thousand miles away, riding on her own toward first grade, a turning point for her, I feel, and I don't know why, euphoric, another Greek word, the separate individual's glee. I think the words Elias tells me, the words I read, the ones inside English words, the inside story, inside play, secret syllables until I came here.

As fast as life changed in Greece and as strange as mine had become in six months, I should have foreseen one more turn before I left. After our last practice, Eleni was waiting for me in a cab outside the Palais. "I want to show you something," she said. Elias heard her and grinned at me. The cab took us up to a sleepy six-table café next to the city walls, where we could look down on Salonika and the sea. The afternoon sun was hot and glaring, but Eleni didn't seem to mind it. She pointed out through the haze to the east and told me about the village there where the secret ceremony of fire-walking originated, barefoot Greeks in a religious frenzy quick-stepping over coals. Closer in were beaches for tourists and Greeks. She then pointed down at the seawalk and said the water-gazers there would have to become water-walkers.

"Even people who stay in one place are tourists now," Eleni said, looking down at the city and shaking her head. "This is the root of the problem. Everybody treats the planet like tourists. Like our priests looking ahead to heaven, people refuse to believe the earth is their home. It's a place they're visiting, a tourist attraction, a temporary entertainment center. This is worldwide Orthodoxy, not just Salonika or Athens. Humans use the earth like a Palais de Sport."

Eleni was angry, and up here with no one around she let her voice rise. That was fine with me.

"The planet is not a greenhouse where life increases. The comparison is wrong, misleading, a lie. We live inside Worlddome, covered by synthetics, walled off by glass in the skyboxes. One admission only, the cover charge. The standing-room-only crowd demands. Entertain us, we scream.

Faster, we holler. We buy out the food stands, spit gum in the water fountains, slosh beer on the floor. We smoke up the air, throw shit under the seats, and piss in the sinks. We're the home crowd. We do what we want: spray the walls, rip up the seats, start fires in the toilets, knock down the ushers. It's a binge. We're here only two hours. Let somebody else clean up the mess, fix the damage, build a new dome. We'll be leaving before the end."

Now Eleni was enraged. From the natural, native way she pronounced "shit" and "piss," I was sure she was American. Possibly Greek-American, but no matter how many times she used "Ellatha" or "we," the words surrounding the Greek were American. Although I didn't know why she had brought me here, and even though her rage now began to worry me, I still felt relieved to know that this woman was an American.

"'Spiti Mas' had the facts right but what good are dead trees and pitted marble? They should have told the human story."

Then Eleni revealed the secret of Salonika's future: a warmed and rising sea will cover this section of Worlddome. First will be storm surges, waves coming over the walls, boats crashing into cafes, the first line of buildings collapsing, people fleeing their homes, everybody running for their lives, literally running through chaotic streets. The natives will return to massive electrical blackouts, sewage forced up into the streets, water contaminated. Later will come the gradual destruction of the seawall and erosion of the parks by the sea, the lower downtown streets flooded, businesses ruined, residents displaced. She gestured out to the plain on the left. Eventually, the water will flood the new apartment buildings there and reclaim the lush farmland to the north and east.

High above the city, Eleni's heat woke up the athlete's mind and I felt size, the player's first principle. Looking down through Eleni's eyes, I recognized how small Salonika is next to the Thermic Gulf. From this perspective, I could see the whole city, most of it spread out on the same plane as the sea. The land is a plain, a low land, a future wetland, Worlddome's Olympic-size tidepool. I could easily imagine the sea overruning the city, making it unlivable. Sitting in the quiet heat, I felt the threat to Greeks below. Athens under a thermal inversion was only a minor disaster compared to a future Salonika under water. The statistics for this flooded city will be huge numbers, both dead and displaced. The statistics will be final. Salonikans won't find their way back to their homes and "volta" ground. For the Greeks below, the change in climate will last until the next ice age.

"Have you heard about the boiled frog?" Eleni asked.

"Not boiled," I told her. "Mom used to fry the legs. Dad and I hunted them at night. I shone the flashlight in their eyes and he whacked them from behind with a board."

Eleni laughed at this and said a frog will allow itself to be boiled alive if the temperature rises gradually enough. Humans are the same, ignoring their surroundings, deceiving themselves, destroying themselves by degrees, small increments, little weights and measures, tenths and inches and micrograms, sitting and croaking in the sun. Something must be done to make them jump onto dry land. Spiti Mas methods were juvenile. Renaming the planet would take a millennium. To move people, you have to make a loud noise, an undeniable stimulus. Like a board hitting water. Or like thunder and heat lightning, a kind of weather prediction. Only cataclysms interest people in the weather. Earthquakes, cyclones, hurricanes. When Chernobyl blew up, we couldn't eat our tomatoes. People in the villages peered at their beautiful red tomatoes, looking for the radiation. Farmers and fishermen used to fear nature, its sudden changes. Now people distrust nature because man's emissions have changed it. We're all passing gas, but it doesn't go away. It rises, it adds up, traces too small to film but still adding up, traces becoming masses spreading over us. Today we all live in our own weather. Nowhere is safe. This idea seems more paralyzing than the old fear. It takes a dramatic event to make people jump.

"I think you know what I mean," Eleni finished up.

At first I thought she might be talking about Drinkman jumping me here. I thought of Henderson and me running out of the Peristeri gym. Then I remembered Ann watching the inversion on TV and bolting the country.

"You mean some massive crowd scene?"

"Not exactly," she said. "Cities are heat islands. We need to disperse the crowd, disperse their cloud, reduce the heat."

While talking about the crowd, Eleni was looking away from me, staring out at the sea and the afternoon haze. She and what she was saying were vague. She asked me what I thought. I told her it was too fuzzy for me. My business was drawing crowds, not dispersing them, and yet I sensed that I was somehow supposed to contribute, help head off the disaster Eleni had described.

"But you know all about the high-light," she said. "We need something for the crowd to hear and see, like a fireworks display or the Sound and Light show at the Parthenon, something to wake up the crowd, get them moving."

Now Eleni turned toward me and, although no one else was at the café, lowered her voice: "I'm going to tell you a secret, Michael. My friends and I are talking about setting up a negative spectacle, like one of those controlled demolitions you see on the news, an old building, no longer useful, collapsing in on itself. We want to use this demolition to frighten people before they boil. We are overbuilt. Now people only pass through what they've built. The buildings dominate. This explains the appeal of the neutron bomb. To change the mass mind you have to attack buildings."

Eleni had been repeating "buildings," the word professional players and coaches use for gyms, arenas, colliseums, stadiums. But when she said "attack," I felt I was suddenly in a movie—not on a coach's tape but in a film. I also felt I was never going to collect the bonus.

"Attack buildings? Just what buildings are you talking about?"

"Banks and embassies are the usual targets, but money and governments are only symptoms of a deeper sickness, the developed countries' treating the earth like a resort. This lie is what creates Worlddome. Our theory is to take down a tourist site."

For some reason, Ann's love of ancient buildings bounced through my mind, the tour we'd taken of the Peloponnese to see piled stones.

"You're telling me you're going to blow up some monument? What kind of bullshit is this?"

"Not blow up," she said, emphasizing the "not." "The word we use is 'deconstruct.' Lay out the site in pieces for the archaeologists to reconstruct. The longer it takes, the more time people will think about the message."

"And just how the fuck does destroying some Greek monument move Greeks away from the water?"

"The action first persuades tourists not to come. When tourism falls off, people will have to move from the islands and the cities. Ellatha will do without tourists. We will once again be a model for the world, an example of moderation, self-sufficiency, recovery."

"I don't see this bombing shit. I also don't know why you're telling me this. I don't want to hear any more about it. This is crazy."

"There are no other means," Eleni protested. Just the slightest note of pleading entered her voice. "This is our last resort. Politicians all go around in the same vicious development spiral: more growth, more people, more demands. Greenpeace and Earth First! give us only temporary entertainment, daring speedboats protecting whales, aging hippies driving spikes in redwoods, throwing monkey wrenches into machines. These are local actions, individual heroics. Only in a crowd do individuals change. The Sound and Light show we plan would draw a crowd, a global crowd."

"I still don't see it. I hate to say so, Eleni, but I'm just a ballplayer."

"Of course," Eleni said, and before she could continue I thought, of course, that's why she's telling me all this: because I'm a ballplayer who changed his name, risked his family, and shaved points.

"That's another reason why I thought you might be sympathetic. Bring down the noble columns."

This was definitely crazy. I was supposed to sympathize with Eleni's show because all those curlicue columns reminded me of museums, libraries, banks, courthouses, and not a single gym in the States? Maybe next she'd suggest some early damage to my psyche. I'd had to dig stones out of the potato field when I was a kid. Or perhaps I secretly resented the order of all my coaches: "get rid of the rock."

I shook my head. "You've got the wrong man," I said.

"Whether you sympathize or not, we need your help."

"Fuck that," I told her. "Find another sucker. If you were a man, I'd kick your ass and drag you down the hill to the police."

I got up to leave. Although I'd been telling myself to stay calm, play along, protect the bonus, this was too fucking strange.

"I'm not bluffing, Keever," Eleni said. "I've got something from Plymouth, Vermont, you better take a look at before you walk away from me." She pulled a piece of paper out of her pocket, and I went back to the table. The paper was a photocopy from the Town Clerk's Office. Eleni had the stats, the names and numbers, McKeever to Keever and the dates. Reading the document, I realized that all along I'd been deceiving myself, hoping that her mysterious name games were educated guesswork, that all her tests were inconclusive. Maybe she didn't have this document when she demanded I throw the Aris game, but there was no avoiding the paper now.

She motioned me to sit back down. "Listen close to what I have to say. You want your bonus, but I'm also convinced you'll like our request. It will prove your celebrity. You will appreciate how a big frog in a small pond will help us."

Eleni was mocking me the way she'd made fun of Greeks that first day in Valtadoros.

"In Cairo," she said, "I will give you something to bring back to Ellatha. Do it and you'll get your bonus. Do this favor for Ellatha and you can stay here as long as you want. Go to the police, and copies of this document will be mailed to all the newspapers."

"Just what will I have to carry?"

"That's a secret until you get to Cairo, but it won't weigh as much as the money and will fit in a film canister."

I got up and walked down the hill toward the city. Fucking drugs. Money to Turkey, drugs back through Egypt. Half my teammates at Rockford smoked crack. It was the only pleasure they could afford on a CBA salary. Now I was going to be a highly paid mule. Eleni could sell the drugs here, buy dynamite, have her bang, and still have money left over. Cabbies honked when they passed me and looked back to see if I was a fare, a tourist they could cheat. I waved them on. It was a long way back to the hotel, but this was a fuck-up I wanted to try walking off.

Chapter 12

On the Airbus to Cairo, packed in with all the other Greek athletes—swimmers, weightlifters, pole-vaulters—and their trainers, I felt again like I was in a movie, this time watching an in-flight film I couldn't leave. Run the tape, check out the players. Vassilis may not be involved with Eleni. A believer in homeopathy, he made me buy my own anti-inflammatories. Eleni kept referring to her associates and used the plural, but that might be a bluff. She could be working alone. As far as I knew for sure, it was one-on-one now and I still didn't know shit about her. She was definitely an American, but the whole ecology spiel might be fake. The bombing part had to be true because I couldn't imagine anything worse. Eleni sent something—money or paper—to Turkey. She could be working with Turks, evening up some old score, trying to fuck up Greek tourism. She could be working against Turks, a member of the fringe group that had been blowing up Turkish embassies in Europe. She may be working for Palestinians and have some American target in mind. If she were Greek, I'd have a better idea of what she might be up to. But she was American, and after listening to her I realized she was more dangerous and unpredictable than any ethnic. Eleni's ideas may have led her anywhere, may lead to almost anything. She was also clever, waiting until the last minute to show me the document. But if this was straight-up blackmail, why the pitch? I realized Eleni had been recruiting me from the beginning, sucking me in, keeping me uncertain, asking for help, pleading altruism. The skittishness before the point-shaving could have been an act. So could have been the anger at tourists. Maybe Eleni thought if she could convince me to join some idealistic group—deceive myself that I was doing something for Greece—then I'd be a more cooperative and relaxed courier, like I'd been when delivering the packet to Istanbul. Now that she had the document— this recruit's binding "Letter of Intent"—she didn't need to pose. She could command.

I should never have lost my temper and threatened her. Now I couldn't play along. But she'd have expected me to be pissed. We were at the second-guessing and third-guessing stage, fakes within fakes. Finally, though, I was a person who accepted defeat, walked away, helpless. My best strategy was repeat the objections and then run for the money. Keep her talking. She still might give away something about herself I could use. Let her talk, make her talk, listen close, try to get inside her.

Our Olympic charter had a private gate and quick passport stamp in Cairo. The Greeks couldn't believe the new, bright airport, high ceilings, glass all around, as cool as Kennedy. Thirty feet of heat and into an air-conditioned tourist coach with Polaroid windows. Now that I was finished, everything was first class. Even the traffic, a four-lane highway right to the Nile Hilton. Thirty more feet of heat from the driveway into the hotel, an American oasis—casino, restaurants, banks, travel agents, and shops all in the same building.

Looking out the window of my tenth-floor room at the other twenty-story hotels up and down the river, I heard a buzz-buzz-buzz. After a few repetitions, I realized it was a phone, my first call in nine months. I figured it's Elias wanting to scout for a bride among the black-veiled women sitting in the lobby. It was Eleni, again. She wanted to talk with me. Talk, I told her. Together, she said. Come on up, I said. "Go out the revolving door away from the river," she told me. "Walk through the bus station and cross Tahrir Square in front of you. Look for Talaat Harb Street. It runs into Talaat Harb Square. Don't be confused. It's not square. It's like a rotary. Walk around and around until you see a man in a doorway motion to you. Leave your camera at the hotel. Wear a tee shirt. It's hot out."

Eleni was rushing me, making me jump. The bitch was right about the heat. Triple digits for sure. I was sweating before I got out of the Hilton garden. Heat and dust. In Athens the Nefos is a distant yellow background. You can see Cairo's shit in the air ten feet in front of you, feel it settle on your skin, stick there on the sweat, keep the heat inside. Just across the Hilton parking lot, dented and rusty buses were rolling in, raising dust off the street, mixing it with their blue smoke. Heads were hanging out the windows. The buses didn't have doors. Sweating men were jumping off before the buses stopped, running and jumping on while the buses were leaving. It looked dangerous in sandals, running and grabbing for a bar at the crowded doorway. The street I was supposed to cross was a gridlock of vehicles, cars from Vermont junkyards, donkey carts loaded with garbage, three-wheeled bicycles carrying families. The lights didn't seem to work. The cars were beep-beeping, not blaring like Greeks demanding movement. The Egyptians sounded resigned to being stuck in crisscrossed lanes. I tagged along with a group of women weaving among the vehicles. On the other side all I could see in the dust and Arabic squiggles were "Iberia" and "British Air." Rubbernecking around for the street sign, I was the only person standing still as thousands of people milled around and past me.

"You are lost," a boy about twelve said to me. For some reason I noticed the kid was wearing low black Reeboks.

"You are right," I said.

"Well-come to Egypt. What do you want?"

"Talaat Harb Street."

"Yes, over there," he said and pointed a couple of streets away. I told him thanks.

"Baksheesh?" he said.

"What?"

"A tip for me?"

"Right," I said and gave him a hundred drachs.

"Sir, this money is not good here. I cannot exchange it for Egyptian money."

"Sorry, but it's all I have right now."

"Would you like to change money? My father will change for you. Dollars, yes? Also francs and yen."

"Not right now," I told him. Twelve years old and he spoke better English than Elias. I guess he had to. He was in the service industry. I wondered if he also spoke French and Japanese.

After walking two blocks in the midday heat and crowds of Talaat Harb Street, I wanted to sit at one of the fresh orange juice stands or hunker down in the shade of a shop door like the old men in robes. Watch the masses pass by. Ann was definitely wrong about Greece. *This* is the Third World. I could tell by the slow-moving feet. Men in lightweight suits ambled in K-Mart dress shoes or leather sandals over soiled white socks. Women in dresses shuffled through the dust in plastic shoes with sequins. Men wearing robes scuffed along the sidewalk in old leather shoes without laces. Some women and skinny-legged kids had on shower clogs or walked barefoot in the street, the dirt and dust working up from their toes and heels to ankles and shins. I saw a woman crawling along the sidewalk. She had pads on her knees and low-cut sneakers on her hands. A girl younger than Sara was following behind carrying a sack. About every tenth person I met, usually a kid, said "Hell-o." An old shoeshine man who looked mute pointed at my dusty white Cons, shook his head, and said, "Well-comb to Egypt."

I walked around the rotary at Talaat Harb Square, where traffic was being controlled by underfed little men with submachine guns slung over their black military uniforms. The second time around I picked out some English signs—Tulip Hotel, Pharmacy—on the old six- and seven-story buildings, once grand but now sooty, balconies crumbling, metal grillwork staining walls with rust. Looking up and looking into every doorway, I must have appeared lost again. A man about twenty came up to me, asked me where I was from, welcomed me to Egypt, and asked me if I was looking for a cool place. His brother owned an air-conditioned perfume shop very close. He lightly touched my sweat-soaked shirt and said, "To cover smell, you understand?" Was this my contact? Had I missed him in the crowd? Was he out here now speaking to me in code? No thanks, I told him and started round again. A white-robed man standing back inside a doorway motioned with his hand. Change money, change smell, change name? When I got to the doorway, he said, "Keef-air queek." I followed him into a courtyard and quickly out another door onto a side street. We walked fast for a block, then turned and entered another building. He steered me out a back door and into an alley where men were sitting at little tables, smoking water pipes and drinking tea. My guide showed me into a small room with four tables. At one of them Eleni was sitting alone, a scarf wrapped around her head. She was wearing sandals. A glass of tea was in front of her. She looked at home, and I wondered if she could be Arab.

"'Welcome to Egypt.' The people are taught those three English words. You'll hear them often."

"What have you got for me?"

"My friends," she started.

"Forget the fiction. Just tell me what you've got."

"Why the rush? I don't think you appreciate the show we're planning. You have to imagine it now, but it will be something you can see as it happens."

The Parthenon. She was going to bring down the

Parthenon. She knew where I lived and knew I'd see it from my balcony. Not just any tourist site but Athena's shrine, a wonder of the world. This had never occurred to me in Salonika. Maybe Eleni wanted to knock over some of those columns out in the country or a local museum but not the Parthenon. Low, Key. Stay low.

"How am I going to see it?"

"Everyone will. Since we know where and when the event will occur, we will tape the columns crumbling, the stones falling down, the dust rising against a blue background. We will give our tape to all the television networks. Viewers will watch the event in slow motion, over and over, columns crumbling, stones falling, dust rising. Like presidential assassinations, but no people. And no voices. We will show a silent film, a loud noise, then silent motion, columns crumbling, symbolic stones breaking up into nonsense, a cloud of dust."

"Just what Athens needs. More pollution in the air."

"The tape will be clear. It's a document that will circulate around the whole world, generating news stories and editorials, features and articles, governmental white papers. When we have the world's attention, we will release our columns of numbers. Statistics are the only way to tell the future. Attached to this event, the statistics will have weight, power. They will be obvious. We, however, will remain a secret. Our group intentionally has no name. Pursuing who is responsible for this film, the curious world will keep coming back to the event and the statistics the event points to, the weather warning."

Eleni sipped her tea, and I thought if there was a group, it wouldn't be secret long, not as much as Eleni loved to talk, to instruct. Eleni was a coach's coach, the kind that flies to other countries and gives clinics. The speech sounded rehearsed, as if she'd made it to others or repeated it to herself. Eleni could be testing herself or maybe she still thought she could persuade me. Was it pride in her knowledge, belief in my obsession with tape, or some of both? The longer Eleni talked, the longer I had to think about what to say next. Exert some pressure. She expects you to argue even if you end up going along.

"This isn't going to work," I said, "The Parthenon is sacred."

"No more. Now we know the frieze depicts child sacrifice, the daughters of King Erechtheus being prepared for slaughter.

It's an old story still true: sacrifice the future to the present."

"Tourists don't know this. You're not going to get the effect you want."

"We invented theater, focusing attention on a small space. There's a plague, an epidemic of building. You don't cure it by having some motherfucker blind himself. People love buildings more than other people. This dramatic event will move the audience, even on tape. We want to change an ideology. To do it, we need an aesthetic effect. Ideology: from the Greek for seeing, the tourist gaze. Aesthetic: from the Greek for feeling, the villager's response. Circulated around the global village, this film will force the audience to feel, make them jump."

"Shoving from behind instead of leading from ahead. Just like the trolleys."

"What would you have us do, build a Biosphere like the one in Arizona? A fake dome, another tourist attraction."

"It's all theory." I quoted Ann, "Hyperbole."

"Here are the facts," Eleni said, rattling off memorized numbers: "Americans make up 5 percent of the world's population, consume 35 percent of the world's energy, release 27 percent of the world's carbon dioxide, and, to balance these emissions in the future, each American will have to plant 4,500 trees every year. Of 250 million Americans, though, only 7 percent hold passports."

"Those may be facts, but your whole strategy is negative."

"The future is negative. Higher temperature, lower life. When the climate changes, scavenger life takes over. Weeds, cockroaches, rats, quick adapters. The planet is in runaway. This is a term you should appreciate. Our action will help slow the systems. We give the world a moving image of negative feedback, the positive 'negative.'"

"'Give'?" I laughed. "Where's the fucking gift?"

Eleni laughed back. "Beware Greeks bearing gifts. We reverse the Trojan horse. It seemed to be a gift but had destruction inside. We turn this inside-out: our destructive act gives the world a better chance to survive, to prevent the Trojan fate, the ruins under ruins. Even America will benefit from our cleverness."

Eleni really did think she could convince me. Then I'd be like one of those mules who take downers to stay low-key through airport security. She was also enjoying this, showing off. Turn it around on her.

"It will all rebound on you. More people will come to see ruins ruined than to see them standing."

"No, you are wrong. We know tragedy, pity and fear, especially fear. The deepest ecology is fear."

Then Eleni completed my language lesson, gave me words I would never have guessed were Greek.

"'Tourism' is, I admit it, a Greek word. To cure it we inspire 'terror,' another Greek word. Tourists will be afraid, fearful that a building with people inside will be next. Tourists will stay away from Ellatha. We will gradually learn to live without them, and we will recover our ancient role as teacher of the world. Viewers worldwide will come to feel that the tourist attitude toward the planet creates our ecological crisis, our future heat."

Eleni had answers for all my objections. It was like arguing with Ann: the positions were all thought out, the causes and effects lined up, the distant past connected to the not-so-distant future, the aesthetic effect canceling the greenhouse effect. It seemed real. So was my money. It was time to get under Eleni's skin.

"You're overlooking one problem."

"Tell me, Keever, or is it a secret?"

"The bomb will never go off. The whole thing is too complicated for Greeks to bring off."

"The famous American organization and efficiency," she said, as if remembering some fact about prehistoric life. "All those time and motion studies are needed by huge corporations to squeeze out profit. We are a small group, like a family. Each has a skill to give the group. All we lack is. . ." She hesitated, as if she were a non-native speaker searching for an expression. It was a little piece of acting. "All we need is a delivery boy."

I was prepared for this. I'd heard it before—from shooters, from Henderson, from Ann. Nothing moved. I was a person who could be insulted without response. A real Greek would have been enraged. For money, I could be used. Let her believe it. It was time to surrender. We were back to the beginning.

"You win," I said, "What have you got for me?"

"Plastic. Plastic explosives."

I couldn't fucking believe it. Something worse than drugs. Leave the United States, show some high-li, get on TV, and I'm assigned a role in the movies I'd been watching for ten years. I suppose I should have anticipated from what Eleni said in Salonika. Maybe I really was dumb. So explosives were the reason for Eleni's long final pitch. Cool, Key, keep cool.

"You want me to smuggle a fucking bomb from Egypt to Greece? This sounds very dangerous to me. Thirty thousand feet and bang. I'd never get it out of the airport. I'd be sweating in the terminal."

"Not a bomb. You can handle the material. This is American-made. We got it from our Libyan friends, who bought it from an American. Don't worry. You can feel it, poke it. Without a detonating mechanism, plastic is harmless even for children. I told you. We are not interested in killing people. Raining down bodies and wreckage on Lockerbie is stupid. The public sees only the aftermath, still photos."

"This isn't the same as taking money to Istanbul. How do you expect me to get this shit out of Egypt?"

"You are a celebrity, a tall and visible person traveling with a group of other celebrities. Leaving Egypt you will receive the same special treatment as when you arrived. In Athens you will be a returning hero. You are famous for your camera. The plastic will fit in your tape canister. You will not be X-rayed or searched in Cairo. Certainly not in Athens. For you, it will be a simple task."

"It's so fucking simple, why don't you do it?"

"You're slow, Keever. Because I'm not a celebrity and don't want to be one."

"But you'll be in the crowd at the Athens airport to take the film off my hands?"

"The exchange is always risky, a time when police might appear. You'll receive instructions on how to turn over the canister."

"You make it sound too easy. Convince me that once you get the canister the document won't appear in the newspapers."

"You want to live in Ellatha next year. We want you to stay. Maybe we can make money together. You might even be more willing to help once you see the effect our film has."

So I'd be willing to blow up the Parthenon to stay and play in Greece. Maybe she thought so, but she also expected me to deny it. What else did she think about the delivery boy? Time to turn up the heat.

"You're no more Greek than I am. The people who invented

the Olympics would never bring down the Parthenon. Why don't you leave Greece to the natives, go back home, and take a shot at the Trade Towers?"

"At-lan-ta," she spit out, syllable by syllable. "America is the fitting place for the golden Olympic Games. Once they were athletic competition and reconciliation of a people, a true holiday. Now they are only gold. All money, television, and advertising like America, the country that exports fakes like you. Speed and greed. For Americans, Atlanta is just another tourist attraction. Like these Mediterranean Games, like Ellatha for you, Keever. Athletes are tourists. We are better off without them."

Eleni had never wanted me here next year. The trips to Istanbul and, now, to Athens were always the payoff. Until this point I'd been poking and pushing and pressing, trying to get Eleni to give away something. I anticipated the insults, even her closing off next year. But to her last comment on athletes I had an immediate and authentic response, a recognition that was useless in my negotiation and, blurted out, maybe even harmful to my pose as skeptical businessman, the man who came for the money. Suddenly my coaches were in my mouth—Kellogg's clock, Matera's spacing, Cater's tape, Z's conditioning. Trainers joined in. I couldn't help myself. It was my first idea, the first time I realized how I'm connected to other people, how I overlap with the rest of the world.

"Athletes are on the road and in the air like tourists. But we're not tourists. When we get out of the bus, we do physical labor. Sure, we love it. From your seat, it looks easy. But peer inside. Athletes are bodies that can't avoid the facts. We're the people who know about air, panting, gasping, choking. We know overheating, not enough fresh water, too much salty water, exhaustion in pools of sweat. Athletes feel chemical traces, how the body's systems balance, how they need to work together."

"Work together," Eleni interrupted with a laugh. "You play with yourselves."

"You plot. We play, improvise together in crowded space. We're always changing, feeling the clock and pressure. We perform in domes but look at our lives, not just our two hours on the floor. We're not close to nature. We are nature, the changing seasons, the changing bodies, the slower recoveries. We're bodies, and they don't lie. Bodies are the present. They sense the future, the sudden end or gradual decline, the forty-year passing on, replacement by the young. Athletes are not tourists. Crazed by too much traveling, we recognize the value of home."

Eleni seemed a little surprised. Maybe bemused is the right word. The athlete speaks. Later I thought that speaking my own mind was not like studying tape but like saying the Spiti Mas lines, not injecting information deep into my body but recovering knowledge from that source, recognizing how the crowded and collaborating inside overlaps with what I'd learned about the crowded, collaborating, competing outside world. Watching tape I tried to bypass language. Writing down these events and conversations, I feel I should jump over words, leap from senses to stats. Players have numbers. We are numbers: height, weight, arm length, hip width, foot speed, hand speed, eye speed, vertical jump, horizontal jump, lung capacity, blood pressure, calories, metabolism, all the numbers trainers can measure with their muscle machines, scopes, and urine analyses. We'd be better players if we watched the numbers the way Olympians do, the pentathletes who figure total intake, total ouput. Maybe we'd be better people, smarter about taking in, passing off.

Players are not artists, competing ballet dancers. We're scientists, compilers of quantities, runners of numbers, collectors of statistics. They are how we represent our day and year and career, the mesh of individual and team, the team's standing, the relation of the smallest detail to the whole changing picture. Statistics predict our long-run performance, help us move up and around the world, carry part of our lives into history. For Eleni statistics were the only key to the future. I've forgotten all the numbers she recited, but she gave me new respect for stats. Although everyone says statistics lie, maybe they are the truth we need to heed.

"Athletes are trained to make quick decisions," Eleni said in the Cairo tearoom. "Will you deliver the package?"

"This isn't something the body decides. You're asking me to carry shit that could kill me. I'll have to think about it."

"Think about your bonus, Keever. I'll give you overnight. We need to make preparations. Or make photocopies for the newspapers. Many people will be angry. You will have to leave, if they let you. And remember, worse things than exposure can happen if you betray someone when you're far from home."

She made a cutting motion with her hand, a gesture I didn't recognize. Then she nodded to the guy in robes, who took my arm and led me out. We twisted and turned through some alleys. When we came out on a busy street, he pointed to the left, gave me a shove, and disappeared into the crowd right. I stood still and waited five minutes for a man in a suit to pass by. I touched his arm and said "Talaat Harb?" He said "Welcome to Egypt," and pointed the same way the guy in robes did. I went round the rotary until I spotted the big blue "H" high in the distance. The Egyptians were still jumping buses when I got back to the hotel, a half hour before our bus left for the shootaround.

Chapter 13

On the bus, I forced myself to think about basketball: leather ball, rubber soles, wool socks, steel rim, cotton net, glass backboard, wooden floor, no plastic components. Tomorrow we'd play France. We were in the easier draw—France, Italy, and Morocco. A round-robin game every afternoon. In the evening Spain, Israel, Croatia, and Egypt would play. After a day off, two qualifiers from each draw played semis and, the next day, games for first and third. We should make the final four. We weren't going to beat Croatia here or anywhere. If we could finish third, we'd qualify for the Atlanta Olympics. That's what the Greeks were here for. Everyone who spoke a hundred words of English had told me about winning the European championship in 1987, the celebrations all over the country, old women in black out in the street waving flags. But the team had never been to the Olympics. With possibly five games in six days, ELLAS needed me at third guard—even if the stadium was fifty degrees, even if it had a plastic floor and plastic seats. Then I realized what would happen if I played: when Eleni dropped the document, Greece could be disqualified from the Olympics. If I didn't bring in the plastic, she'd expose me. If I brought the plastic, got my bonus, and got out, she'd still expose me and disqualify Greece. From what she said about athletes, that was probably a useful byproduct of the whole fucking deal for her.

In the heat between the bus and the stadium, as new and cool as the airport, I thought about Eleni making me jump to Talaat Harb. Her rush to make me sweat gave me an out. We stretched and jogged around the parquet floor. We cruised into a layup line and did a three-point shooting drill. Then Kotopoulos put us into a fast-break drill to get out all the travel kinks. The first time I went to the hoop I grabbed my left hamstring, the million-dollar injury, invisible on an X-ray, no swelling, no bruise, no treatment. Even Kallis looked concerned as I limped to the bench. "Krima," Elias said. The trainer shrugged. Nothing to be done. Ice and heat, ice and heat, but it takes rest and time to recover from a hamstring. In the 1989 NBA championship series, the Lakers lost Magic and Byron Scott to hamstrings. A betting man might be suspicious if national pride weren't at stake.

"Use the crutches if it pains you," the trainer said.

"Not that much pain right now," I told him. After showering, I asked for the crutches. They might come in handy. If I took the plastic out, I'd be pitied at the airport. If we didn't make the final four, I could use them to beat off angry Greeks in Athens. On the bus I sat up front with Kotopoulos. "Take me off the roster," I told him. "You know how hamstrings are. Bring in somebody else. I'll be honorary." He had to check with the officials, see if they'd approve a substitute now. He called that evening to say the officials would allow a replacement because I hadn't played. Georgiades from PAOK was flying down in the morning. Kotopoulos was bringing in another shooter.

The hamstring gave me time to think. An injured player is enraged. He doesn't want to talk to anyone, not even his best friend. Other players stay away, as if hamstrings are contagious. Elias was two doors down. He phoned to ask if I needed anything. Yes, I thought, I need you to sub for me, carry some plastic to Athens. I stayed in my room, flicking back and forth between CNN and an Egyptian soap opera, running through my options. I needed more time. I decided to tell Eleni I'd go along. That would give me a few days to decide what I was really going to do.

The call came in early. I told her I'd do it.

"What are you doing on crutches?" she asked.

"Pulled hamstring. Accidents happen to athletes' bodies."

"You're faking, Keever. What are you trying to pull?"

"I thought the crutches would be a useful prop at the airport."

"Don't try to kid me. You could have injured yourself in the final game. If you try to set me up, you'll be sorry."

"Look," I lied to her, "I get paid whether I play or not. But just in case you get tired of me and decide to release that document next Christmas, I don't want to see Greece barred from the Olympics. I wouldn't get out alive."

Eleni laughed. She appreciated fear. I asked her when and how I'd get the plastic.

"Open your door. Room service will bring it."

I opened the door and stuck my head out. The guy in robes who picked me out of the crowd at Talaat Harb came walking up the hall with a tray. He handed it to me and removed the round cover that keeps your breakfast warm. Under it was a tape canister. I expected the fuckhead to ask for baksheesh.

Eleni was confident. She was also in a hurry. Maybe she wanted to get out of the country early before I could set her up. Maybe she wanted me to get used to the shit, feel comfortable with it, like a fumbling halfback whose coach makes him carry a ball to classes. I opened up the canister. If Eleni wanted to blow up this part of the Hilton she wouldn't have called. The shit looked like Sara's Play Doh. I poked for batteries, transistors, caps, anything that could set off the stuff. I didn't know what plastic was supposed to look like. This could be some new form of coke. It could also be Nile mud, a hoax so fucking complicated I couldn't begin to imagine it.

I was halfway down the hall to breakfast when I remembered my crutches. They were a pain in the ass but a good reminder to hobble. I three-legged out to all the games in the third season. What else would get my mind off the plastic in my room? The mismatched African teams and a round-robin rule created some ugly basketball. If three teams in a draw finished with two-and-one records, the two with the highest point totals advanced. Everybody ran up the score. Egypt was shooter's paradise, except for the host country. It finished zero-and-three, beaten every game by at least fifty points. Kallis got his nose bloodied against France but stayed out there to add his forty-five to the easy win. Italy came back to beat us 98-94 when Kotopoulos refused to rest his starters and they wouldn't sit on the ball at the end. France could beat only Egypt, so Italy at three-and-zero and Greece at two-and-one went to the final four with Croatia and Israel.

Afternoon and evening, I aimed my camera and pointed my eyes toward the action. I wasn't shooting but I wanted to be camera visible, taking lots of film to take home. I also wasn't really looking. In this beautiful NBA arena, built for the Games, I was picturing an Egyptian jail, a flash and fall over the Mediterranean, a Greek prison. I hated these risks, and I didn't want to help Eleni, but I could not think of a way to involve the police and still get my money. I was missing the Games. I wasn't losing that money. I'd put fans in the stands and the ball in Pop's hands in Salonika. Even if I was here under a fake name, I'd earned the money. If I delivered the plastic, Eleni might give me time to collect the bonus. But if she did that, I could then warn the police. So what she'll do is blow up the Parthenon immediately, uncover my secret, and somehow frame me before I can get the bonus and get out. I could bring in the plastic and delay the exchange until I get the bonus. That's unlikely. She didn't give me time to figure out how to do that before I left. When we get back, she'll be in a hurry. She'll be afraid of a setup. It wouldn't be safe to put her off very long. As the teams went up and down the floor, I went round and round in my head. I was fucked if I didn't deliver, probably fucked if I did. Sort of like the Egyptians and Moroccans—overmatched. After the third night of shoot-and-shoot basketball, I went to the Hilton casino. Dollars only. I cashed a traveler's check and lost a hundred playing my number on the roulette wheel. If I'd played for Tark, I'd have known the odds against winning my bonus in a desert casino.

The day off between the round-robins and semis, the team went to see the Pyramids: bus out and camel ride around. I wasn't taking my crutches on a camel. Besides, I'd seen plenty of the Pyramids: the posters in the banks, the guides in the book shop, the mock-ups in the gift shops, the dark interiors of the Pyramid Bar and Grille, the Pyramid Arena in Memphis. The Egyptian Museum was next door to the Hilton. I didn't need to go there either. King Tut, his mummy friends, and their gold cases were everywhere. The Hilton men's room had a picture of Tut on the door. He'd even been on tour in the States. What I never saw pictures of but overheard someone in the lobby talking about was the City of the Dead, the tombs of Cairo where people were now living. It sounded like the way Eleni had me feeling. I asked at American Express. The woman couldn't or wouldn't understand me. Anyway, no bus tour. I asked the desk clerk. He gestured out the window. I stumped down the driveway toward the Nile and the street where the cabbies screamed up to the guests getting into the buses. "Personal tour." "Very cheap." Five drivers gathered around me. "Pyramids, Giza, Saqqara." "Khan al-Khalili bazaar, al-Azhar mosque." "Luxor, Aswan, Sudan," said one guy, playing long odds like me in the casino. "City of the Dead," I said. They buzzed in Arabic. Only one of the drivers recognized this English. "I take you. I am Mahmoud." I made sure he knew where I wanted to go: "cemetery, people live." "I know this place," he said. We agreed on the price. Ten dollars for the rest of the day. For a hundred he'd probably drive the plastic to Greece.

It was a half-hour ride, maybe three miles. Beep, beep.

Beep. In the heat-absorbing black taxi, dust plastered on my skin. Mahmoud first took me up to the Citadel, Cairo's highest point, so I could see how the City of the Dead curled around two sides of this old fortress. The City of the Dead was in the center. From above, one-story tombs with tiled roofs looked like a trash-compacted California suburb. Out farther in the Cairo haze and dust were the domed mosques. "Worlddome," I heard Eleni say inside my head. Minarets shaped like rockets prepare to blast off from the domes, up and out of the yellow dust, but they won't hold many of those bending, bowing, shoe-less masses who gather under the domes to praise Allah's will and a shady paradise.

We drove back down. The City of the Dead was itself a Citadel, surrounded by a ten-foot high stone wall. We drove in one of the entrances, the gate ripped off like the bus doors. I expected to see the Third World's worst, the Sixth World, the Ninth World, the masses in Cairo's streets doubled or squared, crowded like refugees, jammed like prisoners in an Egyptian jail. Instead, the narrow dirt streets were almost empty and still. No other cars, only a few women and children walking in the dust.

I asked Mahmoud where all the people were. "Outside for work," he said. "Or inside." He pointed out the window. An irregular wall ran along each side of the street. Ten- to twenty-foot sections were different heights and were made from different materials—stone, bricks, stucco—but they connected to form a continuous barrier. Each section had its own large wooden door. Some were padlocked. A few were open. Through them I could see into the courtyards. Laundry was hung on five-foot high gravestones. Kids played in the dirt in front of the tombs. They were windowless stone buildings, gray and brown and blackened with soot. The tombs were squat and substantial, built to last. Some were fifteen feet across and had elaborate carvings and decorations over their doors. If the courtyard door and tomb door lined up just right, I could see for an instant inside the tombs, see women tending house by candlelight, see kids standing like little ghosts next to the stacked coffins. Mahmoud explained in English prepared for the Pyramids: "These poor people. They break doors and steal rich family's tomb for home." The Egyptians were living with the dead, other families' dead, people the living had never seen.

When we stopped at a corner, a girl not much older than Sara walked up to Mahmoud's window, stretched her head up to him, and said something.

"What does she want?" I asked.

"Pen," he said, "pen for school."

I didn't have a pen. Even if I had, would this little girl learn to use it and write her way out of the City of the Dead? Write her way into one of the glass-faced hotels along the Nile? She had about the same chance as I did of writing a best-selling travel book. She didn't have a shot.

Mahmoud drove slowly so as not to raise dust. Up one street, down another. The streets were all the same. Just different kinds of walls and tombs. No stores, no open spaces, no trees. A few women hauling in shopping bags. A shirtless sweating man carrying buckets of water suspended from a shoulder yoke, a device I'd seen drawings of in elementary school. He walked barefoot and stooped, as if he were in a rice paddy. His carrying capacity was two buckets. Where the sewage went I didn't know. Maybe into the dry, hot air. Mahmoud nodded at the man and said, "Everything from outside. Nothing inside only dead."

Almost motionless, the City of the Dead was like a place I'd seen on a travel poster in the hotel, an underwater city flooded by the Nile, an occasional fish drifting through the still ruins. Or if not a city of the past, I thought, a city of the future, population thinned by the heat, men gone off to build dikes against the sea, women and children waiting in the desert dust and hot stones. I hadn't lifted my camera off the seat but I wondered why a film of this city couldn't substitute for Eleni's crumbling Parthenon. Because the City of the Dead hadn't ever appeared on TV? Because the tombs didn't move? Or because this was the Third World, already too late for it?

"Let's go back to the Hilton," I told Mahmoud.

Near the gate we'd come in, four teenagers were walking toward us, two in sandals, two barefoot. Mahmoud beeped but they didn't move to the side. They gathered at his window and jabbered. "They say you take photo," Mahmoud told me. Once I saw the City, I was sorry I'd brought my camera. Now I wondered if I'd leave with it. "OK," I said and got out of the car without the crutches. The boys went back in front of the taxi and stood with their arms around each other and stared at the camera while I moved it back and forth. The biggest and probably oldest of the four stepped a little forward, pulled off his headwrap, and covered his face with it like a stone-throwing Palestinian. The others laughed and shouted, "Goha, goha." Then they walked back toward me. I hoped they didn't think my camera was a Polaroid. The leader uncovered his face and said, as politely as the twelve-year-old money-changer, "Baksheesh?" He didn't want film of himself. He was selling his rights for a tip. I gave him ten dollars. At the Hilton I gave Mahmoud twenty. He could go home early. Tomorrow he wouldn't have to go anywhere.

Nowhere in Athens was there poverty like I saw in Cairo. Not just poverty but humiliation, a kid asking a stranger for a twenty-cent pen. And yet I could imagine Cairo present as Athens future. Egypt was once the center of the world. It fed the Mediterranean with its grain before the weather changed. Spiti Mas said the mountains around Athens used to be thickly forested. When the heat rises next century, the olive trees could die and grapes wither. If Greek beaches disappear and the people who have migrated to Athens can't leave, the cleverness Vassilis talked about will be useless. Beggars will be out in the streets, families will start sharing flats, and present Athenians' great-grandchildren could be asking for pens from adventurous travelers willing to brave the crowds and heat to see the Parthenon. "Stylo," the kids will say, a long "e." Their future will have been stolen by the past. Civilization was a pyramid scheme, Eleni had said, the secret the whole world concealed from itself. A centuries-long epidemic of kleptomania. Child-sacrifice. What will future Greek kids write if they're lucky enough to beg a pen or quick enough to pick a pocket? Letters to cooler countries. "Vohethia." Help.

I had four more games to watch, two more days to decide. We drew Israel in the semis. Kallis had had a day of rest. Not even the brothers could stop him. Old brothers, Henderson would have said, desperate brothers who'd agree to be sons of Ham. We'd go to the Olympics even if we lost the final game to Croatia. We would definitely lose. We hadn't given away anything in Salonika.

The Greeks put up a good fight but the Croats took home the cup, a good place to hide explosives. It was our last night at the Hilton. I had to decide. It was too late to call the police. I could walk down the driveway and throw the plastic into the Nile. If I could get the package into Greece, I might still figure out something. A lot of risks for a "might." I poked and squeezed the plastic. I wasn't too worried about the worst, the plane. I was convinced Athens wouldn't be a problem as long as this wasn't a plant. I'd seen the City of the Dead. I was afraid of an Egyptian jail, the airport X-ray camera that sees through every deception. Fear against greed was the way Eleni would call it. I added in justice and pride. I had sweated for that money. Now that little bitch was in my face. This was no time to choke. I thought about the playoff game in Salonika. I thought about Ann and Sara. A house is what we'd come for, a place for Sara to grow in, maybe a family to grow in. I tried to weigh years in an Egyptian jail against years in an American home. "Spiti Mas," I thought. Hospitality. Fuck it, I said to myself, I'm not turning over the plastic. Greece has been a home to me. There was no way I was helping Eleni blow up the Parthenon. That's when I realized the Parthenon is a Greek home. Not "the cry for pity" Ann's guidebook called it, but a model home, up high for the breeze and view of the purple mountains to the north, the blue sea to the south, the other Greek homes all around. The Parthenon is all balcony, open-roofed for the light, columned for shade, big enough to hold a family, flat land around for soccer and parking. The Parthenon is constructed out of dead stone, what the Greeks have in plenty. It's an economic building, a home to keep, a place to pass down to daughters and sons, the Greeks' chief possession. No photograph or film of a desperate act could substitute for the ancient handmade thing itself.

No photograph or film. A desperate act to sell. The boys mugging before the camera in the City of the Dead passed through my mind and I knew what I was going to do. I'll collect my bonus from Eleni. I'd made money for her. Now I'll make her pay. Not only that, I'll fuck her up. I'll make her pay and pass off fake plastic. I'll stick her with a substitute. I didn't know exactly how, but I'd figure a way. "Keever creates in the air," sportswriters said. If Eleni could invent something as fantastic as bringing down a wonder of the world, I could imagine a way to stop her.

The next morning I hobbled slowly toward the gate. If the Egyptians were X-raying charter athletes, I'd have to dump the plastic. "Croatia," I'd tell Elias and throw the shit in a can. I lagged back on the crutches, scanning ahead for the X-ray machines. The airport was cool. I didn't break a sweat. Elias had my carry-on, and I had my camera case with lots of tape. "Many sights," I'd tell a body-searcher. It was no contest. We were athletes, guests, tourists, all Greeks getting on a Greek airplane. Another private gate, decorated with Greek flags. X-ray machines and body searchers would be an insult. The Egyptians wanted us back when we had more time and money. Eleni was right. It was easy. Even the Olympic staff was polite, letting me and a gymnast with a cast board first.

I do have to admit that as much as I had kneaded the plastic my armpits were damp until the plane leveled off at cruising elevation. Don't go in the air without knowing what you're going to do. All coaches agree. Eleni might be at the airport. She or Vassilis, if he was involved, or the guy in robes could be waiting at my apartment. I thought about the apartment, closed up for a month, now definitely closed out for next year. All around me the Greeks were happy to be heading home, leaving Egypt, flying on Olympic, listening to the captain and stewardesses speak Greek, preparing for a Greek meal, looking forward to the welcome "stin Athena." This time I'd avoid the crowd.

After the other athletes pushed down the stairway onto the tarmac and into buses, I told a stewardess I was having a lot of pain. Could she ask an Olympic rep to come out in a car and help me through passport control? "Of course." The driver took me to a door beside the main terminal entrance. He knocked, spoke to the policeman who opened it, and helped me in. "Krimas" for the leg, congratulations for "theftero," second place. A quick passport stamp and I was ready to go. "Taxi?" I said to the cop and pointed to my leg. "Certainly." The cop left, came back five minutes later, and took my carry-on down a corridor. I kept my camera case and the plastic. He showed me out a door. No crowd, one taxi, no baksheesh. Eleni was right about the exit and entry, and I was right about the crutches. The exchange was going to be the tricky part.

Chapter 14

I told the driver Hotel Apollon in the Plaka. I certainly wasn't going home. Out of the crowd, I was just another citizen who might be robbed or worse. I didn't have much reason to go back—some clothes, a couple of tapes, a final view of the Parthenon, tonight lighted up, tomorrow morning in the sun. "Nice to have you back," the receptionist at the Apollon said. At 11:00 I took a roll of athletic tape from my bag and limped down through the lobby. Tourists were eating, laughing, walking back and forth through the alleys. In case any Greeks noticed me, I kept limping until I got up above the cottages at the foot of the Acropolis. I hunted among the olive trees until I found what I needed: the black net farmers use to catch olives. It was early for harvest but you always see one or two in a grove, forgotten or perhaps rotted. I climbed over the low wire fence that separates the olive trees from the Acropolis. No security to worry about down here. Eleni's people would have to scale the rock and the wall. The lightweight plastic would make the climb easier if Eleni planned to go up herself. I walked to the northeast side. In the scrub growth sixty feet almost straight down from the wall where I'd filmed in September is a single dark fir tree, the kind you might see growing out of a cliff in California. It was more like a large bush with thick, up-turned branches. I climbed into the tree. Using my tape and the holes in the net, I rigged a sack about three feet across in the top branches. The net would be invisible from below, barely visible from above.

I limped back to the Apollon. Tourists worried about thieves do funny things with their luggage. My gym bag has two compartments: a large open one reached from the top and an expandable plastic sock reached from one end. The sock for sweaty clothes lies along the bottom of the main compartment. I slit a hole in the sock and taped it back together from inside. In the sock I placed a tape canister taped shut. In the main compartment I put the canister with the plastic. Then I laid in my camera in its case. Then I lay awake imaging, disconnecting, practicing my lines. Keep it simple, Keever. No anger, no loyalty. Just collecting the cash. Admitting defeat, walking away.

In the morning, the first thing I did was call the GM at Panathinaikos to ask about the bonus. He'd have to check all the escalators and calculate it. There was the question of not playing in Cairo. Write that off, I told him. The final figure would have to be approved by the owner, who would have to send a written request to the Swiss bank, which could then transfer my bonus to my Memphis bank if I had the account number to give him. The owner wasn't in today. I asked the GM to get started on it. He wanted to talk about next year. I told him I was waiting to see how they were going to settle this year. Maybe that would speed him up. The written request was still involved. He asked if I wanted Vassilis to look at my hamstring. Tomorrow, I said, I'll be over to the pit tomorrow. Vassilis didn't make any difference anymore. I'd have to do without squeezing him. The bonus also looked like a loss. Eleni would have to pay me.

I was traveling light today, so I had to leave some clothes in the hotel room. I put on a Panathinaikos tee shirt, bermudas, Cons, and a baseball cap—clearly a man recovering in the Greek sun. I got on my crutches, slung my carry-on over my shoulder, and took a taxi to Valtadoros. "Krima," the regulars said. "Then peirazi," it doesn't matter, "Olympiada." No coffee this morning. I wanted to be calm. At ten, the call came in.

"Where have you been?" Eleni asked.

"I don't live here anymore. I'm leaving for the States tonight."

"What about next year?"

"You fucked up in Cairo, Eleni. I know there's no next year for me, so I also know what you will do as soon as I deliver the package. But I got to thinking last night. The delivery boy is paid. He also gets a tip."

"Don't play games with me, Keever."

"I'm off the roster, but I do want my bonus. You want the package. I'm giving you a special price, no mark-up. I'll take the forty thousand dollars I took to Istanbul. No drachmas."

"Don't fuck with me. I can send a man in there and take the package now."

"It's not here. Just a lot of people here, Eleni. All basketball fans." She was pissed. Now I'd call the shots, make her jump, bring her to me. "Come to the Parthenon today at 4:00. The north side. Have the money in an envelope. We'll make the exchange. Be on time. I have a flight to catch."

"What are you talking about, Keever? An exchange in public?"

"That's right. I wouldn't trust you anywhere else. I want people watching."

"I don't believe this. It's a set-up."

"It's too obvious to be a set-up. All I want is the money. I used to love this country, but for the last six months you and the rest of your countrymen have been fucking me up and down. Now I'm getting out. What you do with the package after I leave is your business. And don't forget: when I'm gone, that document you're holding won't be worth shit."

I hung up on her. This was no time for extended debate or subtle misinformation. Keep it simple: money. Eleni had been overconfident, had miscalculated, gotten too close. She'd put the stuff in my hands. She figured I had the telescope on next year. Now it was just a question of how much she wanted to recover the plastic, how big a risk she'd take, how much she believed in my stupidity, how much she trusted my American greed, how much pride she had in her cleverness, how well-trained she was in quick decisions. There was also the money. If she had it, she'd go for the deal. Eleni wanted Greece to be Ellatha, the way it was when gods spoke to men. She feared the future. She was obsessed with doing good for the crowd. Something else too: Eleni was only five-three, but she wanted to be a player, *do* something, test herself, be a secret star, a hidden celebrity. If Eleni didn't show up, I'd hide out, watch the papers, and try to get the bonus from Panathinaikos. Eleni may not have a fallback position. She may have too much invested in me to pull out now.

Valtadoros was the safest place I knew. More orange juice, read the *Athens News*, have a sandwich, watch the people walk by. My last day to watch Greek faces in Kolonaki Square. The shift changed at 3:00. Achilleas always went down to the cellar where the toilet was and never came back up. I was sure he didn't live down there. Just before 3:00 I asked him if there was a back exit. Yes. He took my bag down. By the time I managed the narrow stairs with my crutches, Achilleas had changed out of his waiter's uniform. I told him "ponai," pain, and asked him if he'd get me a taxi. I'd always tipped Achilleas. In five minutes he was back and we went out an alley to a street behind the Square. The taxi was waiting, the meter running, the driver swinging his worry beads, anxious to be in motion. "Avrio," Achilleas said, tomorrow. I gave him a Greek nod, right to left.

The Acropolis was a twenty-five-minute walk and a fifteen-minute ride in the rush hour heat. "Never let them see you sweat" is executive advice. Athletes sweat. Never let them see you ice. Lose your sweat, tighten up, and choke. I knew what I was going to say. I knew what I was going to do.

Between Filopapou Hill and the Acropolis, the buses were emptying their passengers into the diesel heat. The guides were showing their different colored parasols and lining up their charges. This was the tourist way, not climbing through the city and white village and trees as we had in September, but riding to the wide paving-stone path and complaining about the grade. I humped along with a German-speaking group of old people, several with canes. Gypsy kids were trying to sell us postcards. The old, brown guides in lawn chairs were offering their services. Standing in line waiting to buy my ticket, I was recognized by a guard at the gate. He called to me and gestured me up, the hand extended, palm down, fingers pawing backward like a dog paddle. "Ellenas," he said, and waved me through. I thanked him in Greek. I took my time climbing the steps beneath the Temple of Nike, where I'd pointed to the familiar swoosh on Sara's sneakers. I stopped wherever a guard stood and let him see my Panathinaikos tee shirt. Kyvernos visits Acropolis. I wanted everybody to know it. The tourists were oblivious, but I caught some nods from the guards. Fellowship of guards, I thought, and grinned at what I had in the bag.

Limping along the north side of the Parthenon, I was passed by tourists rushing to circle the building, find the best place to shoot the monument. My first visit, I was impressed by how the stones tower. Moving more slowly now, I noticed the black pollution grime that had floated up and stuck to the building's horizontal surfaces. I picked my way across the rocky apron and took my seat on the northeast wall, removed from the crowd going round and round the Parthenon. I was definitely sweating in the late afternoon sun, but it was also cool up here. There was one way up to and down from the Acropolis. I didn't worry about getting shot, not me, a celebrity admiring the view, letting the sun beat on his leg, exhibiting himself. I looked east toward the Olympic Stadium. Don't appear anxious. Pick up Eleni with the peripheral vision. At 4:10 I catch motion right: someone walking toward me, about five-six, a kid, maybe twenty-two. He's wearing sandals and carrying a new leather bag from one of the shops below. A tourist or a sports fan, or Eleni switched off. I thought she might not show up at crunch time. Eleni was a tough little talker, but in these final minutes she choked.

From eight feet away, the kid says "Keever. I have something to give you." The "give" is Greek English: "geeve." I turn and look at him. My eyes tell me the kid is not Greek. He's short and dark. His tee shirt is tucked in. His black wavy hair is combed straight back. But his face is not Greek. I don't know how I know, but I do and I'm sure. This is perfect.

"You came for the package, right?"

"Yes."

"You have the money in the bag."

"Yes."

"Come here and sit on the wall. I'll tell you what we're going to do."

He sits a couple of feet from me. It occurs to me that he may not know exactly what he's been sent for. A package. "Listen close," I tell him. "I'm pressed for time. I'll tell you once. We will put the bags between us. I will open my bag, reach in, and open up the package. You will look in at it. I will close it up and tape it shut. You will put your envelope in my bag. I will reach in and do a rough count. Then I'll pull my hand out of the bag. The wind will blow my cap over the wall and down. I'll look like I'm trying to catch my cap. The package will fly out of my hand. Another fuck-up, a double turnover. I will pretend irritation. We will walk away together to recover my stuff."

"The package must go in my bag."

"This way your hands are clean."

"The package will break on the rocks."

"Look down. See the tree. Do you see the net in the tree?"

"Yes."

"That's where the package will be, safe and sound. We both walk out with clean hands."

"But—" he starts.

"Discussion is over. It's showtime. I show you the package. You give me the money. Decide."

He hesitates. He has to decide. Eleni sent him for an exchange. Now there is this new wrinkle. This kid never wanted the package in his hands. I never intended to put the fake where he could double-check it. He's afraid. He'll go for the drop. He nods his head.

"Yes, but the package must go in the net first."

The fucking kid is dictating to me.

"Do you want this package or not?"

"We want what is inside the package. On the rocks the package is worthless."

I couldn't put the fake in his hands.

Numbers count: his five-six, my six-three.

"Listen here, you little motherfucker. The deal is this. You see the package in my bag. I see the money in your bag. I throw the package into the net. You let me reach in your bag and take the money or I throw you over the wall and tell the police you were trying to plant the shit on me."

The kid's Adam's apple bobs, his tongue fucks up his "i's."

"Eef the package goes een the net, you weel have your money."

We put the bags between us. I show him the goods. I tape the package shut. He opens an envelope in his bag. He riffles through dollars, pounds, and marks.

"What is this shit?"

"It adds up to forty thousand dollars."

"I bet."

Eleni knew I wouldn't have a calculator and exchange rates. She didn't know I'd welcome the distraction to open the slit in my bag. I put my hand on the fake canister. I look straight at the kid. He's sweating over the money.

"This isn't forty thousand dollars."

"It's what we could get together."

Shoot the rock.

I jerk my head to the right, as if the Parthenon were moving or the police were closing in. Look him off. The kid's eyes follow my glance, look into the sun behind the building. I pull out the fake package and flick my head back. My cap flies off. I turn, pretend to fumble, zoom onto the net, and shoot, an off-balance shot with an unfamiliar object and an irregular goal, a high and long shot, almost straight down like jamming from a tower, a high-pressure and long-odds shot, a last-second and a last shot, a one-shot shot for the money, *the* shot, unique, difficult but wide open, no one covering me, no arms or hands in the way, no other choice, no mind to interfere with the eye and hand, the exact calculation of space for this fake shot that will put me in front if it goes down the way I'd imaged it and imagined it since rigging the net. "Wick." Just like the buzzer-beater highlight films. The package settles into the black net and the net closes up around it, hanging in the tree.

I hear the kid exhale. I stamp my good leg and gesture with my hands for any guards that might be looking. The kid gets into the act, pointing down at my cap. I reach into his bag and grab the envelope. I stick the envelope in my bag and check the money inside. Now let's hustle out and find our stuff. The kid walks with me to the exit.

Eleni should have come herself, or sent a Greek. The kid shouldn't have tried to fuck with me. At the gate, with the kid behind me, I speak to the guard: "Xenos einai pousti. Thelei me gameisei. Thelo vohethia. Katalavenis?" The words just came out of me, even the right verb endings Elias had taught me, the little crucial differences between "I," "you," and "he." "The foreigner is a faggot. He wants to fuck me. I want help. Do you understand?" The guard understands. He steps between me and the kid and starts screaming in Greek. "Pousti malaka" are the first words I hear, "faggot faggot."

I duck behind the ticket booth and drop the fucking crutches. A miracle recovery at the shrine. A definite turning point. I sprint down through the bushes on this south side, weaving around the shrubs like the chairs Kellogg used to put on the floor. Out onto the path that Ann, Sara, and I took. Only a few tourists are taking the hard way up to the Acropolis in the late afternoon heat. Greeks are in their beds, out of the way. Two reasons for the four-o'clock meet. I run past the Agora and zigzag through the empty streets and alleys that Ann and I explored. If Eleni wants to catch me, she'll have to run like hell. Vassilis will have to pump those short legs of his. The Egyptian in sandals is out of luck. If Eleni's got some other boys like the "pousti" on my tail, they'll have to be conditioned athletes and experienced Athenians. I cut back toward Monastiraki Square. I'm sweating now like at Talaat Harb Square. Stride past the tourist shops. I go in one and buy *Let's Go Greece and Turkey.* I go into another and buy sunglasses, a Parthenon tee shirt, and a big straw hat, the kind that tourists afraid of skin-cancer now wear. Quick change in an alley: the sweaty Panathinaikos tee for the new white-and-blue souvenir. Normal walk now. Past the old fat lottery salesman at the Monastiraki subway entrance. Push onto the train for Piraeus. If the Greeks recognize me up close, nobody nods. They understand hurt pride. I had failed the national team. I was hiding behind the shades, under the hat. I was probably going to throw myself off a boat for aesthetic effect. I'll be a missing person.

In Piraeus I arranged my own tour, booked a cabin on the eight-o'clock boat to Rhodes, bought a *Tribune* for currency rates, and boarded early. It was a small room but a good place to avoid attention. Eleni was going to be pissed when her boy climbed the tree and found the film. Greeks were shooters. If Eleni had plastic, her people would have guns. "Don't play games," she'd said. My earliest memory of "game" was dead birds, partridges Dad shot. I wasn't showing my famous face at the airport, the obvious place. I also wasn't taking a train or bus west to Patras. I'd go the reverse route: east to Rhodes, ferry over to Turkey, and fly out from there.

Rhodes was a twelve-hour ride, plenty of time to count my cash. Spread around my bag, the different notes looked like a lot of money. Separated, stacked, transformed into dollars, the numbers came to $35,000 and change. Eleni was more honest than I'd figured. I was still short $25,000 from my bonus. No other way to make up the difference, recoup that loss. Who else would buy a fake package from an athlete? If this all works out, I thought, maybe I can sell the movie rights to my story in the States.

Thirty-five thousand in cash was another reason to avoid the airport and its X-rays ready to cancel the profit. I was more than $34,000 over the limit and didn't have time to make a bunch of visits to American Express. When Eleni released the document, she or the newspaper editors might make up a story to go with it. Keever Threatens Parthenon. Keever Attempts Bribe, Tries to Flee Country. I could imagine the headlines even if I couldn't read them. My picture would be in all the papers, not just the sports papers. It was only an hour by plane from Athens to Rhodes. I needed to cross the border before Eleni could react to the double-cross. I'd gotten the most out of my celebrity. Now I wanted to be a tall tourist, lose myself in the annual crowd of ten million.

Getting to Turkey wouldn't be as quick and easy as *Let's Go*'s simple title implied. The Greeks made it inconvenient for tourists to hop over and put money in the enemy's hands. To take a boat to Marmara, I had to buy the ticket a day in advance, leave my passport overnight in the Turkish booking office, and pick it up the next morning at the harbor. *Let's Go* warned

161

against taking excess cigarettes, liquor, or coffee into Turkey, but didn't help on currency. Their readers didn't carry $35. The one book I buy all year, and it's full of problems. I can check other guides in Rhodes, a place *Let's Go* said to avoid. It's the Greek Niagara Falls, the country's most cosmopolitan island, glitzy and overpriced. With $35,000 in my bag, I can afford one night. When the decks got quiet, I walked to the back of the boat and threw the plastic in the sea. Going back to my cabin, I remembered what Dad used to say about kids who couldn't shoot: "can't throw the ball in the ocean."

Chapter 15

At the harbor in Rhodes, I found out the boat for Marmara was leaving at 10:00. I put on my shades and hat and hung around to watch. At 9:00 the passengers started gathering outside the customs house on the quai. At 9:30 a guy about fifty in a white uniform and white shoes unlocked the door from inside and motioned the people into a small room. I stood outside and watched through the doorway as he called names. The tourists went up to his desk, he glanced at what they were holding, gave them their passports, and they left through a side door for the boat. A couple who may have been Turkish were asked to open their suitcases. The guy in white ran his hand through the top layer of clothes. It was a low-tech operation, no X-rays. Who would want to hijack or blow up a little tugboat with benches? If no one was looking for me, I could get the money out.

Before leaving the harbor, I checked the kiosk at the other end of the customs house. Today's papers from Athens were hanging up. They must be flown in. Information moves fast in Greece when you don't want it to. I looked at the back pages for my picture, the tell-tale McKeever. Nothing today. Tomorrow could be different. I asked when the papers came. The news agent pulled down the corners of his mouth: what's the difference? "Ennea, ennea-ke-missi." Nine, nine-thirty. It was 9:45. Tomorrow might be close. Walking from the harbor to the marina down the road, I considered waiting out the coming storm in Rhodes. But once I got in the papers, the Greeks would be talking to each other, reporters would show up, even more pictures would be taken, Eleni could find me, no end of shit. My best chance was to leave early. Tomorrow. I was out ahead. Keep up the momentum. Finish it off. Tomorrow I might still be a secret. The papers might arrive late.

Sixteen of my twenty-four hours in Rhodes I spent with tourists, moving from café to café in Mandraki marina where the Colossus supposedly stood, walking around the market and souvlaki heaven behind the cafes, browsing souvenir shops in Old Town, everywhere looking for the baggy pants or diarrhea-drawn face that would indicate the tourist had been to Turkey. I'd know just where to look in Athens: the Plaka, Filomoussa Square, where the stragglers carrying canvas pouches and rolled blankets met to drink wine and buy drugs. The main dealer was a tall, bearded American who called himself "X-man." Rhodes was no place to find a poor person, or a bookstore for the other guides. If you were in Rhodes, you had planned ahead and saved up your money. Everything was upscale: pastries more expensive than Kolonaki, tablecloths in the souvlaki joints, fur stores and gold shops in with the usual bag and sandal stores.

I have to admit it: Rhodes perfectly illustrates Eleni's arguments against tourism. Everything is smeared by service. In the new city, restaurants have German names and post menus in several Scandinavian languages. The Greeks are cooking wiener schnitzel. Rent Car, Rent Scooter, Rent Bicycle. But not a room in the cool-lobbied hotels that lodge only groups with long-term reservations, the packs of middle-aged white people getting into and out of the oversized tourist coaches that force drivers onto the sidewalk and pedestrians into designer shops franchised from Kolonaki, from Milan, from Paris. Inside the fifteenth-century walls of Old Town, every building that fronts on a narrow street or stone alley is selling something: Italian ice cream, French crepes, Japanese sushi, American hot dogs in Greek pita bread. Film, clothes, blankets, brass, marble, gold. Egyptian papyrus I'd seen in Cairo, Turkish taffy, Russian dolls inside each other, Korean-made Greek tablecloths. Shuffling along hip to hip and toe to heel with crowds of shoppers, I looked up at what *Let's Go* said was the Venetian Palace of the Grand Masters, built in the fourteenth century, destroyed in the nineteenth, and reconstructed fifty years ago. I wondered if it could be a fake, a hub for the shops and restaurants around it. I wondered, too, if *Let's Go* and all the other guides I hadn't read knew it was fake but went along because, after all, writing guides was their business. Deep in Old Town I found an authentic Greek room, advertised as "Let Zimmer:" a little larger than my cabin, a cot and a sink and the family's cooking smells for thirty dollars. No soap or towel, no hot water, no view, pay in advance.

No nap today. I had to stay on my feet, find someone who had been in Turkey. About 5:00 I was grazing a strip of leather shops—jackets, pants, skirts, shorts, halters, even bikini bottoms for Rhodes's cosmopolitan beaches—when I heard two unlikely couples talking about Turkish leather. Tennis-brown Americans about sixty in sailor hats, the round cotton caps the country clubbers wear brim down. Yes, they'd been to Turkey. Everything was cheap but nothing you'd want to buy. I asked if they had trouble getting in or out. The only trouble, one woman said, was spending the hundred dollars each of them had to change into Turkish money. They were in Marmara three hours.

Eating a short souvlaki and a Greek salad heavy on lettuce and cucumber, light on tomatoes and feta, no olives or olive oil, I considered how to cross both borders with my stacks of dollars, pounds, and marks. There was too much to stuff in my pockets. If I posed as a day-tripper, I couldn't use my big gym bag, particularly with its trick slit. No room in my camera case, the sacred tourist space. No room unless I left my camera here. That was the way out. Even if the morning papers had my picture, the case should work. The guy in white would know all about me, my name change, my injury, my camerawork. Keever and his inseparable camera. As long as I wasn't wanted, I'd be able to go to Turkey for a day. I'll buy a round-trip ticket. Be back tonight to explain the whole thing.

That got me out. I couldn't very well show up in Turkey with no luggage and declare $35,000 in three different currencies. They'd ask me what kind of drugs I was there to purchase. I'd use the case to get the money in. Here for the day, take some pictures, do some shopping. Show the round-trip ticket. When I get to a city, I'll go to American Express and buy checks. I can take my time. In Turkey I won't have to worry about seeing my face in the papers, overstaying my welcome. I liked the Greek cash economy, the whiffled piles of drachmas, but transporting bills was a problem. It could be worse. The Greeks could freeze an electronic transfer, a sudden switch from Switzerland to the States. The cash was hot money. They'd have to find it to keep it.

At 7:30 I went back to the new city, bought the two-way ticket, and gave up my passport. The Turk who took it said, "Enjoy your stay in Tour-key-a." I'd never heard a Turk pronounce the name of his country. It sounded to me like a good place to pass through.

I returned to Old Town and waited for the evening crowd. The old folks were back from the Valley of the Butterflies and the Acropolis at Lindos to shop, eat at the front-row tavernas, and watch the young, who had washed off the salt, sand, and oil, slicked back their hair, put imported condoms in their travel pouches, and assembled to turn Old Town into Night Town. They milled around outside the discos, watching who entered before paying the cover charge. They pushed from bar to bar, listening for the native tongue. The pubs were so crowded customers stood in alleys slopping beer from heavy steins and throwing them on the paving stones like plates at a Greek wedding. This was the tourist horde, a Greek word like Eleni's "kosmos." Milling to get in, spilling out, the wall-to-wall people in their shorts and skimpy tees were all inside the balmy, breezy island night. This is what the light-skinned tourists and the Greek honeymooners came to the islands for, non-athletes' action in the Mediterranean darkness, the day's extra period, carnival without costumes, without bats, bare flesh pressing bare flesh, foreign and Greek, Greek and foreign, not sitting in cafes or walking in lines but swarming together to celebrate their bodies and the sun that tanned them, left its heat in the air for this day's overtime.

I circulated through the competing sound systems and the bodies' moisturizer smell. I was taking care of business, one dumb, drunk, melancholy American. Not an imperialist but a parasite. Have to leave Greece early, emergency trip home, sacrificing my professional quality camera. The partiers were a tough crowd to please. The Germans and Swedes didn't appreciate the camera's size or American brand-name. They wanted something they could hold in one hand like a flashlight, so I had to give it away for two hundred fucking dollars' worth of marks. In this deal, I was the mark. Back in my room, I put the marks, pounds, and dollars in the case and covered them with *Let's Go* and a replica of the Colossus, a bowlegged bronze Henderson I'd bought for weight.

Lying in my last short Greek bed, I thought there must be other ways to do this. But I had to leave now, fourteen hours ago if possible. Nine more hours to the papers. Absolutely no problem if I'm not in. If the guy in white wants me, he could cancel my ticket, put me in jail, throw away the key. Always that risk. I kept telling myself: if you can get plastic out of Cairo and into Athens, you can certainly move money from Rhodes to Marmara. I'd fucked up Eleni. The package went in the net. Shooter's confidence, man. Every shot is in. No sweat. What a way to end up, though: clothes on my back, a cheap souvenir, and three kinds of money. No reason to get down. I'd played my minutes, shown the high-li, and collected the cash.

I woke up early, ready to leave, anxious to finish up this third season, Kyvernos against the law, Keever versus the heat. I'd watched the exit process, analyzed my options, arranged the deception. I was exactly what I was pretending to be: a tourist. I'd pass. I walked to the harbor and sat out in the little café next to the kiosk. The weather was warm for this hour of the morning. I was waiting for the news and sports, watching for the guy in white. A panel truck dropped the papers at 8:55. The five Greek customers in the café went over and grabbed papers off the stacks. The kid who waited on me picked up a bunch of different papers and went off into the building, papers in one hand, a tray of Greek coffees in the other. When the news agent got the papers clothespinned on his wires, I went to have a look. The wind off the sea was fluttering the papers on the wires. Nothing in *Hermes*. Nothing in *Vima*. Moving on to the left, I checked the back page of *Ta Nea*, the news. My picture, an action shot, was in the corner. *Rizospastis* had a head shot, the headline "Then Einai Ellenas," and a story continued on the inside, the inside fucking story on Kyvernos.

I pulled the straw hat down and went back to my seat. Still no sign of the guy in white. He didn't need to come out. The kid was back in the building delivering papers and coffees. It was 9:05. Was the guy in white a reader? I'd seen the men crowd together in Omonia Square waiting for the papers, the latest political shit, the newest soccer trivia. I'd waited as bank employees drank their coffee and leafed through a couple of papers at their desks. The guy in white would be reading. What, though? Left, center, right? One of each? It might depend on what he was. A shipping official, customs agent, border guard. To me now he was a customs guard, fully aware of the Greek custom of carrying around cash in a bag. I'm an American. No telling which paper he's reading or how he's reading (front to back, news to sports; the reverse; inside out, starting with the center spreads of girls on beaches) or what this Greek would find interesting (nothing better than a secret revealed, an American fucked-up). No gauging at 9:15 how fast he's reading (sipping and scanning, memorizing faces, reading and talking at the same time, reading and watching a weather report here by the windy sea) or how much time he has left (he might have to leave early to take care of his business) or how his reading could affect me (the time I might spend in jail, Greek overtime). Years, minutes, seconds, tenths. Instant calculation, the moving fence, the solid bars. Odds, probabilities, chance. Still time to decide, change my mind. 9:20. Run it backwards, Old Town, ferry, Athens. Not this time. My passport was in his hands. I couldn't fucking believe it. No pass, sport. 9:21 and no need to split seconds now. The action was over. I just had to wait. Greeks use the same word for "when" and "never." I put the stupid hat on the chair, walked out onto the quai, and stood with the other twenty people going to Marmara.

At 9:30 the door opened and we went inside. The door banged in the wind behind us. Inside it was too dark for sunglasses. The room didn't have windows, just the banging door in back of us, the open door to the left. The man in white stood behind his desk with the stack of passports. As he called the names and people left the room, I felt sick to my stomach. I thought about all the things besides time that didn't make a difference now. My athlete's body and athlete's brains and athlete's skills were useless. Perception, memory, imagination, and statistics were irrelevant. I had nothing to use, lots to lose. No passing now, no avoiding. No one to help. No story to tell. No control, no choice. No cover.

One by one and two by two the tourists collected their passports and went out the open side door. The crowd in the small room thinned and halved and disappeared until I was the only passenger left. The man motioned me up to his desk. He looked at the open passport in his right hand, looked at my face, and said "Kyvernos?"

"No, man," I said, "no more."

He held out his left hand palm down and turned over his fingers like a southpaw throwing a curve. "Klefti," he said in Greek and "You understand?" in English.

"Yes," I said. It was a Greek word hidden with another Greek word in our kleptomaniac.

He handed me my passport and said, "Kalo taxithi," good journey.

I nodded several times up and down, the American affirmation, and said a tourist "Thank you," one word at a time. I was passed over.

Walking across the quai with my money, no hurry now, the boat wouldn't leave early, I thought this was my going away gift from the Greeks, the police who rode without helmets, the guards who did favors, the drivers who shot into your lane, all the shooters and mad bombers, all those proud irresponsible bastards who did what they wanted and respected only other proud bastards like them.

Stepping up onto the boat, I thought my leaving was a reward for telling the truth in my language.

Looking back at the locked customs house, I thought leaving was a secret between him and me.

Why? "Yati." The Greek word for "why" and "because" is the same.

Along with my verbs, I'd been keeping another list: paradox, enigma, mystery, and magic. These were the keywords, words that implied there was no key.

What a place this was. What a time I've had. All over now. I sat on the wooden bench in the rear of the boat and looked back at Rhodes as we pulled out of the harbor. The islands were "stunning," Ann's friends said. Nine months ago, Greece was an unbelievable break, a route out of recruiting, an easy jump into the housing market. Then I became the Greek Key, that zigzag pattern winding around vases and doorways: up, over, down, over, up, over, and then rerun in a circle. The last week I've been like a high-li film on fast-forward, speeding back and forth, taking suicidal chances like a Greek, depending on controlled fear and dumb luck. Maybe the risks were crazy, as Ann said, but I'd avoided Eleni, as Ann used to say I avoided almost everything. In these last months and days, though, I've taken responsibility for myself. You give a pass, take a shot. Mine had gone in and now I was out of Eleni's range. Watching Rhodes recede, I was already homesick for the mainland, for Athens.

I'll never know who or what Eleni is. No matter who she is, she was right about leaving Egypt and entering Greece, right about Rhodes. She could be correct about the time to come. Tourism may well be a false future for a country of fragile islands, even for a cold island like Ireland. It was Eleni's strategy I couldn't go along with, even though the Parthenon has been blown up and reconstructed before. Sending more dust into the air and more noise over the airwaves couldn't be the way to clean up Worlddome. What was there to imitate on Eleni's tape? An act of self-destruction wasn't therapy for self-destruction. Vassilis was the only trainer I ever met who believed in homeopathy. Bodies know better than to take in poison. Unless, of course, the mind overrides and makes up its reasons, like all the reasons for breathing in the Nefos every day. The negatives in Greece multiplied like particles in the air, but even during the inversion the light surrounded us and moved me. For this bright place I loved despite all that happened there, the least I could do was expose Eleni. Security at the Acropolis can be improved. Hire better guards, install some hidden cameras. I'd deprived Eleni of the plastic and a good chunk of her group's money, but she is an angry and insistent woman. She may be back. Realizing that, I decided to write this book, warn Ellatha.

Thinking back about Eleni, I now see that I owe the woman. In Greek, the word for game or contest is "agona." Eleni caused me agony, but she also pressed me into places I'd never have gone, forced me to trade in my zoom lens for the wide angle. And she brought out of me resources I didn't know I had. Natural resources, a connection with the world, a physical overlap and interlock, recognition that being dumb, like playing dumb, could have its benefit, an athlete's sense of the all. Athletes play to trust, to feel how much more we know than we think we do. I know that and know too that we are all athletes, Greeks and Americans. That is the secret people try to conceal from themselves. Greece is the world's reminder, its history, another word given to us by Greeks. Greek names go back thousands of years without changing. Recognized as an imposter, I recognize now that more important than genius is genealogy, who we came from, the archaic athletes that preceded buildings like the Parthenon. We deceive ourselves when we forget that we are all still athletes together within, now, the billion-member crowd of crowds. We all need air and water and livable temperature to exist inside Worlddome. Avoid this body of facts and we'll all be running the suicides together in the future, centers, forwards, and guards, veterans and rookies, shooters and passers, natives and tourists, whites and blacks, men and women, children and grandchildren, Greeks and Americans. When the climate changes and Florida is Atlantis, New York is New Amsterdam, and Los Angeles has no more beaches, the midwest will be desert and Chicago could turn into Cairo. When the weather heats up, Canada will treat us like we treat Mexico, tourist destination and breeding ground for crowds. Our children may try to cross over the northern border like groups of desperate Mexicans in southern California, running through auto checkpoints at midday, weaving across lanes, dodging cars and trucks, scampering away from the police in a suicidal weave. Our grandchildren will be falling over on the floor of this overheated pit we have all made over time and cannot leave, all sweating and choking and puking from our suicidal run to surpass ourselves, mouths gasping and chests heaving overtime in the heat, legs stretched out in the pools of sweat where we will all be lying, our time over.

Trust the body.

That's the skeleton key I learned from and against Eleni. And it was my body that got me safely into Turkey, clarified my future. Sitting on the bench in the ferry, I felt a little queasy from the small boat's bobbing on the windy and warming sea. As Marmara came into view, I knew exactly what I was going to do. Stumble down the plank like a seasick tourist. Stagger across the quai to customs and hold my blue and gold card in front of me, the two-handed bird on the cover of my passport face up and out, the shield a shield. The Turks will take me in, a sick and helpless American. After that, it's all clear sailing. I'll take a bus to Istanbul and exchange the cash for checks at American Express. I saw *Midnight Express*. I'm coming out cool and clean. I'll buy a direct flight on Delta. I can see it all now, a slo-mo iso tape. From my hotel, I'll leave early for the airport. With time on my hands, I won't need to elbow or run through a crowd, my last. Ticket in hand, I'll pass by the policemen with machine guns guarding the terminal. Inside I'll exchange my ticket for a boarding pass and hold onto my carry-on. Passport in hand, I'll pass into the transit area. I'll exchange my leftover lira for dollars. Boarding pass in hand, I'll pass through the electronic scanner, the player-sized keyhole. I'll stand relaxed as the guard passes his hands over my body or turns over my possessions in the carry-on. In the boarding lounge, I'll sit and wait. No surprises now. We'll walk out to the plane. The tarmac will be hot, but inside will be cool. Even if the sun is shining through the windows, each passenger will control his or her own little duct of fresh air. I'll have my numbered and lettered seat, impersonal, exact. The steward will close and double-lock the door. We'll get our safety instructions and slowly taxi out. We'll power up, speed down the runway, and take off. I'll feel the easy uplift of the return, locker-room America, Sara and Ann waiting for me. In a few minutes we'll rise above the cloud cover into the light. We'll pass over Greece. All over now. It will be a straight shot home.

Epilogue

The narrative that you have just finished was first published in Greek as *I Metavivasi*, "The Pass" or "The Passage." Although I couldn't read my own autobiography, it became a bestseller in Greece, I made back my lost bonus, and I became something of a national hero there— "Protector of the Rock"— despite the anxieties of my translator. While doing his "metamorphosis," Greek for translation, he called me about several matters, including Eleni's name.

"She was playing with you," he said. "'Epimeno' means 'insist.' Epimenides was the ancient Greek who gave us the Lying Cretan paradox."

"Eleni said her family was from Crete."

"So did the Lying Cretan. He also insisted all Cretans are liars. Epimenides mocked words. I'd check the facts Eleni threw at you."

"I will."

"Another thing: if you keep 'Epimenides' as her last name, I'm not sure Greek readers will believe all the 'kineses' in the last chapters."

"'Kineses'?"

"Sorry," the translator said, "since you're an athlete, I thought you'd know it from kinesiology: the study of movement. With Eleni's hard 'c,' it's the root of cinema. Move, movies. I'm afraid the moves after Salonika may look like a Hollywood film."

"Epimenides is the name she gave me. You'll just have to work with the words I sent you. I don't have any tape of Eleni and my last days in Greece."

I wished that I did have tape. One of the great pleasures of watching my game tapes was knowing that my opponents were also watching the tapes, listening to their coach point out how I'd deceived them, fucked 'em up with high-li. Lacking tape, I went to the library. If Greek or American readers want to check out Eleni's statistics, they can look up *The End of Nature*, a black-covered paperback shelved in the nonfiction section along with autobiographies and travel writing.

Americans who don't trust an account with so many strange words can take the tour, the detour. Not the islands, but the city. Not the mountains of Delphi for the future, but the pit. If you sit in the heat, breathe air you can see, and watch hundreds of helpless people die in silence, it's not so hard—no matter what your name may be—to imagine Eleni's projected film, a loud noise and the Parthenon collapsing. The movie wasn't shot, but lying in bed some night in the future, waiting through the news and weather for the 11:25 sports highlights, you may still see Eleni's short nightmare of bright light, blue sky, and yellow cloud. Although that tape is now merely words—"columns crumbling, stones falling, dust rising"—I'm no Lying Cretan. I faked "Kyvernos" and learned other deceptions from Eleni, but all the words after this pro's "Prologue" are, I insist, true.